The Naming of Girl

Praise for The Naming of Girl

If you like pithy dialogue and vivid evocations of the underbelly of life, if you like characters who make you howl with laughter and who break your heart, if you like a novel that reminds you of everything that is wrong with the world and then reminds you of everything that is right, you will love *The Naming of Girl*.

— Mark Spencer, winner of the Faulkner Society Faulkner Award and author of *Trespassers, A Haunted Love Story, The Weary Motel*, and others.

Rhonda G. Williams's fresh voice catapults her boisterous, foul-mouthed, half-feral, larcenously irrepressible, and ultimately sweet heroine, Girl, right off the page into readers' hearts. Girl is lawless by necessity, and her intrepid can-do attitude made me laugh. I loved *The Naming of Girl*.

— Margaret Hawkins, Author of one memoir and three novels, most recently, *Lydia's Party* from Penguin Press. Senior lecturer at the School of the Art Institute of Chicago

As Flannery O' Connor's ghost haunts this book, it will haunt you. The strange, fantastic South is the main character in this novel, which is the vivid story of a stubborn girl, persistent in her wildness, lawlessness, bountiful in her rage and will to live. Rhonda Williams' writing is ferocious, and this taunting creature she calls "Girl" will come to live permanently in your imagination.

— Kate Gale, author of *The Goldilocks Zone*

Rhonda G. Williams lives in south Arkansas where she is an online composition instructor for Virtual Arkansas. She received an MFA in playwriting from the University of Arkansas, and an MFA in creative writing from the University of Nebraska at Omaha. When she's not writing or teaching, she is busy with a vast menagerie of rescued animals, and she enjoys traveling to places off the beaten path.

THE NAMING OF GIRL

RHONDA G. WILLIAMS

Upper Hand
PRESS

Bexley, Ohio

Published by Upper Hand Press LLC
P. O. Box 91179
Bexley, Ohio 43209
U. S. A.

www.upperhandpress.com

ISBN 978-0-9964395-1-0

Cover by Natalee Michelle Brown
Printed by Bookmasters, Ashland, Ohio

For Flossie

ACKNOWLEDGMENTS

I would like to thank Ann Starr and all the folks at Upper Hand Press for believing in this book. Here's to a long and prosperous relationship!

To my mentors in the writing program at UNO: Catherine, Pope, Kate, and Amy, you helped me shape this book in the earlier stages, and I thank you so much for your help and guidance. You guys rock!

To my LFB for always being there, talking through the problems, reading the many drafts, and for just being. I love you more than my luggage.

To Peter, who introduced me to Marylake and told me stories that fueled my imagination.

To my co-workers who keep me laughing and make sure I don't get above myself.

And to anyone and everyone who has ever believed in me, from the very bottom of a very full heart, I thank you, and I am so happy our paths have crossed and my life is brighter for knowing you.

Always be kind. Kindness is free, yet it becomes a priceless gift when bestowed on those whom society deems "different."

The Naming of Girl

ONE

Last summer when I was eight, fixing to be nine, was when everything changed. Seemed like it all started early on a Thursday morning, on August 29, 1968. See, the reason I knew the date is 'cause it was the day after Tracie'd bought a bunch of groceries at the grocery store in Lakeside, and I marked a big red X on the calendar that hung on the kitchen wall so I'd know how long it'd be till she bought some more. She only bought a lot of stuff once a month and sometimes when it would be almost time for her to go again, there wouldn't be much to eat but the stuff in the green cans we kept hid in the fruit cellar. Now, the food in them wasn't all that bad, but we didn't have a whole lot left and Antoe could eat everything up in one meal if I'd let him. Chuck brought them and when I asked him what they were he said, "Shit the government called food." So I took and hid them and when the next grocery day was a lot of days past the big red X, well, we'd have something to eat besides ketchup or mayonnaise sandwiches.

This morning though, I knew there were pop-tarts. I put them way up in the top cabinet. Tracie wouldn't let me get them usually, she said they cost too much, but Bettes was with us and they were laughing and carrying on so she didn't notice I snuck them in the buggy.

I jumped out of bed with the pop-tarts on my mind, and ran down the stairs as fast as I could, but being careful to be quiet. Tracie didn't like to be woke up early. First thing I did when I got down there was run to the windows in the front hallway and push aside the heavy red velvet curtains that had so much dust on them they looked white.

After peeking out in the driveway, I let them fall back in place and boy, was I relieved. Chuck's old rusted car wasn't there, which meant he was gone somewhere. His shiny red car was out there, but he never drove it much, 'specially not in the daytime. Chuck being gone always meant a good day.

I went to the kitchen and there was Antoe, cracking two eggs and mixing them up with what he'd already put in a bowl. I could see he'd got the flour out, and some chocolate milk, and now on top of the eggs, he was shaking in some Cheetos.

"Antoe, what're you doing?" I asked as I took the

Cheetos from him. I hopped up on the counter by the sink with the Cheetos bag in my teeth, and climbed up on top of the icebox, being careful not to knock off the horse skull that set up there. I fished around in the very top cabinet over the icebox and got the pop-tarts.

"Making waffles," Antoe said, and I watched while he poured his batter in the old toaster that set beside the stove.

"There's waffles in the freezer," I said, but I knew it wouldn't do no good. See, those waffles had holes in them, and Antoe didn't like holes in his food. He wouldn't even eat donuts unless I pulled them apart so he wouldn't see the holes.

Since our stove had to be turned on by holding a lit match to the burner, Antoe wouldn't dare try. I wasn't 'posed to but I did 'cause I liked the whooshing noise it'd make when it lit. So he poured that batter in the only place he could think of: our old rusted toaster. He knew that's where the holey waffles were cooked. He pushed down the little lever on the side of it and pretty soon the inside of the toaster started to glow bright red.

After it was glowing real good, it started to pop and sizzle and smoke like crazy. Big, smelly, black clouds were rolling out of the toaster and pretty soon, sparks started to shoot up towards the ceiling. I ran over and yanked the cord out of the wall and that made more sparks fly and then everything went pitch black. It was the kind of black where you couldn't even see your hand if you held it up in front of your face.

The thing is you'd think I'd be used to it, since it was always dark in our house, even on the brightest days. This was mainly 'cause Tracie said she was a night creature and she hated the sun. In the blackness after the lights went out, I waited to see what was gonna happen. It was real early in the morning and Tracie'd be mad as hell if someone woke her up before the sun was way, way up in the sky. If Chuck'd been home, I would've stopped Antoe from cooking and making a mess. Chuck always wore a big thick belt and he could yank it loose and have it whistling quicker than you could blink. I kinda liked it when Tracie would get mad though, 'cause she would cuss up a storm and I always liked to learn new words or new ways of saying them.

Our house was real, real old and the lights would go off a lot. Sometimes when me and Antoe were home by ourselves, we'd get scared. When Tracie was home, she'd wake up when her fans stopped going. She kept fans going in her room all the time. Even in the winter.

In the black kitchen, Antoe squawked like a chicken; he was more scared of the dark than I was.

"Antoe, it's alright, I'm here, and Tracie'll come in a little bit."

"Dark. Tonio not like." I couldn't hardly hear him 'cause he was whispering, and then I heard Tracie's bedroom door slam open.

"Goddammit. Shit. Shithelldamn...Girl! Tonio! I smell smoke, are y'all burning the goddamn house down?"

I heard her stumbling down the hallway, still cussing. I knew where she was going, too. She'd gone to the end of the hallway and into one of the bedrooms that didn't have nothing in it but junk. In there was an old, rusted looking box on the wall, and I heard the clicking sounds the same as always when the lights were out and Tracie was getting them back on.

I was trying to figure out if I should stay in the kitchen or go hide somewhere. If Tracie didn't see me, she'd blame the whole thing on Antoe, but then again, she might be mad at me for not stopping him from cooking. She always told me it was my job to watch him and not let him do stupid shit. Sometimes we didn't agree on what stupid shit was.

"Goddammit, why can't y'all let me sleep? I got a splitting headache." She made it down the stairs and in the kitchen, not in a hurrying way, but in a stumbling, not ready to be up kinda way. She looked like what she called the back roads of hell. Her long blonde hair was all over the place, and it was full of sticks and grass. She had black smudges over and under her eyes, just like the coons that came and dug around in our trash cans after dark, and the white parts of her eyes looked like there were red threads glued all over them. All she was wearing was a tee shirt and her underwear.

I thought Tracie was real pretty, and always compared the way she looked to me. I had curly black hair that wouldn't ever lay down right and I was so bony Tracie said she couldn't ever hug me 'cause it hurt too bad. But this morning I looked better.

Antoe's lip was poking out and I knew he was about to have a hissy fit. He was the world champion hissy fit thrower and if somebody yelled at him, it usually meant he was gonna have one.

"Antoe was making me waffles and the toaster blew up," I said, jumping out of my hiding place. She didn't need to know what kind of waffles he was making; let her think it was the toaster's fault.

"Goddammit. Throw it away, then. Shit, what a mess." She leaned against the cabinets and rubbed her forehead back and forth with her thumbs.

"We'll throw it out and clean up, won't we Antoe?" I nudged him with my elbow and he nodded "yes."

"Y'all do that. I gotta get rid of this shitty headache." She started out of the kitchen, then turned around and went to get a chair and pulled it over to the ice box and crawled up to fish around in the horse skull, and she pulled out a pink cigarette. She always went to the horse skull when she was trying to get rid of a shitty headache. Somebody had brought it for her a long time ago, before I was born even. When I was little it'd scare me, but I was used to it now. Sometimes I would tell Antoe it was gonna come alive one night and it liked to eat people. Tracie told me not to ever touch it; so of course, I checked it out from top to bottom. There were only pink cigarettes and little bags of green stuff in it, nothing very interesting. I did lick one of the pink cigarettes once and found out they tasted like strawberries.

She put the cigarette in her mouth and lit it and sucked in. She held the smoke in her mouth for a long time, then let it out, real slow like, and she put her head back and watched the smoke float up toward the ceiling. She did that a few more times then she went over to the icebox and got out the jar that always had tea. Tracie loved tea and she drank it all day long. I didn't like it much and neither did Antoe. We liked to drink Tang, 'cause it was what the spacemen drank. Plus, it tasted good.

Tracie sat down at the table and just drank tea out of the jar while she kept smoking her pink cigarette.

"Girl, get me the aspirin."

I went to the drawer where the aspirin always stayed and got the bottle out, opened the lid and shook two pills out in my hand. I handed them to Tracie.

"Give me two more," she said, so I did.

I watched her swallow two more pills then went and unplugged the toaster and picked it up. It was still a little warm, but not too much to hold. I hauled it over to the counter by the sink and opened up the cabinet door under there and got out a sack and stuffed the toaster in. I grabbed the dish rag out of the sink and wet it and handed it to Antoe to start wiping up all the mess.

"Is Chuck here?" I asked, knowing he wasn't, but I always liked to double-check.

'No, he went into town for a little while. You better be glad, too. He wouldn't like all this mess."

No shit, I thought to myself. See, we'd do something and Tracie'd get pissed off and she'd holler and cuss, but she never whipped either of us. I don't think she was big enough to whip Antoe, and if she started after me, I'd run like hell. All I had to do was stay gone for a while and she'd forget all about it. She forgot things a lot.

"You need to go take a bath," she said, as she carefully put out the pink cigarette. I stared at her.

"What for?" I asked.

"We're going to Greenville after while."

"Who?"

"Me, you, and Chuck." She left the kitchen and started back up the stairs. I followed her.

"Why?" I asked. I hated going anywhere with Chuck, 'cause he didn't like what he called "sassy-mouthed kids," and he told me I was the sassiest one of all. Traci went to her bedroom.

"Why do I gotta go?" I asked her again.

"Just 'cause. Now go 'way. I wanna go back to sleep." She stripped off her tee shirt and crawled back under the covers. I stood in her dark bedroom listening to the fans whirring. It was cool and dark in there and it made me feel sleepy myself. I knew Tracie wouldn't mind if I laid down beside her; I did sometimes when Chuck was gone. But I was too busy wondering why I was gonna have to go to Greenville with them so I left and pulled the bedroom door closed behind me and went back down the stairs.

Antoe wasn't in the kitchen and he hadn't finished cleaning up the mess so I got the rag and went back to wiping down the black gunk that was all over the counters. I was just finishing up when he came back in the kitchen from the washer room. There was a back door in there and he'd been outside peeing, like he always did. When he came back in his pants were still down and his tallywacker was flopped out.

"Antoe, you gotta remember to pull up your pants. Nobody wants to see your tallywacker." I don't know why I bothered 'cause I knew it didn't make no difference to him.

"Tonio hungry."

I got the box of pop-tarts down and got a package out for him and one for me. I'd eat one of mine and save the other one, but I knew he'd eat both of them. He opened up the package and stuffed both of them in his mouth and took a huge bite. He went back through to the washer room and I followed him. At the back of the room was a door and on the other side was skinny stairs that went down to the bottom and opened up to a big room that was always called the fruit cellar. This was our special place. We'd dragged a bunch of quilts down from upstairs and made a thick bed in one corner. An old coffee table was in the middle of the room and we used that for a table. The box of green cans of food was in the corner with a blanket over the top. We kept our stuff down there, stuff we didn't want other people to find. I had a box that I sometimes kept candy bars in, 'cause of Antoe and the mice, and I kept my money in it. There was always coins and sometimes dollar bills laying around in the front room, and I would gather it up. Antoe's favorite thing was a white statue of a lady he had setting on the coffee table. The lady was wearing a long dress and she had her hands out. She was standing on snakes. I don't know where he got her from but he loved her. He also had an old battered radio, a huge key ring that had a bunch of keys that didn't fit nothing, an old green bag, and some picture books. Along the sides of the walls were old jars that had stuff in them from a long time ago and Tracie told us not to ever eat any of it 'cause we'd get sick and die. She kept telling me to haul all those jars out and throw them away, but I liked to look at them and wonder who put them there.

Antoe was looking at one of his books, so I got out my box to count the money in it. I had eight dollars and forty-three cents in one dollar bills, quarters, dimes, nickels and pennies. I put it back in the box 'cause if I took it to Greenville, then they'd wonder where I got it from.

"Girl go play?" Antoe had gone through all his books, one at a time, and I was half-asleep when he jumped up. He was like that. He'd be doing something then all at once he'd jump up to go do something else. I didn't mind, either. I shoved my box back under the pile of quilts and followed him up the stairs, through the washer room and kitchen, into the hallway and out the front door and down the steps. I was careful, like always, not to fall in the holes on our front steps. Both of us headed out to our swing, and let me tell you, it was the best swing in the whole wide world. It was a big burlap sack filled with hay and tied at the top and it hung from a huge, huge tree. We had a bunch of trees in our yard, and they all had this long dangly moss that blew around. Sometimes at night I'd tell Antoe the moss was monsters and it was gonna jump out of the trees and follow us. I scared him so bad one time he peed his pants.

I got on the bag and wrapped my legs around it and Antoe started to push me. He would really get going and run under the swing and I'd be so high in the air it'd feel like I was flying!

See, that was the good thing about Antoe: he was big and strong, like a grown-up, but he liked to play just like I did. Sometimes I'd get us both in trouble 'cause I would think up something to do and he'd help me do it. Last summer we were playing circus, where I'd get to going real high and I'd stand up on the bag and jump off and try to land on my feet, only I didn't land right and broke my arm and had to go to the hospital. But that was before Chuck was living with us and we got to eat lots of ice cream when we got back home.

"Girl, wanna play circus?" Antoe asked me, like he could read my mind. I was about to tell him yeah, but then I heard a car coming and I knew it was Chuck. I could always tell the sound everybody's car made when it was coming up the driveway.

"Chuck's coming."

As soon as I said that, he started to look around and it wasn't but a second later that he said, "Tonio tired. Go sing." And he headed around to the back and from there I knew he'd go back to the fruit cellar and turn on his radio. That's what he called singing.

Chuck pulled up, got out of his car, and went hopping up the steps. I played like I didn't see him but I was watching out of the corner of my eye. He didn't pay me no attention, well, he never paid me much attention unless I was doing or saying something that'd cause his eyes to bug out and get after me.

I stayed out on the swing, using my feet to twirl the rope on the swing around and around till it was wound up tight then I'd let it go and spin in a circle so fast it made me dizzy. When I finally came to a stop, I heard another car spitting and backfiring up the road. I couldn't see it yet, but I knew it was Bettes.

I watched her little car chug up the driveway. It was mostly yellow, but there were some rusty spots all over it, and over the rusty spots she'd painted pink and white flowers. I thought her car was beautiful. When she came to a stop I hopped off the swing and ran crookedly over to where she was getting out. I nearly fell on her.

"Bettes!" I grabbed her around the middle like I hadn't seen her in years, but she'd been to our house a couple of days ago. I didn't care; I loved Bettes. She was real tall, and kinda big, and she had long black hair she wore in two braids like an Indian. She always wore long, bright dresses and they were always so low in front her ninnies hung out the top.

"Hey, Girl!" She shouted, grabbing me and swinging me so my legs went flying around like the top of a helicopter. She must've turned in three circles before she got dizzy and put me down. I was too, and when I tried to walk, I fell down on the grass.

"Damn, that's a cheap high," Bettes said and she laughed and laughed. That was another thing about Bettes: she laughed all the time, and even if you were in a bad mood, just hearing her would make you laugh too. She held out her hand and pulled me up.

"Call me Sally."

"OK, *Sally*, whatcha been doing?" She asked as we walked up towards the house swinging hands.

"Me and Antoe were swinging just now." I told her. "Are you going to Greenville with us?" I was hopeful, 'cause if Bettes went, then it might not be so bad.

"No, I'm gonna stay here with Tonio and knit." She laughed and held up her big bag of what she called her knitting only I never saw her knit one thing.

"Then I don't wanna go neither." I knew staying home with Bettes and Antoe would be a lot more fun. I knew what would happen on this trip: I'd say something "sassy" and Chuck would yank his belt out so fast it whistled and beat me half to death.

"You got to," Bettes said.

"Hellshitdamn." Bettes just laughed.

"It won't be so bad," she said. "Just try not to say nothing."

"I always try, but it's hard."

"I know, but I'm gonna make a cake for when you get back, OK?"

"What kind?" I asked.

"What kind would you like?"

"Chocolate!"

She laughed some more. "Chocolate it is! Tonio'll help me."

"OK, but you gotta promise you won't let him eat it all before I get home."

"I promise!" She laughed some more and grabbed my hand and we walked up the front steps holding hands and swinging them. Right when Bettes was fixing to open the door, Chuck slung it open and walked right into her, bounced off her huge ninnies, and fell back in the house flat on his back. Even though I wanted to laugh so bad I bout busted my britches, I bit the inside of my cheek, frowned, and looked down and my bare feet that were so dirty it looked like I was wearing brown sandals.

"Goddamn, Chuck, you trying to break my neck?" Bettes asked him as she went on in the house without making a move to help him up.

One thing about Chuck was he only had one leg. Well, he had two of them but one wasn't real, it was made out of wood, or plastic, or something and he tied it on, but I never knew how. He didn't walk real good on account of it and he used a walking stick.

He got his real leg shot off someplace they were fighting. *Be it Calm* or something like that. And the person who did was named Charlie or Gook, I couldn't figure out which. Chuck'd get to cussing and carrying on about Charlie and Gook whenever he'd drink his brown stuff. I overheard them talking about it, but I sure never mentioned it. I acted like he had two good legs same as anybody.

Another thing about him was it was real hard to

know what kind of mood he was gonna be in. Sometimes he was pretty nice and he would bring us candy and stuff. But then there were times when he'd grab his head like it was hurting him bad and whenever that happened I would get to the fruit cellar as fast as I could.

Even though he didn't say nothing to Bettes about knocking him down, I could tell he was mad on account of how red his face got. He used his walking stick to help him get up and came outside and slammed the door so hard it shook the windows. He jerked his head around to stare at me to make sure I wasn't laughing then he made his way down the steps and out to his car. I watched him walk, laughing on the inside, about how he went up and down kinda like that merry-go-round that was on the parking lot of Perone's store last summer.

Before he got to his car I went on in the house and Tracie was coming down the stairs. She was wearing her holey blue jeans with the flowers going up one leg, the red top that tied around her neck and looked like a handkerchief, and the shoes that let her toes show. She had put on her makeup and looked real pretty.

"Girl, I told you to take a bath!"

"Oh."

It's too late now, go get in the car. Chuck's already out there and you know he hates to wait."

I did know this so I followed right behind her and hopped in the backseat as she was getting in the front.

Chuck had put on those stupid mirror glasses that meant I couldn't see his eyes and I hated that. He threw his arm over the seat and turned around in the car to look at me.

"Where're your shoes?" He asked.

Hellshitdamn. I didn't even think about putting on shoes, Tracie never made me.

"Aw, nobody cares if she wears shoes, it's summer." Tracie told him as she was lighting up a pink cigarette. She sucked on it for a long time then handed it to Chuck. He did just like she did and I wanted to laugh cause I'd never seen him smoke the pink cigarette and it looked funny to me.

We pulled out of our driveway and the first thing we passed was Perone's store, then the store that had the huge big bottle out in front, the one Tracie'd go to buy beer and Chuck's brown stuff. I didn't know how they drank it 'cause I'd tried both and they were nasty.

I was sitting in the back and I was real careful not to put my dirty feet up on the seat, even though the seat looked dirtier than my feet did. Chuck'd beat me half to death for that once and I wasn't looking for it to happen again.

"Hand me that lighter," Chuck said and Tracie started scratching in her purse to find it. Whenever Chuck said for Tracie to do something, I noticed she did it in a hurry. I wondered if he ever used his belt on her. I knew he yelled at her sometimes, and they'd make all kinds of noise whenever they went to the bedroom to take a nap. Personally, I didn't think they were napping.

"Hey runt," Chuck said, looking up in the mirror so he could see me. "You excited about school?"

I didn't know what he was talking about so I just looked at him.

"You gonna answer me?" His voice got quiet and loud all at the same time and he started slowing the car down.

"I don't know what you're talking about. What about school?" I asked him in a hurry, before he stopped on the side of the road.

"You didn't tell her?" He asked Tracie and he started driving fast again.

"No, I was gonna wait till tomorrow." And she looked over at him.

"That's what's wrong with her. You baby the hell outta her." He looked up in the mirror again, well, I could tell he was looking up by the way he raised his head but I couldn't see his eyes on account of those stupid mirrors.

"You fixing' to start school on Monday. Get you some learning so you won't wind up a retard like—

"Don't Chuck." Tracie raised her voice just a little bit and Chuck jerked his head around towards her. I thought he was fixing to yell at her some but he just grunted and went to fiddling with the radio. Tracie set back in the seat and rolled the window down a little bit and lit up a cigarette, just a white one this time. I scooted over behind Chuck so I wouldn't have smoke and ashes blowing in my face and I could think in peace.

I knew about school from seeing shows on our old black and white television that worked sometimes, if the weather was clear, and you wacked it just right. When I was real little, I used to bug Tracie about going. It looked like it would be fun, and everyone who went got school supplies. I'd do just about anything for some notebooks, colored pencils and a big huge box of colors.

But whenever I'd asked Tracie about it, she'd told me that they taught hate and bullshit there and that there was too much of that going around and I could learn stuff just fine on my own. Then she said they'd be mean to me, for a lot of things, but mainly 'cause of my name. See, I knew Girl wasn't really a name. It was kinda like if you had a cat or a dog or a horse, you wouldn't call them cat, dog, or horse 'cause that would be stupid. But for some reason, somebody'd named me Girl, and that was the stupidest name of all. I asked Tracie if she'd named me and she laughed and said, "Hell no, I ain't ever been that high."

So after a while I just forgot about going, and really, I was happy staying home with Antoe. Seemed like going to school would take away a lot of my free time.

"I'm really going to school?" I asked.

"Yeah, we're gonna get you some new clothes

and stuff."

"Can I have some notebooks and pencils?" I asked.

Tracie nodded and said, "Yeah, all that shit."

"Can you tell them my name is Jeannie?"

"What?"

"I don't wanna be Girl no more."

She turned around to answer me but Chuck started talking to her and she never finished.

I sat back in the seat then and didn't say no more 'cause they were talking and I knew better than to butt in. Pretty soon we got to the big, big bridge and I leaned up so I could see it better. It seemed like the car was gonna go right over the edge of it, it was that high. It kinda scared me but I liked the feeling all at the same time.

"Welcome to Mississippi," I said, reading the green sign on the side of the road. Tracie turned around again and stared at me.

"Since when can you read?"

I shrugged. "I don't know." I really didn't. Seemed like I always knew how.

She stared at me awhile longer then turned back around in her seat. I was thinking maybe I'd be in trouble by the way she was acting, then I saw the big Woolworth's sign up ahead and Chuck whipped in the parking lot so fast I was slung on the other side of the car, but instead of parking the car, he pulled up right in front of the store. Tracie opened the door to get out but I beat her.

"I'll be back in a coupla hours; y'all be out here, 'cause I ain't waiting." He squealed his tires out of the lot and was gone.

Me and Tracie watched him leave then we walked up to the store and pushed open the door that jangled as we went in. It seemed dark in the store after we'd just been outside where it was bright sun and I had to stand there for a second to let my eyes get used to it.

"Will Chuck leave us?" I asked Tracie as we both stood inside the door. There were little bells hanging on the inside door handle and I ran my hand over them, making them jangle again.

"Na, he knows better." She laughed. "He can't live without it."

"Live without what?" But she was already heading back to the back of the store where the clothes were. I would've rather gone to check out the toys first, but I followed Tracie.

I loved Woolworths 'cause all the stuff was on low shelves, and I could pick up and touch anything I wanted to. Maybe the clothes buying wouldn't take long, and I could go check out the good stuff.

Tracie came to a rack of dresses and started to look through them. She pulled out three or four and held them up for me to see.

"I don't wear dresses."

"Tough. They won't let you wear pants to school."

Hellshitdamn. Another reason not to want to go. As far as I could remember, I'd never once had on a dress. Tracie didn't wear them either.

"You don't wear dresses." I reminded her.

"Girl, just don't. I didn't make the rules so try these on." She pushed the dresses at me then shoved me through this little door that had a curtain covering it.

I stood there in that little room, and it had a huge, huge mirror in it, and it was the first time I'd seen all of myself at once. We had mirrors, but you could only see your top half, or if you stood on something, your bottom half. I saw that I looked kinda raggedy, my shirt hung down to my knees, (it was an old one of Tracie's) and my pants were dirty and holey. And my bare feet had rings of dirt caked up around the toes. I just stood there holding the dresses.

"Do they fit?" Tracie called out to me.

"Yeah." I told her. I knew she wouldn't check.

"OK, well here's some more, try these." And she stuffed an armful of dresses in through the door. They were pure-d ugly. All of them. Dark, boring colors, grey, black, dark green, and one had a wide plaid color and a plaid skirt, another one had a huge bow at the neck, and another one was the color I called shit brown. I didn't know if Woolworths maybe didn't have pretty dresses, or if Tracie just didn't care if I wore ugly stuff.

"These don't fit." I told her, coming out of the dressing room. I wanted to try and find something not so ugly.

"Shit." Tracie looked like she was about to get pissed off; I knew she hated shopping, and I didn't especially want her to pick out more ugly stuff for me to try on.

"I could look for some that fit, and you could go," I said.

"Are you sure? You can't wear pants, they won't let you, it has to be dresses." I could tell she was thinking about leaving.

"No pants, just dresses."

"And you need some shoes too." She looked around. "No tenny shoes. You gotta have some school shoes. OK?"

"OK." I agreed, but not knowing exactly what "school shoes" were. She picked up her purse and dug through her wallet and from a secret pocket she pulled out two bills: a twenty dollar bill and a five dollar bill.

"OK, but this is all you got to spend, and you need school supplies too, remember? I'm going to go get some coffee in that diner right beside here. When you get finished, come over, OK?

"OK."

"Don't be late either, 'cause you know Chuck'll be mad." And with that she turned around and walked out the door. As soon as she got outside she lit a cigarette, and I watched her take off down the sidewalk towards the diner.

Now I could get something I might wear. I wandered over to the rack of dresses that Tracie had gotten the ugly ones from, and I saw one that caught my attention. It was beautiful: all white and lacey, and it was full and swingy and I knew if I twirled around it would fly out. If I wore it I would look pretty as Tracie. I pulled it off the rack, and put it carefully over my arm so I wouldn't crush it. I knew I had to find some more, but after the beautiful white one, the rest were even uglier.

"Hi there, can I help you with something?" A voice called out, nearly scaring me to death, and I wheeled around and there was a girl with a blue coat and a name tag. She was chewing gum and kinda looking me up and down. She didn't look very old and she was wearing a real short skirt and real high heeled shoes. She had bright red lipstick on and there were red smears down her chin and on one side of her face, and when she talked I could see red stains all over her teeth.

"My momma sent me in here to buy some clothes, so that's what I'm doing." I told her, smiling up at her like I didn't have a lick of sense and trying not to stare at her red smeared chin.

"Oooo that's pretty, is that gonna be your first communion dress?"

"Yeah," I said, but I didn't know what first communion was.

"Well, you need the veil that goes with it don't

you?" And she pulled down from the top shelf a little box, opened it, and showed me this beautiful little veil that had flowers and a little comb that went in my hair so that it would sit on top of my head. I'd look so pretty wearing that I wouldn't even mind going to school.

"Thank you ma'am," I said, reaching out for that beautiful thing. She handed it to me and then: "What else can I help you with?"

"Well, I need some dresses...for school; they won't let you wear pants. Only all those dresses are ugly."

"I see," she said, and then, "maybe some skirts? We have a lot of skirts and tops in your size." She motioned me to follow her and we went to the back of the store, and folded up on tables were shirts and skirts of all colors, with bright flowers and all kinds of pretty things. This is better, I thought to myself.

"Do you know what size you need?"

"Yeah," I said, but I didn't know. She started going through the skirts and pulling out the ones in my size, and then she started pulling out tops. I picked out four of the brightest skirts; one green one the color of lime popsicles, one with pink and white flowers on yellow, ('cause it reminded me of Bettes car) one that was striped red and white like a candy cane, and one that had all kinds of shapes, squares, triangles, and circles, that were all different colors. Then I picked out four of the brightest tops I could find, making sure I got different colors than the skirts. I found a striped green and yellow top that I thought would look good with my striped skirt, a red top, a pink top, and one that had balloons all over it in all different colors.

"These are the ones I want," I said.

She looked at them. "You want to get some that match better than these." And she started to put some of my shirts back.

"No, I want these." I snatched them back from her and she stared at me, then sighed and gathered them up.

She shrugged her shoulders like she really didn't care and turned around to go back to the front.

"I need school supplies first," I said, wishing she would leave me alone.

"Do you need any help?"

"No."

"OK, I'll put your clothes up front on the counter; just bring the rest of your stuff when you're finished." She left me then, and went to help somebody else and boy, was I glad. I intended to get me and Antoe a lot of candy. I had worn my baggiest pants with the biggest pockets, and I had my big bag slung over my shoulder, the one Tracie'd given me when she got tired of it. It sure didn't take me long to fill that bag up with as much candy as I could grab, and I even managed to get us two cap guns and caps that I put in my pockets. I got wax lips, wax bottles, candy cigarettes, suckers, and candy bars.

Then I walked over to the school supplies and stuffed a huge box of colors in my bag, along with a box of colored pencils. I figured that was enough to steal, and then I'd pay for the rest with the money Tracie'd given me.

That was the thing to keep from getting caught: you had to buy stuff, too. If you just walked around swiping stuff and not buying anything, they'd follow you around and even check your pockets.

I found two notebooks, a box of pencils, and a beautiful shiny, black and pink book satchel. I got scissors, glue, a pencil sharpener, and a little box of colors. This was all I could come up with as far as school supplies went, and while I still wasn't too happy at the thought of going, I had wanted the supplies for as long as I could remember. I took my stuff up to the front and laid it all on the counter, stretching on my tiptoes to reach. There was a different lady up there, she had grey hair and wore glasses that had little chains with beads that dipped down on either side of her face. Her name tag said Clara.

"Well, hey there little girl. Did you find everything you needed?" She asked me as she was taking stuff out of my arms.

"Yes Ma'am, I sure did," I said. Bettes had told me that if I was trying to get away with something, always say yes ma'am and no ma'am, she was also the one who'd told me that some grownups liked it if I acted like I didn't have a lick of sense. And you know what?

It worked every time. Not with Tracie though. She said whenever I said ma'am to her, her bullshit detector went off. I asked her what that was exactly and she just laughed and said I'd figure it out 'bout the time I got my first boyfriend.

And then I remembered: shoes.

"Oh, I'm supposed to get school shoes, only I don't know what they are." I told the lady as she was punching numbers into the cash register.

"Marla," the lady called to someone behind her, "will you help this little girl find some shoes for school?"

Marla came out, and she was the same one who'd helped me with the skirts. She didn't look too happy to have to put out her cigarette, either. She didn't say anything to me, just walked back to the back of the store and pointed out some shoes. There were some black ones, and some white ones, and there were some that were black and white together that had laces, sorta like tenny shoes.

"I like them," I said, pointing at the black and white shoes.

"Do you know what size you need?"

"Uh-uh." Marla went rooting through some boxes and came up with one pair.

"All we have left is a size one and a half." She looked down at my bare, dirty feet and wrinkled up her nose like she smelled something bad.

"That's the size I wear," I said, reaching out my hand for the shoes she was holding up. I wasn't fixing to take a chance 'cause the other ones were pure-d ugly.

"OK, then," she said, and I guess she went back to finish her cigarette.

I put the shoes back in the box and took them to the counter. All the rest of my stuff was up there, waiting on the grey haired lady named Clara to sack it up. I wondered if Tracie had given me enough money for all of it, and then it came to me.

I put the shoes on the counter and Clara picked them up and punched in some numbers on the cash register. Then she started folding up the skirts and shirts, the beautiful white dress with the veil, and then the school supplies. When she finished she said, "That's gonna be eighteen dollars and eighty three cents."

I looked in my purse, careful not to let the stuff I'd swiped show, and pulled out the five dollar bill Tracie'd given me, leaving the other one, the twenty, way down in the bag. I set it down on the floor and started digging through it like I was looking for more. I put my hands in my pockets then, making sure I didn't pull out the cap guns I'd stashed there, and I pulled out the inside of one pocket that I knew had a hole it, and I just stared at the hole.

"Oh no," I whispered. "My momma is gonna kill me 'cause I lost my money." I made my face look as sad and scared as possible, like I was about to cry.

"I guess I better put most of this stuff back, and just get the school supplies, will five dollars be enough?" I kept the sad face, and I blinked my eyes real fast, and I could feel tears beginning to puddle up, and then one slid down my cheek. Even though I made it a point to never cry, I could, and found out that it came in handy sometimes.

I stood there staring down at the pocket hole, that I still had hanging out, like I didn't know what on earth I was going to do. Clara looked like she was about to cry, too. She came around from the counter and squatted down and put her arms around me and hugged me.

"You poor little thing," she said. "Don't you worry about it, you just give me the money you've got, and it'll be our little secret, hush your crying now."

I managed to smile up at her and wiped my eyes on my shirt. She took my five dollars and then she handed me the sacks full of my stuff.

"Here you go, remember it's our secret now." She winked at me.

"Thank you ma'am, thank you so much. My momma would've beaten me half to death, 'cause that's what she told me. If you lose this money I'll beat you half to death."

"Does she beat you?" Clara asked me then, looking all worried.

Hellshitdamn. "No ma'am, she don't, but she

would've been really mad that I lost that money. We don't have a lot see, and that was all she had."

I needed to shut up and get out of this store. I looked out the window and then said, "Oh I see momma now, thank you again ma'am!" I grabbed my sacks and went running out the store careful not to drop anything.

As soon as I was outside, I tore off down the sidewalk towards the diner Tracie said she'd be at. I saw her standing outside talking to a man on a motorcycle. I slowed down then, 'cause she hated for me to come up to her when she was talking to somebody, so I stood on the sidewalk with my sacks, but out of sight of the ladies in Woolworth.

Tracie was laughing with the man and I saw her shake his hand, and then I saw him drop something in her purse. I wondered what it was, but I wasn't gonna ask. She didn't like it when I asked too many questions.

The man roared off on his motorcycle then, and I got a tighter grip on my sacks and went over to her. She looked like she was in a good mood.

"There you are, right on time. What the hell is all that?" She asked me, looking at all the stuff I was carrying.

"Notebooks and school clothes." I started putting the candy in my pockets in one sack and I dumped out what was in my bag in one of the other ones.

She leaned down and opened up a sack, the one with the book satchel and notebooks, and poked around.

"You had enough money to buy all this?"

"Yeah."

She looked at me and I grinned and she bust out laughing. "When they lock your little ass up, don't call me to bail you out. I hope you got some decent shit to wear, 'cause I don't wanna deal with them up at the school."

"Can I go get some ice cream?"

"There's Chuck now." She pointed to the far side of the parking lot, and I saw the clouds of black smoke that always came from his car.

He pulled up in his car that was huffing and puffing, and Tracie had the door open before he stopped completely, and I did too, and slid in the back seat.

"Hey, babe." He leaned over and kissed her on the mouth. "I gotta lead on a helluva business opportunity. Tommy told me about it." He was in a good mood, which meant that I would probably be OK.

"Yeah? What? Tracie asked.

"Can't say right now, but if all goes as plan, we're gonna be shitting in tall cotton!" He looked at her and winked.

"Well, I got the horse some hay!" She said, digging in her purse, and she pulled out a little bag of what looked like dried up grass and held it up and shook it. They both laughed then, and Chuck looked in the mirror at me. "How 'bout you runt? Didja get some clothes for school?"

"Yeah," I said, and smiled, 'cause that was the best

thing to do when he was in a good mood.

"Get you some lady clothes and get you an education so you won't wind up a retard like your—

"Chuck." Tracie sounded like she was about to get mad.

"Aw, the runt knows I'm joking doncha runt?" He looked up at me again and winked and I smiled back at him.

I had to play along when he felt like playing, 'cause if I ignored him, he'd think I was "sassing" him and that's when he'd yank out his belt.

They talked on the way home, but I didn't really listen, and when we drove up our driveway, Chuck didn't turn off the car, so I knew they'd probably be gone most of the night. I got out carrying my bags and I saw Bettes coming out of the house and walking kinda sideways like she sometimes did.

"Hey Bettes, you going to Jimmy's?" Tracie asked her.

"Na, not tonight, I got company coming," She laughed.

"There's a big ole chocolate cake with your name on it, Girl!" I grabbed her for a quick hug 'cause nobody made cake like Bettes did. Tracie met her on the steps and I heard them talking as I was going on in the house.

"Well, come over tomorrow and we'll take the horsey out for a ride!"

They both laughed then and Bettes shook all over. I carried my bags down the steps to the fruit cellar where I knew Antoe was. He was carving on one of his soap bars.

"Girl back!" He threw down his carving and hugged me like I'd been gone a million years.

"Lookit what I got." I dumped the stuff on the floor: my clothes, the school supplies, and all the candy I'd swiped. We spent the rest of the day wearing candy necklaces, wax lips, eating candy bars and drawing and coloring with the new colors. Then, later on that night, we ate that entire chocolate cake. It'd been a pretty good day.

TWO

The next few days were so busy I forgot about the whole school thing. Antoe and I played outside all day long, and Chuck only whipped me once, for using up all his matches lighting a fire in the burning barrel. He told me he was doing it 'cause playing with matches was something the devil told me to do, but I knew he was just mad 'cause I'd used all his matches. Plus, he'd been drinking the night before and it had been raining all day. I noticed he was always in a bad mood the day after he'd been drinking and whenever it was raining.

Monday night we came back in from playing under the trees and Tracie told me I needed to go upstairs and take a good bath, 'cause tomorrow was the first day of school.

"Do I have to go?" I asked, knowing the answer. "I already know how to read and write."

"Do you?" She asked. "How'd you learn that?"

I just shrugged. I really didn't know how I learned, it seemed like I'd always known how. I was even trying to teach Antoe how to write his name, but I wasn't having much luck. He'd learn some letters and words one day and then by the next day he'd forget them.

"Can Antoe go too? He needs to learn."

"You know how bad he'd hate that. And don't say anything to him about it."

"Do I really have to go?" I asked her, hoping that like she did sometimes, she'd all of a sudden change her mind.

"Yeah, you gotta go." You're already gonna be older than all the other kids, but you're so little it won't matter much."

"How old will they be?"

"Six I guess."

Well, that was just great. Not only would I have to go to school, I'd have to go to school with a bunch of babies.

"Why can't I be with kids my age?"

"Cause you're starting late. Now go take a bath."

I wanted to argue some more about being with younger kids, and ask her if I could tell them my name was something else, but I did like she said and went to take a bath. I scrubbed real good, too, and even washed my hair. I thought about asking Tracie to braid it, she did sometimes, but then I heard Chuck talking in the hallway and heard the bedroom door slam so I figured they were going to bed. I got out of the tub and put on my cut off shorts and tee shirt, which is what I slept in most nights, and then I went down to my bedroom and made sure my book satchel and all the notebooks were in order. I pulled out my white dress and veil and laid it on the little dresser where I kept some of my clothes. Now that I was about to wear it, I wasn't sure I liked it as much. Or, maybe I did, but I didn't want to wear it to school. It would be a lot more fun to wear it at home.

The next morning, I woke up while it was still kinda dark out. I knew Tracie wouldn't get up and I wasn't exactly sure what time the bus would be there so I put on my white dress, and stuck the veil on. I meant to ask Tracie for some bobby pins to keep it on my head, but I forgot. Then I sat down on the bed to put on my black and white shoes but I couldn't find any socks. After I was dressed I went downstairs and got me a banana that was all black and squishy but would taste alright and went out on the porch. I knew I'd have to go wait for the bus at the end of our driveway. I'd seen it pass by for years.

As I was walking down the driveway eating my banana, my feet were already hurting in the black and white shoes, so I took them off and put them in a hollow stump at the end of the yard. They'd be alright there and I could put them on when I got home and Tracie wouldn't know. I knew she wouldn't care, but I knew

Chuck would and she might tell him on accident.

I got to the road and waited. And I waited. Tracie would kill me if I missed the bus, but since it didn't come, I guess that's what I'd done. I could hide out all day, but they might look for me or something and I'd get in worse trouble than if I went back and told her I'd missed the bus.

I looked up the road towards the Perone's store and didn't see a thing. I knew where the school was, it was straight down the road past our house. It never seemed like it was a long ride in the car, but I didn't know how long it would take me to walk there. There wasn't a thing to do but take off walking.

It was a narrow road, and curvy and not many cars ever drove by, and this morning, only two passed me. They didn't offer to stop either. I was beginning to get really hot and sweaty, and I knew my feet were getting real dirty, when I heard a loud sounding something coming up behind me.

I turned around and saw the yellow school bus chugging up the road. I wasn't sure it would stop for me since I wasn't standing at the driveway, so I put my book satchel down and jumped in the middle of the road and waved my arms.

Even though it was still a good ways up the road, the driver must've stomped on the brakes 'cause I heard the most awful screeching and moaning you could imagine.

I grabbed my satchel and jumped off in the ditch when it got to me. The driver opened the door, it was an older lady wearing overalls, with black and white hair, and she looked like she was in a real bad mood. She jumped out of her seat, still with a cigarette dangling from her mouth, down the steps, and grabbed me by both arms and shook me so hard my teeth rattled like the dice Antoe liked to play with.

"Don't you ever jump in the road when I'm coming, you little idiot!" The lady had a deep scratchy voice and all her shaking was causing me to feel dizzy and it knocked off my veil.

"Who the hell are you anyway?"

"Girl Bro-Bro-Brown, I'm starting school today." I managed to get out between shakes.

"Well why'n hell didn't you wait for me at your driveway?"

"I thought I was late, and you left me."

She let go of me and grunted.

"Well, get on and don't ever do that again. I'm gonna call your mother and make sure she waits with you from now on."

She told me to go sit my little butt down and she picked up my veil and handed it to me before she climbed in her seat that was way up high, and she watched me through the mirror as I made my way down the aisle. There were kids in every seat and they were laughing and staring at me. The kids who were sitting by themselves scooted over so I couldn't sit with them. I didn't want to anyway. I kept going till I found an empty seat in the very back. The driver had watched me go all the way back and then she hollered at everybody to turn around and the bus took off.

I stared out the window, and even though I had been down this road a bunch of times, it seemed like it was different 'cause I was in a big school bus instead of Chuck's old car. We turned on a gravel road that had so many holes in it I had to grab hold of the seat in front of me to keep from getting bounced off in the floor.

We pulled up in front of this crazy house that looked like something Antoe might've built out of his blocks; there were parts stacked on top of parts and it was all leaning everywhichway. The big bad wolf could've blown it down as easy as he did the straw and stick houses. There were a bunch of dogs running around, some goats and chickens, and old rusted cars setting everywhere. There was even an icebox that didn't have any door on the front porch, too.

Three boys were out in front, and they were push- ing and shoving each other out of the way, and then I remembered: I had come with Tracie here one time. It was where Chuck's momma and daddy lived and those three boys pushing and shoving each other were his baby brothers. One time, they came out to our house when me and Antoe were playing on the swings. They'd seen us out there and told us to get off, they wanted to swing, so Antoe ran down to the fruit cellar and I went with him.

When the driver opened up the doors of the bus, they ran down the aisle, still pushing and shoving, towards the back. Since I was sitting by myself, the biggest one plopped down beside me and the other two took the empty seat across from me. I gripped my book satchel even tighter and scooted way up against the window. I could tell he was looking me over.

"Hey Richie, lookit her feet! She ain't got no shoes on!"

He whacked the boy sitting across from him. Richie whacked him back, looked at my bare feet, snorted and elbowed the boy sitting next to him.

"Lookit her bare feet, Tiny!" The youngest one leaned out to look at my feet, and I pulled them up under me and kept staring out the window. Richie grabbed his nose like he was smelling something bad.

"God, I smell nasty feet!" The one beside me laughed. The little one, Tiny, just went to looking out the window.

"Hey Dale, what's she got on her head?" Dale was the big one sitting beside me.

"Let's see!" He grabbed my veil and pulled it off. I snatched for it but Dale was too quick.

"Hey, I know who she is." Dale still had my veil held up high so I couldn't reach it. "It's Tracie's kid, the one that's always with the big retard."

They all laughed then, and I didn't know what to do. I wanted my veil back, but I didn't wanna fight them for it, and if I did, they'd probably tear it up. So I just ignored them and hoped they'd get tired of it. But they didn't. They didn't like that I was ignoring them, and Richie leaned over across Dale and grabbed hold of my book satchel and started tugging on it.

"Whatcha got in here?" He kept tugging and I held on for dear life.

"Ain't she got nigger hair?" He let go of my bag and stared at me.

"Yeah, she does!" Dale agreed.

"Lemme see this bag, nigger hair." Dale reached over and started pulling, and he was stronger than Richie was, and he pulled it away from me.

He had it in his lap and was about to open it up when I grabbed for it. I managed to get it, but he started trying to pull it back and in the tug of war, the handle broke. Well, I got mad then and flew into him with my fists, punching and scratching.

"Leave me alone you goddamn bastard!" I screamed at the top of my lungs, still pounding anything I could reach. I managed to get my veil back and I was hitting him with the part that went on top of my head. It must've been sharp 'cause it scratched him all down the side of his face. Next thing I knew, the bus had stopped and the bus driver had jerked me up out of my seat, plopped me in the aisle in front of her, and marched me down to the front of the bus. I wondered if she was gonna throw me off, but she shoved me down in the first seat that was right behind her.

"Don't you move," she said, so I didn't.

When we finally got to the school, I jumped up to get off, but she put her arm out in front of me and made me wait until all the kids were off the bus. She got out of her seat and stood in front of me with her hands on her hips.

"Don't you know fighting is against the rules?"

I nodded, and then looked down at my poor veil, that was now ripped in half and covered in dirt. My book satchel was missing one of the handles, too.

"Then why'd you do it?" She asked.

"They took my stuff and wouldn't give it back," I said.

She didn't say anything for a second, then, "Look, I don't wanna get you in trouble on your very first day, just remember you can't fight, OK?"

I nodded again.

"And watch your language, too. Go on to your classroom, do you know where it is?"

"No."

"See that red brick building?" She pointed out the window. "Go through those big orange doors and somebody will be there to help you, OK?"

I nodded for the third time, stuffed my book satchel under my arm and wobbled off the bus. If there had been somewhere I could've run and hid, I would've. But I knew the driver was watching me, and besides that, I was already tired. I made my way through crowds of kids and grownups and opened up the big orange doors. When I went though, there were a lot of people, so I just stood off to the side. It smelled funny; like the place where I went to get shots when I broke my arm. A lady in a yellow dress with red hair came up to me with a notebook and a pencil and asked me my name and where my parents were.

"Well, my name is Girl...Girl Brown, but would you call me Cathy?"

"Is that your name?" The lady asked, still looking at her list.

"No, it's Girl, but-"

"Here you are!" She used her pencil to mark something on her list. "Where are your parents?"

"They're not here."

"OK, well..." She looked back at her notebook then she noticed my feet.

"Where on earth are your shoes?"

"They hurt so I took them off."

"Oh. Well...just come with me, we'll worry about your shoes later."

She took off down the hall without looking to see

if I was following or not. She was big, like Bettes was big, only Bettes wore long dresses, and this lady had on a real short skirt and you could see her fat jiggling as she walked. She also made a screetch-screetch noise, too, and I wanted to laugh it sounded so funny. Then the screetching stopped and I almost bumped into the back of her.

"Here you are, sweetie; this is Mrs. Huitt's class-room. She is your homeroom teacher, so just go on in-side and have a seat. I noticed that there were pink and blue kittens outside the room, running up and down the wall. All the kittens had names on them so I looked for mine. I found it, GIRL, and wouldn't you know it? My kitten was cross-eyed.

I went into the classroom then, and saw all these desks lined up in a row. A little tiny grey haired woman came over to me.

"Welcome, young lady. And what is your name?"

"Girl Brown. But you can call me Cathy."

"Is your mother with you?" She asked, looking around the room for some lady who looked like she might be with me. She didn't even answer about calling me Cathy.

"No, she couldn't come. She had to work."

"Well, aren't you the brave girl to come by yourself! Now go find a seat, anywhere you like, and the bell will be ringing soon."

I wandered back towards the back of the room, and there were grownups standing all around, and the kids were mostly sitting in the desks. A few people looked at me, but they didn't stare like the ones on the bus. I saw an empty seat, next to a little girl who was the color of a Hershey bar. I put my broken book satchel down beside the desk and slid into it.

The desk had a groove at the top, where you could put your pencil and it wouldn't roll off, and there was a little drawer that opened up. I pulled it out and all it had in it was broken chalk pieces and some chewed up gum.

I looked over at the chocolate girl and she was staring right at me. She had on a faded pink dress that looked old, but was clean as a whistle. I looked down and noticed my white dress was sorta brown in places now. The girl had tiny braids all over her head, and they all had little shiny pink balls on the ends of them. I made up my mind to ask Tracie for some of those pink balls for my hair, too.

"You ain't got no shoes on." She told me, like I didn't know.

"I don't wear shoes," I said. "They hurt my feet."

She looked at me for a second longer, and then turned her eyes back towards the front. She didn't have a grownup with her either. Or at least, I didn't see anybody who could've been her mother. I'd seen chocolate people around Lakeside, and when we went to Greenville, but I didn't know any of them, so I was kinda interested in looking at the girl. She was so black she was shiny, and I wondered if I touched her face, would the black rub off on me.

I was thinking about asking her something, so she'd talk to me some more, when I heard a loud bell ring. The grownups started to hug and kiss their kids bye and then they all left. One little girl, who was wearing a fancy blue dress with ribbons and lace and bows, started bawling at the top of her lungs. But as soon as the lady with her left, she flounced her shoulder and looked mean-eyed around the room. She noticed my bare feet and snurled up her nose like she was smelling something bad.

"OK boys and girls, let's be quiet please. We have a lot of things to talk about today, the first day of your educational journey."

Mrs. Huitt was one of those grownups who talked to kids like she really liked them, but you just knew she didn't. She kept on going about all the things we'd be learning, but I stopped listening to her. I was busy thinking about Antoe, and wondering what he was doing, when I heard her call my name.

"Yeah?"

"Girl, you're supposed to say yes, ma'am and you're supposed to say present when I call your name, weren't you listening to me?"

"I'm sorry. I forgot." I said.

"OK, we'll remember next time, won't we? Now why don't you stand up and tell us something about yourself."

So I stood up. But I didn't know what exactly to tell them.

"I live with Tracie and Antoe. And Chuck. But only him sometimes. We live in a big house with fun trees to climb. And we have the best swing in the world." And then I sat back down.

Mrs. Huitt didn't say anything; she just went on to call the other kids' names. When they stood up, they told things like "I like to color," and "I have two brothers and a sister," and "I like helping Mommy cook for Daddy." When she called out the name Cerese Miller, the little black girl beside me stood up.

"Present, ma'am. I have an older brother, and a Mommy, only I ain't got a daddy. He's up with Jesus. I like to play with my dolls." Then she tossed her head and all the little pink balls clacked together.

This went on for a good while, then Mrs. Huitt got up and said we were gonna learn the alphabet. Well, I already knew all that so I pulled a book off the shelf that was behind me and opened it up to read while they were making the sounds of the letters. It was a pretty stupid book, though, all about Dick and Jane, and they had a dog and a cat named Spot and Puff. If I had a dog, I sure wouldn't name it something dumb like Spot. That was almost as bad as Girl.

As I was reading that book, I realized I had to pee bad, so I got up and went down front to ask Mrs. Huitt where the bathroom was. She didn't like that one little bit.

"Young lady, we do not get up and wander while we are having class. Now go sit down this minute!" I thought about telling her how bad I had to pee, but it probably wouldn't do no good. As I was going back to sit down that bell rang again and she told us all to line up for recess. I stood up and followed the kids in front of me, and when I got to Mrs. Huitt's desk, she noticed my bare feet for the first time and snatched me out of line.

"Where are your shoes? She asked me, looking back to where I had been sitting, like I might've taken them off or something.

And for what felt like the hundredth time, I had to tell somebody that my shoes hurt my feet and I didn't wanna wear them.

"Well, you simply cannot go outside with bare feet. You might step on glass and cut yourself. You'll have to stay here and I'll have to go see if there are some shoes in the lost and found for you to wear."

She went sailing out of the room before I could ask her where the bathroom was. I had to pee so bad by now that I had to hold myself and jump up and down to keep it from coming out. I saw a big trash can that was setting by the door and I grabbed it, pulled my skirt up, and squatted over it and just peed and peed and peed. After I yanked my underwear up, I looked in the trash can to see if you could tell pee was there, but you couldn't. Anyway, it was better than peeing in my pants like Antoe.

I was sitting in my desk when Mrs. Huitt came back with a pair of muddy old tenny shoes with no laces.

"Here, put these on. They might be too big, but it's better than cutting your feet on something. I want you to give this note to your mother when you get home."

I didn't want to put on those smelly old shoes, but Mrs. Huitt looked like she was in a bad mood by now so I just took them from her and jammed my feet in them. They were way too big and they stuck out a mile. They were ugly, too, shit brown with yellow stripes down the sides.

I thought maybe I might get to go outside, but the bell rang again. The rest of the kids came tromping back in and they were all sweaty and red faced from running and playing. I was mad when I thought about how much more fun I would be having at home with Antoe, and I made up my mind that this was the last day I'd be going to school.

Mrs. Huitt started talking again and I went back to reading the stupid book. Pretty soon she said for us to take out our crayons 'cause we were going to color. She called Jennifer to come pass out the color sheets, and announced that Jennifer was the teacher's helper for this week. It was the girl in the fancy blue dress who'd looked at my feet and made a face. She made a big deal about putting every color sheet just perfectly on the desks, but when she came to Cerese's desk, she dropped it on the floor. Then she walked behind her desk and came over to mine and just stood staring down at my feet in those ugly brown shoes.

"You better pick that up," I said, but she just stuck her nose in the air and threw mine down, too. I got up and picked up both of the sheets and handed one to Cerese. She grinned at me then, and I saw she had a nice big gap where she was missing her two front teeth. I'd lost mine a while ago and was mad when new ones grew back.

I picked up my sheet and saw it was a dumb looking picture of a school house with kids playing in front. I turned it over and started to use my colors to draw a picture of birds, and trees, and a lake, with a big rainbow over it all. I even drew a big turtle sitting on a log. I had just finished it when Mrs. Huitt told us to hold our pages up so she could see how well we'd done. She started to walk around the room, and she was saying how pretty they all were, and she made a big deal out of putting a gold star on everybody's page. Then she stopped at my desk. She picked up my paper, then turned it over and saw that I'd left the front blank.

"Why didn't you color this?"

I shrugged and her mouth got real tight like she didn't much like that.

"I told you to color the picture. You did not follow my directions. Therefore, you do not get a star today."

Well, big fat deal, I thought to myself. I could get me a whole big box of stickers and I could put as many as I wanted to on it. That bell rang for the fourth time that morning, and Mrs. Huitt told us it was time to go eat lunch. She said she would take up our lunch money at the door. Tracie must've not known about me needing to bring money. I didn't have any and I was sure hungry. When I got to Mrs. Huitt, I told her I'd forgot my money.

"Just like your shoes, I suppose." She walked over to her purse and got some money out. "You'll have to bring fifty cents tomorrow," she said. "Twenty-five for your lunch today and twenty-five for lunch tomorrow. I'll explain it all, again, in the note I'm writing to your mother."

She was mad; I could tell. Her cheeks had two bright red spots.

"Come on boys and girls, let's get in line and walk to lunch. No pushing, no running and no talking."

She went to the head of the line and all the kids got in behind her. I waited until I was the very last one. We walked all the way down a long hallway, where there were other rooms full of other kids, and out two big doors at the end. When we got outside, there was a sidewalk with a roof over it and we walked down that until we came to another building with two big doors, dirty white ones, and we went through that to the place where we would eat. It smelled good.

We all stayed in that line until we got to a counter where ladies were putting hamburgers, French fries, some kind of fruit, cookies, and an apple on these square metal trays that had little scooped out places for the food. I got a tray and a carton of chocolate milk and went to find me a seat at long tables with metal chairs. I looked around at all the kids sitting together, and I didn't want to sit with people I didn't know. So I was about to go to a table way in the back and sit by myself when I saw Cerese sitting with an older black boy, and two older black girls. I walked to where they were and asked:

"Can I sit with you?"

The older boy said, "Hell no, I ain't sitting with no honkies."

"Shut up Brady, I'll tell momma," Cerese said.

Brady just gave her a look, jumped up and grabbed his tray and left. The two girls just ignored us and kept on talking to each other.

"He's my brother," Cerese said, "and he's stupid. What's your name?"

"Girl Brown." I told her.

"That's a funny name. Why do they call you that?"

I shrugged my shoulders. "You can call me Susie."

"Is your name Susie?"

"Not really, but I like that better'n Girl."

Cerese was staring at me and I went back to eating

my hamburger.

"Do you have a daddy?" She finally asked me.

"No," I said, through a mouthful of french-fries.

"I don't either, he passed," she said. Then she asked, "Did yours pass too?"

"Uh uh, I ain't ever had one. "

"Are you a bastard then?" It was one of the older girls who'd stopped talking to her friend long enough to listen to us.

"No. That's what Chuck is. Tracie calls him a drunk ass bastard, or sometimes she calls him a god-damn bastard."

They all just stared at me then, and I heard "Ooooo I'm gonna tell!" It was Jennifer: the fancy dress girl who'd thrown Cerese's color sheet in the floor.

"I'm gonna tell Mrs. Huitt you said bad words!"

And off she ran to tell on me. She leaned down and whispered in Mrs. Huitt's ear, and then pointed over to me. Mrs. Huitt jumped up and made a beeline to where I was sitting. She grabbed me up out of my chair and didn't even give me a chance to pick up my tray, but I managed to snatch the apple. She pulled me out the dirty white doors and down the sidewalk without say-ing a word. Then she yanked those second doors open like they were on fire.

We walked all the way past the room where I'd sat all morning, turned a corner and headed down another hallway. We came to a door that had glass on the front and Mrs. Huitt pushed me through it. There were black chairs lined up against the walls and she pointed me towards one, then walked over and said something to a lady who was sitting behind a big counter. The lady got up and walked into another room and Mrs. Huitt left without giving me one look.

I sat down in one of those metal chairs, and they were cold and hard. I was thinking about standing up and waiting when the lady came back and motioned me to follow her. I walked around the counter and into another room that had more chairs, only these were wooden ones and had cushions, and a desk that was almost as big as Toomie, and there was a white haired man sitting behind the big desk. There were furry grey rugs on the floor that reminded me of Toomie, too. I thought about taking off the ugly brown shoes so I could feel it on my feet. The man stood up then walked around his desk and held out his hand to me. He was so tall, way taller than anybody I'd ever seen before, and his hair was just as white as it could be, and it was kinda long, but not all the way long like Chuck's was.

"I'm Mr. Pat, and what is your name?

"Girl Brown."

"Is that your real name?" he asked.

"Yeah, I mean, yes sir, but I don't know why that's my name, it just is. If you don't like it, you could call me

Cindy." I told him.

"I see," he said. "Why don't you sit down and let's have a little talk?"

So I sat down in one of the big chairs that were in front of his desk, and he stood in front of his desk and leaned back on it.

"It seems like you've had a pretty rough start to school, haven't you?"

"I guess so," I said.

"Why don't you tell me about your day?"

I thought for a minute.

"Well, I didn't wanna wear shoes, 'cause they hurt, then I thought I was late, but I wasn't. We had to sit all morning, and Mrs. Huitt wouldn't let me go outside 'cause I didn't have on shoes, and I had to pee in the trashcan, and I know I wasn't supposed to, but I had to go that bad, and then we went to lunch and a girl asked me if I was a bastard, and I told her no, that Chuck was a drunk ass bastard or a goddamn bastard, at least that's what Tracie says he is, and now I'm here."

"I see." He said again, and he pulled out his handkerchief and wiped his face with it, and he was kinda shaking all over and making snorting noises. I was about to ask him if he was alright, when he looked up at me but he kinda kept his handkerchief over his mouth and his eyes were all crinkled up at the corners.

"Well, Girl, I think that you'll be fine, but I want

you to understand you cannot go to the bathroom in a trashcan, and you cannot say ugly words at school, and you must wear your shoes, even if they hurt. Now if you can do that, I don't think you'll have any more problems. Will you promise me you'll try?"

I told him I would and then I heard the bell ring again. I jumped up to go, 'cause I knew by now that's what that sound meant, but he told me to sit back down.

"I bet you didn't get to finish your lunch, did you?"

I shook my head.

"Are you hungry?" He asked me, and I told him I was. He told me to just have a seat and he would bring me something to eat.

So I did, and he left. I kicked off those ugly shoes then, and rubbed my bare feet on the rug. It was soft like Toomie was, and then I got down in the floor and stretched out. I was about to drift off to sleep when Mr. Pat came back in and I jumped up like I was shot out of something.

"Taking a nap?" He asked me. "I'd like to do that myself. They'd already put up the leftovers in the cafeteria, so I went across the street to the dairy bar and got you something. Would you like a hot dog, hamburger, or a corndog?"

"Yes," I said.

He laughed and laughed and handed me the sack and I sat right down and ate it all. There were even

French fries. When I finished, he walked me back to class, shook my hand, and told me he wanted me to have a good day. I liked him; he was a nice man, and he was the first nice person I'd met, besides Cerese and the bus driver, all day long.

THREE

Nothing else bad happened the rest of the day, it was just long and boring. When the last bell rang, I was glad. We had to get our stuff and walk outside in a line. They liked kids to be in lines, I could tell that. There were teachers with pieces of paper they were looking at and they were telling all the kids which bus they were supposed to get on. I already saw my bus, 'cause I'd noticed it had a big dent in the front that had red and white paint on it, but I stayed in the line until a lady told me I was always to get on bus number 4. I took off towards it and since the seat behind the driver was empty, I sat down behind her. Chuck's brothers got on but they didn't see me.

It didn't take long to get to my house. I waited till the bus driver stopped and opened the doors and I flew down the steps and up the driveway.

Chuck's old green car was gone and when I was on the porch I heard an awful racket. I went through the front room to the kitchen and Antoe had the big skillet and was beating hell out of the cabinets and squalling at the top of his lungs. Tracie must've been gone, too, or she'd have been downstairs trying to kill him.

In the middle of a squall he looked over and saw me and dropped the skillet and grabbed me up and hugged me half to death.

"Ow, Antoe, you're squishing me!" I said, and he put me down.

"Where Girl go? Girl not go 'morrow. Tonio not like being 'lone."

I didn't tell him I had to go to school every day from now on, 'cause it'd just make him cry more, and he wouldn't remember it anyway.

"Did you shit your pants?" I could smell something bad.

He didn't answer, but I knew he had. Sometimes when he'd get worked up, he'd shit his pants. I would have to get him to take a bath before he went to bed. Or else hose him off with the water hose behind the house.

I pulled out the apple I had grabbed from my lunch tray and handed it to him. He took it and immediately carried it downstairs. I knew he wouldn't eat it. When he came back upstairs he said, "Tonio hungry, we eat?"

I wasn't really hungry after all the food Mr. Pat

brought me, but I started looking for something for Antoe. Most everything we liked to eat was already gone,
but I fixed him three mayonnaise sandwiches and a
glass of ice water. He sat down at the kitchen table, gobbled them down, and then went back downstairs. I was
putting up the bread and mayonnaise when I heard a
car door slam. I ran to push aside the dusty curtains in
the front room window and peek out. It was Bettes and
Tracie, only Bettes didn't get out. She just stopped long
enough for Tracie to jump out then she was gone. I went
out on the front porch to meet her.

"Hey, school girl, how'd it go today?" She said as she
was coming up the stairs and then past me through the
front door.

"OK." I followed her thinking about the letter I had
in my book satchel but I already knew I wasn't giving
it to her.

"Do I have to go tomorrow?

"Yeah, you'll have to go till you're eighteen, I guess.
Or is it sixteen? I forget."

"That long?"

"That long. Longer if you go to college." She
stared at me.

"Did you go to school that long?" I asked just to
change the subject, 'cause she was looking at me weird.

"Nah, I quit."

"That's what I'm gonna do then." She just smiled

and went to the icebox to get out her tea. She sat down at the table and lit a cigarette.

"Where's Chuck?" I asked, although I didn't care.

"He went to his parent's house. Why?"

"I just wondered," I said.

She was staring at me. "What the hell are you wearing?"

Hellshitdamn. I forgot to change clothes and I forgot about my shoes in the stump.

"It's one of my new dresses."

"That's a communion dress."

"Yeah, the lady said. What's communion?"

"Why'n hell would you want a dress like that? What else did you buy?"

"Some skirts and tops."

"And where're your goddamn shoes? Don't tell me you didn't wear any? Goddamn, Girl." She pushed her cigarette down in the ashtray to put it out and looked like she was about to get really mad.

"No, I just took them off when I came home," I lied. "They were hurting my feet."

She sighed, picked up her tea glass and went towards the front room. I followed her and she flopped down on our bright blue, furry couch that I'd named Toomie a long time ago. I stood behind Toomie now, picking at a piece of tape somebody had put over a place that was torn open and part of his insides were sticking out.

"What else did you do?" She asked.

"Not much, it was boring. I sat with a girl who was nice," I said.

"That's good, run upstairs and get me my other pack of cigarettes, please." So I ran upstairs and got her brown case that had her other cigarettes in it, the regular white kind, not the pink kind, and took it downstairs and handed it to her. I was wondering how much about the day I should tell her, and then I figured if I told her a little bit, she probably wouldn't find out about it all.

"I got in trouble," I said.

She looked at me. "For what?"

"Some girl, Jennifer, she told on me for saying a bad word."

"Girl, you can't say cuss words at school, 'cause I don't wanna bunch of nosey bastards coming around trying to find out why you talk like you do. Zip it, OK?"

"OK. Did I have a daddy who passed?"

"Why're you asking that?"

"Everybody was talking about Momma's and Daddy's and they all asked me about mine, and I told them I didn't have either one. You're sure you're not? My momma, I mean?" I thought I'd check just one more time.

"Nope, I'm not momma material. Just don't pay any attention to them when they ask you shit like that, you hear?"

"Do you have a momma or a daddy?"

"Nope. Mine've been dead a long time. Now go play

so I can drink my tea in peace, OK?"

"Oh yeah, I gotta have fifty cents for lunch money tomorrow. Mrs. Huitt said she already told you about lunch money." And then before she could get mad, "Can me and Antoe go down to Perone's?"

Both of us loved going to the Perone's store, just right down the road, and I still had that twenty dollars from the trip to Greenville. We needed some candy to make up for the bad day both of us had.

"OK, but be back before it gets dark. You know Tonio will freak out if he has to walk past the trees."

I went down to the fruit cellar to get Antoe and to get my money from my secret box. He was always glad to go to the Perone's 'cause he loved both of them. And Antoe didn't like most people.

"C'mon Antoe, we're going down to Perone's." He was sitting on his bed of quilts and he had something in his hand.

"Here. Made for Girl." He handed me the apple I'd given him, only it wasn't an apple anymore, it was a little woman. Antoe could carve anything; he'd swipe all the bars of soap from the house and I'd have to get them back from him and wash with cows or dogs or ducks or whatever he'd carved them into.

"That's pretty." I told him, and it was too. "I'm gonna carry it to show Mrs. Perone, OK?"

"Yeah, show Perone's." And he held out his hand for

me to take it, and we left the house and started walking down the road in the direction of the Perone's store.

I got another whiff of Antoe then, and I remembered that he still had on shitty pants. Well, there wasn't nothing to do but go on and hope nobody else smelled him. I knew it wouldn't make no difference to Antoe if he stunk or not.

It wasn't far, just down the road and around a real sharp curve, but it was still hot so we took our time. The great thing about Antoe was he didn't care if we talked or not. It was kinda nice to be quiet after the day at school. I had a feeling that school would always be like that, too. It was kinda like when you wanted to be quiet, they wanted you to talk and then when you wanted to talk, they wanted you to shut up.

We rounded the curve and saw the store up ahead. It was the place where all the fishermen came to buy their fish bait and snacks and gas. Tracie sometimes bought stuff for us there, only she never gave them any money but wrote her name down in a little book.

There were places behind the store where the fishermen could back their trucks up to the water and get their boats out. I liked to sit out there and watch the boats go by; some were great big boats with loud motors and some were just little ones that they had to paddle with big round wooden paddles. Antoe loved the boats too, and he'd get so interested in watching them that I'd have to make sure we were way out of the way so nobody would run over him.

The Perone's store sat back from the road, in a big parking lot that was black and lumpy, and the black lumps were hot and rough on my bare feet. The store wasn't very big, and it was all peeling paint and grey boards. There were red gas pumps in front, two of them, and the gasoline smell was strong—sweet smelling, but it burned my nose at the same time. Kinda like the way Tracie's pink cigarettes did. There was a bench outside the store, and Mr. Perone was sitting there in his overalls like he always did.

"Hey there, Girl, 'Tonio, what y'all up to?" Mr. Perone had a huge stomach that stuck way out in front of his dirty green overalls, and he didn't have any teeth at all. He said he had some false ones but they hurt so he didn't wear them. Mrs. Perone said they were his Sunday teeth. Mr. Perone was a preacher, like Chuck, only he wasn't nothing like Chuck. Him and Mrs. Perone told me and Antoe we could come to church with them sometime. I loved to watch Mr. Perone eat potato chips with no teeth 'cause it was a real mess, worse than Antoe even.

"We're gonna buy us some candy," I said, as Antoe plopped down right beside him. Mr. Perone was whittling away on a stick and Antoe wanted to watch him.

"What doin?" Antoe asked him.

"Oh, I'm just killing time, whittlin' on this here stick."

"Antoe whittle, made doll. Show doll, Girl."

I pulled out the doll Antoe had carved from the apple. It had started to turn dark. Mr. Perone took it and looked it over carefully.

"You do this?" Mr. Perone asked, and Antoe nodded.

"Well, I be dog. That's good, son, real good. Lemme go out here and see if I can't find you some good wood to work on. You gotta have the right kinda wood, not too soft, not too hard. That'd be better than an apple."

He huffed up off the bench and motioned Antoe to follow him out around the store, out towards the back, where he and Mrs. Perone had a trailer house they lived in. I thought about following them, but decided I'd rather go and pick out candy without Antoe. Sometimes he'd open it up right there in the store and eat it, and Mrs. Perone never made us pay for it, but I felt bad whenever he'd do that. That's the thing I never, ever did: I might swipe from Woolworths or the dime store, but I never did from the Perone's.

I pushed open the door to the store, and it was real cool in there. Mrs. Perone always wore a sweater, even when it was so hot you couldn't breathe outside. She always said she had to keep it that cold on account of Mr. Perone had trouble breathing. I figured it was 'cause he was so fat; he always sweated something awful.

"Well, hey there, little Miss Girl. Or am I 'posed to call you something else today?" Mrs. Perone was a little bitty woman, not much taller than me. She was skinny as a stick, too. I wondered if Mr. Perone ate up all their food like Antoe did.

"Hey, Mrs. Perone, you can just call me Girl for today."

"I hear you went to school today, how'd you like it?"

"I didn't. But I gotta go back, for a long time, till I'm eighteen."

"Well, yeah, you wanna be smart doncha?"

"I guess."

"What can I get for you today?"

"I'm gonna get me and Antoe some candy." I pulled out the twenty dollar bill I'd been saving since the Greenville trip.

"My, you'll be sick if you eat that much candy."

"We won't eat it all at once. Or at least I won't. I'll hide it so Antoe won't either."

I started to look around the store then. Mrs. Perone went back behind the counter; 'cause she knew I liked to look at everything before I settled down to choose my candy. I went back and looked at the box where they kept all the crickets, watching them squirm and jump all over the place. They stunk to high heaven, and there were all these raw potatoes in the box. I asked what they were for and Mrs. Perone told me that's what they ate. I didn't blame them, either; I liked to eat raw potatoes myself.

Then I wandered back and looked at the little bitty fish swimming around in the water. It was almost like a little pond, there was so much water in there. It was lots bigger than our bathtub and I thought it might be fun to play in. Only thing was, I wasn't sure if those little fish would bite or not. They were called minnows, and the fisherman used them for bait on the ends of their hooks. Mrs. Perone let me throw some food to them 'cause I liked seeing them jump up out of the water to grab those little brown bits of food. They acted like they were starving to death. I fed them a couple of handfuls then I made my way back out to the main part of the store to finally begin looking over the candy and deciding what to get.

I didn't have to ask Antoe; he liked it all. I was standing in front of the wire racks, where all the bags of candy were hanging. I was trying to make up my mind between a bag of Bit O' Honeys and some Slapstix. I finally figured the Bit O' Honeys would last the longest, and I had just pulled the bag off the hanger, when I heard screaming, hollering, and yelling from outside the store. I could tell it was Antoe so I dropped the candy and went tearing outside wondering what he'd gotten into now. Mrs. Perone was right behind me, and she could move pretty fast for an old lady.

We both ran around towards their trailer and there were Chuck's brothers, Richie, Dale, and Tiny, and two older boys I didn't know. They were circled around with Antoe in the middle, and they were grabbing him and spinning him around to make him dizzy. Tiny, the youngest one would wait until he was staggering and run up and whack him across the head with a big stick.

"Stop it this minute, you boys get out of here and leave him alone!" Mrs. Perone was yelling at them, but they sure didn't listen to her. I thought for a minute she might sail in the middle of them but then she took off towards the trailer to get Mr. Perone.

Well, I just stood there for a second trying to figure out what to do. I knew I couldn't help Antoe by myself, so I looked around to see what I could use. I saw an old rusted can that was sitting beside the house, and I ran over to it and picked it up. It was full of something that smelled like gas. I ran over to where the boys were beating up Antoe and screamed, "Get down, Antoe!"

He immediately fell to the ground and covered his head. I threw what was in the can straight at the boys and I hit Richie smack in the face with it. Richie grabbed for his eyes and started hollering and screaming like you wouldn't believe. He was jumping up and down and rubbing his eyes with his shirt. I hoped he was blind. They shouldn't have been beating up Antoe.

The rest of the boys were trying to figure out what was wrong with Richie, and they were all yelling at him, when I saw Chuck come hopping around from the front of the store. I didn't know he was there, but he flew into the middle of the boys, and grabbed Richie and tried to figure out what was wrong. Richie just kept screaming and rubbing his eyes. Chuck finally dragged him over to the side of the store where there was a water faucet. He turned it on and stuck Richie's head under it and started to wash out his eyes.

Mrs. Perone came flying back around then, and right behind her was Mr. Perone, huffing and puffing, and moving as fast as he could. Antoe was still on the ground curled up in a ball. I went over to him then, and moved his hands away from his face.

"It's OK Antoe, they're gone," I said, and he peeked up at me and grinned. He had a bunch of scratches on his face, and his nose was bleeding. I held out my hand and he got up just as Mr. and Mrs. Perone got to us.

"You poor little lamb, come on with me and I'll clean you up." Mrs. Perone took Antoe by the hand and started to pull him towards the store. I knew Chuck was still washing out Richie's eyes, so I made sure I was on the other side of her, as close as I could get. I peeked out of the corner of my eye and I could see Chuck straighten up and stare at me. I walked a little bit faster. Mrs. Perone was grumbling.

"I swan, I don't know what's wrong with them Carter boys, they're all hellions, just plain old hellions." I didn't know what a hellion was but decided it must be bad. I wondered if she thought Chuck was a hellion, too.

She led Antoe into the back of the store, where the minnows were, and sat him down on a bench and went and got a wet rag. She started to wipe his face and clean up the blood and I couldn't believe he let her. Usually Antoe hated having his face washed. While she was cleaning him up, I remembered dropping the bag of candy, so I went back out to the store to get it. I got the Bit O' Honeys, and I got a big bag of Now N'Laters, and some Smoothie Bars, 'cause I liked the little cardboard coins that came in the back. I took it all up to the front and put it on the counter and waited for Mrs. Perone to come tell me how much money I needed to give her.

I was just waiting at the counter when someone grabbed my shoulder, hard and turned me around so that I almost lost my balance.

"You threw gas in Richie's eyes! Don't you know that could've blinded him?" Chuck was so mad he was only talking in a whisper. His eyes were red, and he smelled like the brown stuff in the bottle.

"You better get your little ass home, you're gonna get it, do you understand me?"

He was hurting my shoulder in a bad way, but I just nodded my head. He let go of me then, and turned around and I watched him make his up and down way out the door. Mrs. Perone led Antoe back in, and went behind the counter to total up our candy. She put it all in a bag for us, and I gave her the money and she gave me change, but my mind was on what was gonna happen when we got home.

"Thanks Mrs. Perone." I remembered to say and me and Antoe started the walk home. He didn't look too bad, he just had some scratches on his face, but he was real happy 'cause Mr. Perone had given him a shiny pocket knife to carve wood with and he'd given him some chunks of wood.

"Girl, look!" He dug around in his sack and pulled out the knife and opened it up and showed me the huge blade.

"You better not let Chuck see that," I said, and wished I hadn't, 'cause he started to look around like Chuck was right behind us. When he didn't see him, he closed the knife up and shoved it in his pocket. The walk home wasn't nearly as long as I'd liked for it to be.

"Antoe, go to the fruit cellar." I pushed him towards the side of the house, where the back door was that we used to get down to the fruit cellar when it wasn't safe to go in the front door. I knew he'd hide until I told him it was OK. This was the only way I could keep him from getting beat up by Chuck. Chuck would take it out on whoever was closest and that was usually me.

I took my time going up the steps real slow and I stopped on the porch and took some deep breaths. Chuck slammed open the door like he was waiting for me, and grabbed me and dragged me inside, causing me to drop my bag of candy on the porch. He didn't even wait to take me in the front room like he usually did; he already had his belt off and swinging. Sometimes when he smelled like the brown stuff, like he did now, he didn't aim very well and I was able to get off without bruises. Not this time though. He might've not landed every lick, but he was swinging twice as hard as he usually did. I made a point to never, ever cry when he whipped me, but this time I thought I was gonna disgrace myself by screaming and begging, when all of a sudden he stopped. That was both a good and a bad thing. The good thing was, it wasn't hurting anymore, but the bad thing was, I knew what was gonna come next, and really, I'd rather he kept on beating me till I was dead. It was quiet except for his breathing, and I heard the belt jangle on the floor where he dropped it.

Next, I heard him go to the cabinet where he kept the brown stuff. I thought about running like hell, but I wasn't sure how much he'd had already. Sometimes it was just better to stay there and get it over with, 'cause if he had time to think about it, it made it worse.

I heard him swallowing, and then he came up behind me and put his arms around me.

"You know how bad I hate whipping you, don't you?" He asked but I didn't say anything.

"It don't make me feel good at all. But you could've

blinded Richie by throwing that gas an' shit in his eyes! Why'n hell you do that for?" He gave me a little shake and I knew I better answer.

"They were beating Antoe."

"Yeah, so what? He's big enough to take up for himself, and if he ain't, tough. But I'll forgive you this time, 'cause Jesus forgives, even the most miserable of sinners."

He shoved me on my knees and yanked my arms around in back of me. He made sure I was kneeling where the floor was warped and coming up in places, and there were splinters all sticking up and they were sticking straight in my knees.

"You're gonna kneel there and think about what you've done and pray for forgiveness, 'cause Jesus'll forgive you. He forgives everybody, most everybody. Jesus and me are like this." He held up two of his fingers that were wrapped on top of each other.

"We're thick. He don't like no gooks an' he don't like no shit from no sassy kids." He took a big deep drink from the bottle. All I had to say about that, if Jesus was so thick with him, then I didn't want no part of Jesus.

He made me kneel there for what seemed like hours. My knees felt numb and sore from all the splinters, plus my legs and behind hurt like crazy from the belt. Chuck stomped and snorted and talked about Jesus, and how he was a "chosen one" whatever that meant. Finally when I thought I was gonna have to beg him to let me up, he put the empty bottle down and hauled me up to my feet.

"You know I don't like doing this, don't you?" He hugged me tight to his chest.

"Don't you? I think about you like you're my own daughter, you know that don't you? He asked again and shook me a little.

"Yes." He laid his face on mine and that beard scratched something awful, then he kissed me on my forehead, and I felt like my face was on fire. He let me go then and I was about to run downstairs when there was a horrible BAM! BAM! BAM! from outside. It was probably some of the people who came to our house; their cars would always make sounds like a gun shooting.

Chuck heard that noise and he jumped like a mile in the air then he fell down on his belly and wiggled across the floor with his fake leg thumping like all get out. It was so funny looking I forgot to run and just watched to see what he'd do next. He got to the window and pulled himself up to peek out, all the while looking around the way Antoe did when he thought something was gonna jump out of the dark. Then there was sounds of boots tromping across the porch and he hopped over to the door and yanked it open. Well, I didn't hang around after that but hightailed it to the fruit cellar.

I remembered on the way down, that I'd dropped my bag of candy on the porch, so I went out the back door in the washing machine room, around the house, and I looked around the corner to make sure whoever it was had gone in the house. Nobody was out there and my sack of candy was laying right where I dropped it so I snatched it up and ran downstairs as fast as I could. Antoe had the door locked, like I'd taught him to do, and I knocked on it and whispered as loud as I could, "It's me Antoe, I got candy." Well, he opened it up quick and I gave him the bag of Bit O'Honeys and he was real happy. I plopped down on our quilt bed to work on the Now N'Laters, while I checked out my bruises.

There wasn't that many of them, the only bad thing was they'd show when I wore those stupid dresses to school. Antoe was smelling bad by now, and I knew we oughta go upstairs to clean him up, but I could still hear Chuck and somebody out in the kitchen talking and laughing.

They were probably drinking more brown stuff, too. And after whoever it was went home, Chuck would be all worked up. He'd holler and carry on something awful about Charlie all night long. See, whenever he wasn't yelling about Jesus, or acting like something was trying to get him, he'd be hollering about Charlie and I didn't know who Charlie was, but I figured it was somebody who'd done something pretty bad to Chuck. Whoever Charlie was, I wished I could thank him.

FOUR

After that first day, nothing really happened at school, good or bad. I didn't like it much and it was real boring. Even though I was as little as the rest of the kids, I knew a whole lot more than they did. I found out I should've been in the third grade, but they wouldn't let me go there on account of me never going to school before.

On the bus I always sat behind Mrs. Kat, the bus driver, and Dale, Richie, and Tiny always sat in the very back of the bus, like on that first day when we got in a fight. They stared at me real mean whenever they saw me, but they didn't bother me. I wondered if they'd got in trouble for beating up Antoe, but figured they didn't. I was just glad they were leaving me alone.

Me and Cerese sat together in the lunch room every day, and nobody ever sat with us. Not even her brother Brady, 'cause she told me he was in tenth grade and he just came to check on her that first morning. The other two girls who were sitting with them never sat with us anymore either. Cerese said they were in the sixth grade and the only reason they were there that day was 'cause they liked Brady. She said her momma said girls like that were fast and that wasn't a good way to be.

Jennifer, the one who'd told on me, acted like she couldn't even see us. She was always with a big crowd of girls, and they sat up front in the cafeteria, by the teachers. They were always bringing dolls and stuff to school, and they always played with them at recess. Me and Cerese would swing, or if the swings were all full, we'd just walk around the playground.

I was always real glad when Friday afternoon came 'cause it was the best time of the week. Chuck and Tracie would usually go somewhere and be gone all night so me and Antoe would have the house to ourselves. Most times we'd sleep down in the fruit cellar, but sometimes we'd go upstairs and camp out in one of the empty bedrooms. We'd found an old tent and put it up and we'd play like we were in a different country. I liked Africa, 'cause of all the animals we were learning about in school. Antoe always wanted to be somewhere it was cold so he could play in the snow. He didn't like hot weather 'cause he was pretty fat and sweated a lot, like Mr. Perone.

On Saturday mornings we'd watch cartoons on our

old black and white TV set. I loved Penelope Pittstop, and Batman, and whenever I could, I'd make Antoe play Batman with me. I loved being Batgirl, only Antoe wouldn't be Batman, he only wanted to be the Penguin so he could wobble from side to side, and if I could find it, he'd use Chuck's cane. I was always real careful to put it back where I found it.

So Friday nights and Saturday mornings were the best, and Sunday was pretty good, too. Chuck would go to church on Sundays and it was way out in the country. Tracie and me and Antoe would go to Bettes' house then, and we always had the best time. Bettes and Tracie would look at these weird cards for hours, and then Bettes would make a cake or cookies or something and we'd stay till it was almost dark. The only thing was, Chuck would usually be in a real, real bad mood when we got home so Sunday nights were always spent in the fruit cellar.

Sometime in October, real early on a Sunday morning, Tracie came in my room and said, "C'mon Girl, get up."

The reason I knew it was October was 'cause I just couldn't wait for Halloween, Bettes told me she'd make me the best costume ever, and I decided I was gonna be Wonder Woman, with the bracelets and the gold rope, and maybe even the tall white go-go boots, if I could talk Tracie into getting them for me.

Anyway, when she came in my room and said that, I

rolled over and cracked my eyelids open to stare at her. She was wearing a dress, which she never did, and she had on makeup, and her hair was all piled up on top of her head. The dress was black, and it was all the way to the ground. Tracie normally wore skirts way up above her knees, or ripped holey blue jeans.

"Why? It's still dark outside." I sat up to get a better look at her.

"We gotta go to church with Chuck today. They're having something special today, a homecoming, and we're gonna eat dinner there. Chuck wants to get there early. You better get a move on; you know he hates waiting."

I sure did know this so I got up. I went to get some clothes off the chair, or off the floor, and Tracie pulled out a black dress from a sack she'd had with her that I hadn't noticed.

"What's that?"

"A dress Chuck got you."

I took the dress from her and got some underwear from my dresser drawer and headed towards the bathroom to take a bath. I washed quickly, then dried off and put on the dress. It was pure-d ugly and I'd have hated it even if Chuck hadn't bought it. It was long, almost down to my ankles, and it was scratchy and stiff with ugly brown checks and it had a huge white collar around the neck. It had sleeves down past my wrists, and they had white around them. It was so big it looked like I was being swallowed up in ugly brown checks. I stood in front of the mirror after I put it on and made faces at myself.

"That's a goddamn ugly dress," I said out loud, and pictured myself saying it to Chuck, and I got tickled. I tried to brush my hair then, but it was sticking up in all directions, so I dug around and found a hot pink head band of Tracie's and used it to push my hair back. It made my hair look a little better, and it even made the dress look a little better. When I came out, Tracie was waiting in the hallway.

"Here." She handed me a pair of white socks that had lace on them, and a pair of black shiny shoes.

I looked at the shoes and then looked at her.

"C'mon girl, we ain't got all day, just put the damn shoes and socks on!" She plonked them down on the floor and headed downstairs.

I sat down in the hallway and pulled on the socks then jammed my feet in the shoes. They were too tight and they pinched my feet. I limped downstairs and in the kitchen to see if Antoe was down there. He wasn't, but Bettes was, and she was cooking eggs. I was surprised to see her up that early, but she was still wearing clothes so I figured she just hadn't been to bed yet.

"Hey!" She turned around when she heard me come in. "Want some eggs and bacon?"

"Yeah!" And I ran over and grabbed a plate out of the cabinet and took it over to Bettes and she piled up scrambled eggs and bacon on it.

I sat down at the table and started eating fast, 'cause I wasn't sure how long it'd be before Chuck came down and was ready to go.

"Slow down! You're gonna choke!"

"I gotta hurry, Chuck don't like to wait."

"Chuck can go to hell." Bettes snorted and I laughed.

"Why'm I having to go today? Did Tracie say? Is Antoe going too?"

"Nah, I'm gonna stay here with him."

"Did Tracie say why I had to go?"

"Where'd you get that ugly ass dress?" If I didn't know Bettes better, I wouldn't have thought much about her asking me that. But I knew she only kept asking questions whenever she didn't wanna answer something I'd asked her.

I was still shoveling down my eggs when I heard Chuck's up and down thump on the stairs. I grabbed up my bacon and was about to run when Bettes caught me.

"Keep your mouth shut today, OK?" I nodded and she gave me a quick squeeze and then I galloped to the front room and out the door before he could get down the stairs. Tracie was sitting in the car already and she was smoking. I slid in the back seat and it wasn't but a minute or two that Chuck came out and climbed in the driver's seat. He looked over at Tracie.

"Put that out." She threw it out the window. "Don't

smoke today; you know they don't like it." Tracie didn't say a word.

He started the car up then looked in the mirror at me.

"You look real nice, runt." I managed to smile at him. "That's a real pretty dress on you." He waited a second. "Can you not say "Thank-you?""

"Thank you," I said and I finished it off in my mind. "For this ugly damn dress nobody in their right mind would wanna wear."

Sometimes I thought he might know what it was I was thinking in my mind, 'cause he turned around and looked at me.

"You being smart?"

Chuck, she said thank you, what more do you want?" Tracie asked.

"She had a sassy tone."

"She did not."

He started the car and we went down the driveway. When we got to the end of it, we turned like we were going towards the school. I didn't have no idea where this church was so I just sat back and stared out the window. Chuck was fiddling with the radio and he kept changing it.

"Why're you doing this again?" Tracie asked him.

"I told you. It'll make me look good, like a family man."

"She's not gonna understand."

I kept on staring out the window, but I sure was listening 'cause I had an idea I was the "she" Tracie was talking about.

"Don't matter. Kids ain't got to understand, they just got to do what they're told." I looked up and Chuck was watching me in the mirror.

"Ain't that right, runt?"

"Huh?" I acted like I didn't know what he was talking about and he laughed.

"Nothing. Nothing. We're gonna have a fine time today, and you be on your best behavior, hear me?" I nodded, but I really wanted to spit in his face.

Nobody said much more and it was a long way there, and the roads were all dirt, and they were rough. It felt like my teeth were gonna shake right out of my mouth, and I was being jounced around in the back seat something awful.

When we finally drove up to the church I saw that it was real little, and the paint was all peeling off, just like on our house. There were some men standing around out front and when Chuck got out of the car and walked up to them, they all shook his hand and threw their arms around his shoulders like they were glad to see him.

Tracie got out and I followed behind her. We went past the men and in the two big doors that were like the ones in my school, only these were peeling white paint and grey. There were bench seats lined up all the way up to the front, and Tracie went down to the very first one. So I sat down right beside her and checked everything out. There was a raised place up front, and a big wooden thing in the middle, kinda like a desk, but way taller. There were little flat benches down in front that had red cushions on them. Behind the wooden thing in front, there was a giant picture of a man with long hair. He was holding an airplane in his hand and there was a storm going on. That picture must've been about a thousand feet tall.

Pretty soon people started coming in then, and it was mostly old ladies and stuff, and they all came over and said something to Tracie and then they hugged me. They smelled like the bedrooms at home that nobody went in.

"Ain't you just the cutest little thing ever?" One of them said to me, and I smiled the best I could but she was pinching both of my cheeks so it was kinda hard.

I cut my eyes back to see if anymore coming, but about then Chuck came walking up the middle through all the people, shaking their hands and putting his arm around them.

"Good morning Brothers and Sisters in Christ! The Lord loves you. I'm so blessed to have my family here today, my wife Tracie, and our sweet baby Girl."

Well, I didn't know what the hell he was talking about 'cause Tracie wasn't his wife, I knew what wifes were, and I sure as hell wasn't his baby anything. I didn't listen to him after that 'cause just like Bettes always said, he was full of shit. He was acting real important and you should've seen how those old ladies looked at him. Like he was a big bag of candy they couldn't wait to eat up. I sure felt like telling them they just oughta see how he acted after he'd had that brown stuff.

Then everybody got a book and started singing and it was so bad my ears felt all crinkly on the inside. After the singing, Chuck got up in front of the big wooden stand, and opened a book and started reading from it. All those people would holler out "amen" from time to time. Then the singing would start again, and then Chuck would talk again. Every time he started talking he'd get louder and louder and it seemed like all those people were getting worked up, too. Pretty soon, a couple of them started to holler and carry on and then they started to run around the church like something was chasing them. I saw one big fat woman come tearing down the middle of the church, and all of a sudden she stopped and fell out on the floor.

Well, I thought for sure she was dead, but nobody else seemed to be worried and sure enough, she went to rolling around and then she got back up and took off running again.

They were all talking too, low at first so I couldn't make out what it was they were saying. Then they got louder and louder and it sounded like they were all going gobble, gobble, gobble, like a bunch of turkeys. It was so funny; I had to bite the inside of my cheek to keep from busting out laughing. I cut my eyes at Tracie and she was frowning and sorta looking at her lap.

Chuck kept talking and those people just kept running around like crazy, falling in the floor and rolling around and gobbling. Finally he shut up and waited till they calmed down. When they were all back in their seats, he cleared his throat.

"And now we have a special, special thing. One of the lost has come home to the fold. A poor sinning lamb has come home. My sweet baby girl, who I recently adopted, has realized she's worthless and doomed to a devil's hell, and she wants to get right with God. Girl, come on up here, honey."

I sat there and didn't move and wondered what he was talking about. Tracie reached over and pinched my leg.

"C'mon baby, don't be bashful, we're all sinners in Jesus' eyes." Since Tracie was bruising my leg she was pinching so hard, I couldn't think of nothing else but to get away from her fingers so I got up and went to where Chuck was standing with his arms out, waiting for me.

When I got to him he hugged me tight and then he shoved me down at the bench in front and put his hand on my head, making me keep my head bowed down.

"Sweet Jesus, take this sinnin' lamb and make her clean, AMEN."

I couldn't look up but I could hear everybody getting worked up; I could tell they were running around and gobbling again, and Chuck was holding me down and talking and talking till he finally pulled me up to stand beside him and he kept his arm tight around my shoulders so I couldn't leave.

"Folks, there'll be rejoicing in heaven tonight! Now why'n y'all come forward to welcome this lamb to the fold?"

Then I was nearly smothered by all those people coming up and hugging and kissing me. Tracie came up there too, and she hugged me quick, but wouldn't look at me. That shocked me worse than anything. When everybody finally sat back down, I went to go, too, but Chuck grabbed me by my wrist, hard.

"Now y'all, I'm gonna ask Brother Bobbie Wayne to offer thanks for this fine meal, then afterwards, we'll go down to the pond and wash Girl in the blood of the lamb."

What? I wasn't gonna have lamb blood on me, no matter how bad Chuck whipped me. I just wasn't gonna do that. I didn't care if I had to run away.

Brother Bobbie Wayne prayed then, and Chuck finally let me go and I didn't waste no time getting back to my seat and out the door. I made it down the steps on the porch and around the side of the church before anybody even got outside. There was an old broken down picnic table at the edge of the yard, right before it turned into woods and I went over there and sat down. My wrist was all red where Chuck had been holding it so tight, and I knew it'd probably turn blue later on.

I could hear noises around back, and I wondered what everybody was doing, but I didn't wonder bad enough to go see, I'd been hugged enough. There was a bunch of little girls in uglier dresses than what I was wearing running around the side of the church. They looked like they were playing tag. I wondered if any of them went to my school.

I noticed there were huge, huge pinecones laying all over the ground; we didn't have any like this around our house, so I started to gather some up figuring I could use them for something. I was over by the edge of the woods using the bottom of my skirt as a basket for those pine cones when I heard something. I turned around right quick and saw that Dale and Richie had snuck up behind me.

Hellshitdamn. Not only did I not hear them, I hadn't even *seen* them in the church. Tiny was with them, but he was far behind, just watching what they were gonna do. I let my skirt fall and those pinecones rolled everywhere.

"Hey Richie, it's the little nigger-haired bitch, the one who damn near blinded you with that gas," Dale said.

"Tiny, you go stand watch and tell us if anybody's coming. She's fixing to get her ass whupped." Richie looked mean as hell, and he made a fist with one hand and started punching his other hand with it. Dale grinned and sat down on the picnic table. He was just gonna watch Richie beat me up.

"Y'all better leave me alone, I mean it, or I'll tell."

"Oh yeah?" Dale sneered, "Who you gonna tell? I know Chuck whupped your ass for throwing that shit on Richie." And they all bust out laughing.

I was just about to take off running when Richie jumped at me and slung me to the ground. When I hit it I just kept rolling 'cause I knew I had to get away from him. He jumped on me then and started punching me in the stomach. It hurt and I started bucking and kicking my legs for all I was worth. That stupid long dress was all up around my waist and my panties were showing but I just didn't care. I was too busy trying not to get killed.

I guess Richie didn't think I'd fight that much and I was able to get him off me for a minute. I tried to roll away again but he grabbed me by the legs and yanked me back. I felt something scratch me awful bad and it was those stupid pinecones. Richie flipped me over on my back again but I managed to pick up a pinecone and I hauled off and drug it down the side of his face. He hollered and grabbed his face and I could see that pinecone had scratched it all to hell. I started kicking for all

I was worth then and landed a real hard one and I heard him squeal like a pig. I jumped up as fast as I could and he was rolling around on the ground holding his tally-wacker. Dale jumped up from the table and started towards me but I dodged him and flew around the back of the church where everyone else was.

When I got around there, I didn't see Tracie. Everybody was lined up at the big tables that they'd set up and they were filling their plates with food. I wasn't the least bit hungry so I went over to the back steps of the church and sat down on the bottom one so I could catch my breath. About that time I saw Tiny coming around from the back, when he saw me he changed directions so he was heading straight over to where I was. Well, I didn't think he was stupid enough to start something with all these people everywhere, so I just watched him.

"You hurt Richie. You kicked him right in his nuts and he's around there puking."

"He started it," I said, even though I knew that excuse never got you anywhere.

"Yeah." He agreed. "They beat me up all the time."

"Why?"

He shrugged. "They're just mean that way."

"You helped them beat up Antoe at Perone's that time."

"Yeah. Sometimes you have to do what they say."

We just sat there then. I wasn't completely sure I liked him, but I figured he was probably telling the truth about having to do what they said.

"Hey Girl, why're you so damn filthy?" Tracie had come up with a glass of tea in her hand and she looked like she was hot and she looked like she could use a cigarette but I knew she wouldn't smoke one 'cause Chuck had told her not to.

"We was playing out back," Tiny said, and I looked at him real quick but I didn't say nothing about Richie jumping on me.

"Well, y'all go get something to eat."

Both of us got up then and went over to where the food was. Some lady handed us a paper plate and we got in behind some grown-ups who were filling their plates. I looked everything over, and if I didn't know what it was, I didn't get it. I wound up with a chicken leg and a biscuit. Tiny loaded his plate up, though. There was so much on it he had to carry it with two hands back to the steps. He started to shovel it in as soon as he sat down. He ate worse than Antoe even, spilling stuff all down his front.

I ate my chicken leg and my biscuit and hopped up to throw the plate away in a big trash can somebody had put by the tables. I was about to go back and sit on the steps with Tiny when I saw Dale and Richie coming from around the front. Richie looked kinda green and I was real glad. Tracie was sitting over by some ladies so I went over to where she was. There wasn't a chair so I sat down on the ground. She turned her head to look at me sideways and made a face. I knew she was bored out of her mind and would rather be anywhere but here. See, that's what I didn't quite get. Normally if we were doing something or going somewhere and Tracie got bored, then she'd just quit or go home. Seemed like she was doing a bunch of stuff she didn't really want to these days.

"Did you get plenty to eat?"

"Yeah, I said.

"What about dessert?"

"There's dessert?" Those women laughed then.

"Sure is, honeychile, you wanna go with me to see what all there is?" The same big fat women who'd fallen out in the floor and had a fit got up out of her chair and held out her hand to me. Well, I didn't like holding hands so I just nodded and followed her. We went around to the very end of the table and there were pies, and cakes, and cookies of all kinds. I grabbed a plate.

"What kind you want, darlin'? She asked.

"Chocolate." I told her.

"Pie or cake?"

"Yeah."

She laughed and laughed and cut a huge piece of chocolate cake and a huge piece of pie and slapped them on my plate.

"This'll put some meat on them skinny bones o'yours!" And she winked at me.

I went back and sat on the ground behind Tracie and ate every crumb of that pie and that cake. It was better than candy was, but it wasn't better than Bettes' cakes.

After all that, I felt sleepy, so I just laid back on the grass and was thinking about taking me a little nap when I heard Chuck talking.

"Folks, now you've all gotten your bellies full, we're gonna fill the soul a little more! Since my baby girl came into the fold this morning, we're gonna take her down and wash her in the blood of the lamb."

There he was, talking about lambs and blood again, and I was so full from all that cake and pie, there was no way I could run fast enough to get away. I sat up and looked over at Tracie and she wouldn't look at me, which was a bad sign. Chuck came right over to where I was sitting and grabbed my wrist and pulled me to my feet and led me past all the tables where there was left-over food still setting there, and down a little trail that was full of weeds and briars that kept catching on my dress. I glanced back over my shoulder and saw that all the people were right behind us, but I didn't see Tracie.

All of a sudden, we came to an open place, where the woods thinned out, and there was a pond there. It looked like it was almost dried up, and just as muddy as it could be. Chuck stopped then, and all the people sorta lined themselves up on all sides of the pond. I was too busy looking around and trying to figure out what was going on, to pay attention to what Chuck was saying, but I should've been, 'cause the next thing I knew he'd picked me up, and was walking out in the middle of that pond! I started to fight to get down, 'cause I didn't know what he was doing. As I was wiggling trying to get loose, he whispered in my ear, "stop fighting and I'll get you a big sack of candy when we go home."

Well, I couldn't enjoy no candy if I was dead, so I kept on trying to get away from him. I managed to scratch him and bite his arm and he grabbed me by the hair on the back of my head so tight I couldn't move without it feeling like he was gonna snatch me bald.

"Folks," he called out, "see how the Devil's working here? He's in my sweet little girl so bad she don't even know what she's doing, and she's fighting salvation for all she's worth!"

All those people were shouting and hollering, and he still had me by the back of my hair with my head pulled back and he started to lower me right down in that muddy water and held me under. I couldn't hear what he was saying, 'cause water was in my ears, nose and mouth, but he kept on talking and hollering and just when I thought I was gonna pass out, he pulled me up. I was coughing and spitting out that nasty water, and I was so mad; I wished he would fall down dead, right in front of all those people! I was mad at Tracie too, 'cause she let him do it.

Chuck walked out of the water and put me down, and all those women came around me hugging and carrying on. Somebody wrapped a blanket around me, and grabbed me by the hand and led me back up the path towards the church. When we got there, somebody fixed me a glass of tea, and I drank it, just to try and get that muddy water taste out of my mouth, and then I went and sat down on one of the chairs. All the women started packing up the food then, and Tracie came over and pulled my hair back out of my face.

"Why'd you let him do that?" I asked her.

She didn't answer me, but kept trying to straighten out my hair.

"We'll have to wash your hair tonight," was all she said.

After they got all the food packed up, Chuck had to pray some more and then everybody started leaving. I went and got in the back seat of Chuck's car and I laid down back there, partly 'cause I was real tired and partly 'cause I didn't wanna talk to them.

"Here," I heard Chuck say and I peeked just a little bit and saw he was handing Tracie a lit cigarette. I could see her take it from him then I heard the air blowing in so I knew she'd cracked her window to let the smoke out.

"Count that." I heard him say, and I could tell he'd handed her something. She didn't say nothing for a little bit then she said, "A hundred eighty-seven and forty-three cents."

"Not a bad haul. And it wouldn't even been half of that if I hadn't baptized her."

"I still don't think you should've done it. She didn't know what the hell was going on."

"She don't need to know. That's part of her problem; she's too damn growny for her own good."

They didn't say no more then and I guess I must've fallen asleep 'cause next thing I knew was the car stopped and when I sat up, we were back at home. Bettes' car was still parked there so I hopped out first and ran in the house. I heard the TV going in the living room so I ran in there, and Bettes and Antoe were laying on Toomie watching something.

"Girl, look!" Antoe had a bunch of beads around his neck and he held them up so I could see. "Bettes made!"

"Those are pretty, can I have some?"

"Hey, I didn't hear y'all come up. What the hell happened to you?" Bettes was staring at me and I must've been a sight with my hair all dried and muddy and sticking up in all directions.

I was about to tell her Chuck tried to drown me when I heard the front door slam so I just went over and sat down by Antoe. Tracie came in and sat down in the big chair over by the window, and I heard Chuck tromping up the stairs.

"What the hell happened to Girl?" Bettes asked Tracie.

"Oh, Chuck baptized her."

"Well, goddamn, Tracie. Have you lost every bit of your fucking mind?" Bettes stood up then, with her hands on her hips, and she was staring a hole in Tracie.

"Girl, take Tonio out to the kitchen and y'all get something to eat," Tracie told me.

Hellshitdamn. I wanted to hear what it was that Bettes was about to say, 'cause I knew she had a tone in her voice, but I did like she said.

Bettes had made a big pot of soup of some kind, and there was a box of crackers on the counter. I got two bowls down and fixed me and Antoe a bowl and I got out two packages of crackers. I knew Antoe would eat an entire one by himself. I wondered what Bettes was saying to Tracie. It wasn't but a little bit till I heard the door slam and then her car start up in the driveway. I knew she was mad 'cause she always told us bye before she left.

I looked over at Antoe slurping down the last of his soup. He was still wearing the bead necklaces, four of them.

"Can I wear one of those?"

He put his bowl down and looked down at them and took all of them off and reached over and put them around my neck.

"Girl wear. Boys not wear necklaces. Girls do." And then he grinned at me and I grinned back and looked down at them. They were real pretty.

Chuck didn't get me any candy and we never did wash my hair after all.

FIVE

It was a little bit later, right before Halloween, on a Wednesday night when me and Antoe were sitting at the kitchen table, coloring in a coloring book Bettes had brought us.

"Your birthday is coming up." Tracie walked in and told me like I didn't know it already.

"Yeah, it's Saturday," I said, "October the 26th."

"Well, what do you want? For a present. "A doll? A book? I don't even know what you like. Clothes?"

I thought about it. "Could I have cupcakes? And maybe a new book satchel?" I was still carrying the one I'd broken on Richie's head the very first day of school.

"And can the cupcakes have candles and little crunchy flowers on top?" I knew all about these, 'cause Jennifer's mother had brought a bunch of cupcakes in to our classroom one day, and they were the best things

I'd ever eaten.

"Yeah, sure, cupcakes and a book satchel. I can do that. You'll be eight, no, nine years old. Wow." Tracie got that same weird look she got the last time she was talking about how old I was. She was looking straight at me, but she acted like she was really seeing something else.

"Instead of a book satchel, could I maybe have a radio?" Sometime last week Chuck had come in and started messing with Antoe. He would tell him stuff like he was gonna put him outside and make him sleep in the woods with wild animals. Or he'd tell him he was gonna drive him somewhere, push him out of the car, and leave him there. He kept on this way for hours and Antoe got so worked up he went down to the fruit cellar and smashed hell out of most everything he could get his hands on. The radio was now in a million pieces and it made him sad to see it. He'd tried to fix it but it wasn't any use.

"New Raid-O!" Antoe was excited.

"Yeah, a radio. OK then, I'll get Bettes to take me to Greenville Friday so we can get everything."

"Friday's not my birthday."

"No, I know. But I thought you might want them Friday." She thought a minute. "Do you have any friends at school? You could ask somebody to come home with you to spend the night if you want."

"Really? Somebody could stay all night?"

"Sure."

"Will Chuck get mad?"

"Nah, he won't mind if it's only one. Just one, OK?"

"Yeah, there's only one I'd wanna ask. I'll ask her tomorrow."

"OK," Tracie said. "Just be sure and let me know if she's coming. Y'all put this stuff up now, and go on to bed. There's people coming over."

Well, she didn't have to tell us twice, we grabbed up our coloring books and colors and hightailed it to the fruit cellar.

I couldn't believe Tracie had told me I could ask Cerese to come to my house and spend the night! I planned out exactly what I would say to Cerese the next day, and then I planned out everything we might do on Friday night if she got to come. I would definitely want to show her our fruit cellar, so I knew I'd have to clean it tomorrow. Then, I'd take her down to the lake, to see if we could maybe see the old alligator that lived there, and we could play under the trees and scare each other with the moss. And I'd take her down to the Perone's store. I hoped she'd like Antoe, and for once, he wouldn't get all worked up about strangers. I fell asleep still planning out everything we were going to do. I had so many things planned; Cerese would've had to stay a month for us to do them all.

The next morning I woke up bright and early and

put on my candy cane skirt, 'cause it was my favorite, and my orange t-shirt. Tracie would see what I'd worn to school when I got home, and most times she'd laugh and say that I must be Bettes' kid, 'cause both of us had shit for taste. I didn't care, I liked everything as bright as possible and I didn't care who laughed at me.

I got off the bus and hurried into the classroom, but Cerese wasn't there yet. I put my book satchel down beside my desk, and settled in to wait. I didn't have a sweater or a coat to hang up on the hangers that were in a line all around the room. Jennifer floated into the classroom then, and normally she ignored me, but today she flounced right over. She always wore dresses that had tons of ruffles and her hair bows were always matching. Today she had on pink.

"Why do you play with niggers?" She asked.

"Shut up and mind your own business." That was all I could think of to say.

"My momma says you're trash, and your family is, too. She told me never to talk to trash." And she prissed back to her seat. I was thinking about whupping her good when Cerese got there. She came to her seat that was right across from mine, and put her stuff down.

"Hey," I said, getting up and going over to where she was hanging up her sweater. I had to ask Tracie for a sweater to hang up, too.

"Hey." She said back to me, and I could see that her

blue dress had a sewn up hole in the back of it. But she had matching blue balls in her hair, so who cared about a patched up hole?

"Saturday is my birthday, and I want you to come home with me after school tomorrow, maybe even spend the night if you can, or if you want to?" It was hard to look at her all of a sudden.

"Is it a party? Who else is coming?"

"Just you. And there's not gonna be a party, but Tracie is gonna get cupcakes and we'll have hamburgers too. From the Dairy Queen." Tracie didn't say anything about the hamburgers, but I was sure I could talk her into it. Or maybe Bettes would bring us some.

"Yeah, I'd like to, only I gotta ask my momma. She might not let me stay all night 'cause she don't like me to stay with folks she don't know."

I thought it was a good thing she didn't know us, 'cause she sure wouldn't let Cerese stay if she knew Chuck. Mrs. Huitt came in then, and the bell rang, so we both sat down, then, real quick, Cerese turned to me and asked, "Why're you asking me?"

"Tracie said I could ask a friend to come home with me."

She grinned at me, and said, "OK, I wanna come, but I gotta ask Momma."

I grinned back at her and we both turned to face the front so we wouldn't get in trouble. I felt pretty good. I felt so good I thought it might be a good time to tell on Jennifer for saying nigger. I gave her a look and got up out of my seat and went and stood beside Mrs. Huitt's desk.

"Yes, Girl?"

"I have to tell you something."

"Go ahead."

"Jennifer said a bad word earlier." Mrs. Huitt looked at me, and then looked at Jennifer sitting, all prim and proper, in the front row, looking at a catalogue she'd brought from home. She sighed.

"What is it?"

I leaned in closer to her and whispered. "She asked me why I played with niggers, and she was talking about Cerese." I stepped back to wait for the mad look to come over her face, but it never did.

"Girl, it's not nice to be a tattle-tale. Now please go sit down. I'm going to send a letter to your mother about your tattling."

"I don't have a mother." How many times did I have to tell this lady that?

"I said go sit down." Mrs. Huitt raised her voice a little and the mad look was there, so I went back to my seat. Jennifer had told on me, and I had gotten hauled away to see Mr. Pat. And I knew by now that only the real bad kids got sent to Mr. Pat. I knew nigger was a bad word, just like goddamn bastard was; only Mrs. Huitt didn't send Jennifer to Mr. Pat. I decided that there really wasn't a whole lot of fairness in the world.

We started our lessons then. I generally did pretty good in reading and writing, but not so good in math. Mrs. Huitt wouldn't call on me to answer in reading and writing, but she always called on me in math and I couldn't get the right answer for nothing. Math was first today, and sure enough, she called on me, and since I didn't know the answer, I had to go up front to the board and work out problems till I got them right. I stayed there for a long time, till the bell rang, and then, since I still didn't have the right answer, Mrs. Huitt told me I couldn't go out for recess till I got the answer and that if I still didn't have it right, I'd have to stay in at lunch recess too. I figured I'd be standing there till I died. I watched all the kids leave the room and I was feeling mad at the world, when Cerese came around the other side of me, pulled the chalk out of my hand, and wrote a number under the problem I was trying to work.

"That's the right answer, now come on, let's go play!"

When the bell rang to go home, Cerese promised me she'd ask her Momma and let me know in the morning. On the way home I got to thinking about how we could go down to Perone's and buy some candy. I still had some money left, and maybe Tracie would give us some more. Maybe I should've asked Cerese if she had some money and if she did, then she might wanna bring it with her.

Pretty soon, we were getting to my house, and I stood up and held onto the big silver pole before we got there. Miss Kat let me do that, but she didn't let the other kids do it. I told her that my birthday was Saturday, and that I might have a friend coming home with me tomorrow.

"That's OK, ain't it?" I wondered if there was a rule about nobody else riding the bus but the ones who rode it all the time.

"Sure, that'll be fine. How old will you be?"

"Nine."

"Well, happy early birthday."

"Thanks," I said, and then I flew down those steps and ran like hell up the driveway. I had to tell Antoe we were maybe having company tomorrow but I should've known better.

He was down in the fruit cellar carving on a piece of wood.

"Antoe, I might have a friend coming over tomorrow.

"Who friend?"

"A girl I know."

He stopped carving and looked at me.

"Mean?"

"No, she's real nice."

"Take Tonio's wood? Take knife? Hit Tonio?"

"No, she's nice, you'll like her, I promise."

"She mean. Tonio no like mean."

Well, don't you know he was getting all worked up? "Antoe, I was playing. Nobody's coming, I just wanted to trick you so you'd clean up down here."

"No clean."

"Yeah, we gotta. It's nasty." I knew Cerese would be coming down here and it *was* dirty. We shook out all the quilts we used for a bed and dusted off the coffee table and the lady statue. I made sure the cans of food were covered up in the corner, and I gathered up all the trash where we'd let it just pile up. The last thing I did before going to bed was to get the broom from the kitchen and sweep the floor. It probably needed mopping, too, but I was too tired.

The next morning, I woke up earlier than usual and got dressed extra carefully. I wore my orange skirt, the one with the shapes all over it, and put on my pink tee shirt. Over this I put an old green sweater of Tracie's, 'cause even though I told her I needed one, who knew when she'd finally get around to getting it? Her sweater was way too big, and the sleeves hung a mile off my wrists, but I rolled them up and thought it looked just fine. I also got one of her old headbands and tied my hair back with it. It was my favorite 'cause it had bright colored beads, kinda like what Cerese wore in her hair, hanging down one side. It was just like the Indian girls Mrs. Huitt had been telling us about. They always wore lots of beads.

I ran downstairs and found the last pop-tart I'd hid a long time ago and just now remembered. I ate one, and decided I would save the other one for Cerese. I heard the bus chugging up the highway before I saw it, and I stepped back out of the road to wait. I hoped somebody might say something about my headband, or that I looked nice. I wished Tracie had been awake to see me.

And then I started thinking about something that'd been bothering me lately. Since I'd been going to school, I realized I wasn't like other kids. They all had mommas and daddies. Well, Cerese didn't have a daddy, but that's 'cause he'd passed. Whatever that meant. But the other kids had one of each, and to hear them talk, their momma's were always fixing them snacks and breakfast and stuff, and making them do their homework at night. And the daddies would work all day then they'd be there at night to eat supper and help with homework and play with them. And some of the boys talked about their daddies taking them fishing and hunting, things like that.

Not that I wanted to go fishing or hunting, but sometimes I wondered why Tracie didn't do any of that fixing me snacks and making me go to bed. I really didn't mind most of the time, but there were those nights when me and Antoe had spent too much time by ourselves, and there wasn't any food in the house except for what was in those green cans, or something had scared us, well those times, I thought it might be nice to have a Momma or a Daddy. I figured I didn't need both of them, just one would be OK.

I wondered every now and then, if maybe Tracie was really my momma and was just lying about it. You just never knew sometimes. There were a lot of things I wanted to ask her, and I was writing them all down as I thought of them. Sooner or later, maybe when I got older, she'd have to tell the truth.

The bus got there, and I got on, and just sat and wondered about things all the way to school. We pulled up in the big circle like we always did, and I hopped off first, like I always did. I ran across the playground to the schoolhouse, opened the door, went inside, and then I had to walk. They sure didn't like it if you ran inside the building. I got to my classroom and put my things away, and today I had a sweater to hang up, too.

Jennifer was sitting with all her friends, and they started whispering and laughing when they saw me. Cerese was the only friend I had; none of the other girls would have a thing to do with us. They were always having parties and stuff, and I think everybody got asked to them but us.

A tall, older boy came through the door then, and I remembered he was Cerese's big brother, Brady. I hadn't seen him since that very first day he was sitting with her in the cafeteria. Cerese was always talking about him.

She said he left school every day at lunch to go to the Vo-Tech to study welding. I asked her what welding was and she didn't know, either.

Cerese dragged him over to my desk. "Brady, this is Girl Brown. She's the one who asked me to her house to eat cupcakes and hamburgers." I nodded.

"Where you live?" Brady didn't smile, he just looked at me.

"Ummm..."

"Your house? You got a house, doncha?" Where is it?"

"Well, I ride bus 4, and it's a long driveway right before you get to Perone's Bait Shop." That was pretty much all I knew for directions, and I couldn't have told you my address if my life depended on it.

"Don't you even know your own address? White folks. Shit."

Cerese pushed Brady. "Imma tell Momma on you!"

"You do that an' Imma tell her you going to white folk's house and less' see which one gets in the most trouble!"

"Are you gonna come?" I asked Cerese hopefully.

"Yeah, but I can't stay the night. That's why Brady wants to know where you live, so he can pick me up at seven. Momma works in Greenville and she gotta work late Friday."

"Does she know you're coming to my house?"

"I forgot to ask her," Cerese said, and Brady made a noise and rolled his eyes. "But she won't care."

This sounded like the same kind of thinking I'd used myself when I was doing something Tracie didn't know about. I would make it seem OK to be doing whatever it was by telling myself that Tracie wouldn't care, and knowing Tracie, she probably wouldn't. But I wasn't sure about Cerese's mother.

"Are you sure she won't care? Shouldn't you tell her? I don't want you to get in trouble."

Brady snorted and rolled his eyes again. "Like Baby ever gonna be in trouble. I been to that Bait Shop before, it's on the lake landing, ain't it?" I nodded. "And you live on the same road? OK, then, there ain't but one mailbox on that road so I guess that one is your house. Ain't nobody gonna shoot me if I drive up there, are they?"

I told him no, but I didn't know if he was joking or not, and I wasn't real sure Chuck wouldn't shoot him. He looked at Cerese then, "OK, I'll be there at seven. If you need me before then, call." He looked at me.

"I guess you white folks HAVE a phone?" I nodded again. "I don't guess you got any idea what your number is?" I didn't. Brady sighed.

"Cerese, if you gotta hang with white folks, will you tell them they need to know their damn phone number and where they live?" He turned around and walked out of the door without looking back.

Me and Cerese grinned at each other. I didn't even feel bad about her not getting to spend the night. It was probably better this way. This way, Antoe would get to know her before she spent the night and this way, maybe he wouldn't freak out so bad. Plus, you never knew who might be over. Chuck had friends as bad as he was, and sometimes they got to carrying on something awful.

"I don't think Brady likes me."

"He don't like nobody. An' I don't like HIM. He's mean to me an' he always tells me to leave him alone and get out of his room."

"Are you sure your Momma won't be mad?"

"Well, she might, but she won't know about it. See, she works a lot, and we don't like to bother her much. Brady has to take care of things when she's gone, so that's why I asked him. If Brady says it's OK, then Momma won't care. 'Cause he'd get in worse trouble n'me." She laughed.

"I'm glad you're coming," is all I could think of to say, and it was all I had time to say 'cause Mrs. Huitt tapped her ruler on the black board, which was her signal that we were going to start.

The morning went by pretty quick and then it was lunchtime. It was pizza day, which was our favorite day. We always ate the food in the cafeteria but a bunch of kids brought little sandwiches and fruit and stuff. The only good thing about bringing your lunch is you got to go to the front of the line and get your milk first.

We ate our pizza and didn't talk much. Cerese was

like Antoe that way; she didn't care if there was quietness. We finished eating and took our trays to the front and handed them to the ladies washing them and then we went outside. While we were wandering around the playground, I found a rock that looked like a block of wood so I picked it up to take to Antoe.

"Why you keeping that old rock?"

"I'm taking it to Antoe."

"Who's that? Your brother?"

"No, he's...just Antoe. You'll get to meet him." Here was a new thought. Even if Antoe didn't get all weird when he met Cerese, maybe she wouldn't like him. What if she called him a "retard" like Richie, Dale, and Chuck did? I wasn't completely sure what "retard" meant, but I knew it was something about the way Antoe was. Like how he was a grownup, but he would shit his pants sometimes and cry like he was a real little kid.

The bell rang then and we swarmed back to the building. The afternoon passed as slow as it could. I generally liked afternoons best 'cause we got to do arts and crafts. I always chose construction paper for my projects, 'cause I liked to make pictures with cut-outs. Today I decided to make a lake, with fish jumping and swimming in the water. I made trees and birds, and I even made a turtle, like the one I caught last summer, but let go. I thought about making an alligator, but I didn't really know how. I made the lake blue, and the fish were all different colors: green, yellow, brown, blue, and red. I was really happy with the way it turned out, and especially when Mrs. Huitt came around and asked if I wanted to hang it on the wall. The only pictures that got hung on the wall were those she picked, so I was glad she picked mine, but I really wanted to take it home and put it on our icebox.

"Thank you ma'am, but I wanna hang it on our icebox. Maybe I can make one for the wall tomorrow?

"Well, you can, of course, but I just thought this one was so good you'd want to have it there when we have parent's night."

"Yeah, well, I still wanna take it home."

"Fine." She wheeled around and went off to her desk.

I knew I made her mad again, but I didn't really care, and it was too close to going home time to worry about it. I carefully put my picture in my book satchel and sat quietly until Mrs. Huitt told my row we could get our things and leave. I tied my sweater around my waist the way I'd seen some of the other girls do, and I left the classroom and waited on Cerese in the hallway. I was so excited I could hardly stand it. I really wanted to tell everybody I saw that tomorrow was my birthday and I was having company over. Cerese came out then, and we walked together to bus 4 and got in line with the rest of the kids.

When we got on, we sat in my usual seat right behind Miss Kat. She turned around in her seat and stared at Cerese. She looked at me then and asked, "Does your mother know she's coming home with you?"

"Yeah, I told you yesterday, remember?

She was still staring at Cerese. "Yeah, I remember. Well. Takes all kinds, I guess. Make sure your little friend behaves herself." And she turned around and didn't say another word, but started up the bus.

I noticed that all the kids were staring at Cerese, but Cerese didn't pay them any attention, she just looked out the window all the way home. She told me she didn't ride the bus, that Brady drove them to school every day. She said he'd had to get special permission to be able to drive them, but 'cause her Momma worked so much, they'd let him.

When we got to my driveway, I nudged her and she jumped up to get off with me. I told Miss Kat 'bye, but she just grunted something at me. As we were walking up the driveway, I stopped and dug around in my book satchel for the rock I'd found.

"Here. You can give this to Antoe. Sometimes he don't like people he hasn't met before, and if you give him this, he'll like you."

"OK. Why don't he like people?"

"He just don't."

She took the rock from me, and I noticed her staring at the moss in the trees. I told her it wouldn't hurt her, it was just old moss. We rounded the corner that hid the house from view and she stopped in her tracks.

"Is that your house?"

"Yeah, that's my house."

"Is it haunted? It looks haunted." She still hadn't moved from where she stopped and I had to turn around to look at her.

"Haunted?

"Like ghosts and stuff. Do you have ghosts?"

"No, there's no ghosts, ghosts are dead people. There's just me, Antoe, n' Tracie. There was no point in telling her about Chuck, he was a lot worse than any ghost. "C'mon, let's go."

I wanted to get her walking towards the house, 'cause she was staring at it in a way I didn't like. She looked like she was scared of it. I guess our house was kinda scary looking, if you didn't know it. It had moss growing up all alongside of it, and the porch was sagging in the middle. The window that was in the kitchen had been broken out and there was a big board covering the hole. I didn't notice these things every day, but now I was seeing it through Cerese's eyes, it looked like hell.

I also noticed that both of Chuck's cars were there, and a couple more cars, and a truck, and a van. I didn't want Cerese to see all of his friends, so I grabbed her hand and led her in to the front hallway; the front room door was shut, so I was glad about that, and past the stairs into the kitchen. When we got to the kitchen, I smelled a lot of smoke. There was overflowing ashtrays sitting on the table, and all kinds of bottles and cans on the floor and on the cabinets. There was a pile of balloons laying on the side of the sink. They were all ripped up like they'd been blown up then popped. There was also a needle there, like the one they used when I got shots.

I hoped they were all sleeping now, 'cause that's what they did sometimes when there was a lot of smoke in the house and needles laying around. There was music playing really loud and Antoe was nowhere to be seen. I saw a white box on the table, in the middle of all the trash, and I was sure it had the cupcakes, but I didn't see any sign of hamburgers, but Tracie promised she'd get them for when we got home. The horse skull was setting on the table, and Cerese was standing still and stiff like a board, staring at it.

"It's just old bones, it won't hurt you." She still didn't move.

I grabbed her hand and pulled her through the kitchen and down the stairs to the fruit cellar to find Antoe. He was fiddling with the broken radio, and I wondered if Tracie had bought the new one. He dropped his head when he saw Cerese, but before he could make any noise, I nudged her and motioned her to give Antoe the rock she was still holding.

She stepped forward and handed it to him. "Here."

He took it and smiled at her.

"T'anks." He turned the rock over and over in his hand, checking it out.

"You can't carve that though, it's a rock. Antoe, this is my friend Cerese. This is Antoe."

"No Antoe. 'Tonio. 'Rese. Hi. T'anks."

Antoe put the rock carefully on the coffee table.

"Let's go eat cupcakes." I shooed her back up the stairs, and I could hear that the music was still playing, but nobody had come out and I hoped maybe they wouldn't. I opened up the white box, and I could see where there'd been cupcakes, but all it had left was a smear of pink icing, a few crumbs, and some crumpled papers. Then I went to look in the icebox but there was no sign of hamburgers, either. Nothing was in there but some old milk and a bowl of something that was once spaghetti.

"I thought there was gonna be cupcakes," Cerese said, looking around the kitchen. "Are you sure there ain't ghosts here?" I looked around, too, and there sure was a big bunch of trash and mess, but I didn't see anything that looked like ghosts.

"There's no ghosts here."

I was mad. I went back and looked in the box again, just to make sure nothing was there. I picked up a crumb and popped it in my mouth.

There was a crumpled white sack beside the cup-cakes, I opened it up and smelled the inside. It smelled like there'd been hamburgers there once, but not anymore.

"Let's go swing, we got a great swing." If we went outside and played for a while, maybe somebody would bring some more food.

"I'm hungry," Cerese said.

"Tracie's gonna make us something when she gets up." That was a lie, 'cause I didn't even know if Tracie was here.

"Why's that man so weird?"

"What man?"

"The one downstairs."

"Antoe. He's not weird."

"He's big," Cerese said, like I didn't know.

"Yeah, he's big. He can push you really good on the swings. I'll go get him and he'll push us, OK?"

"I wanna eat first."

Well, I couldn't blame her, 'cause I did too, but I didn't really know what we were gonna eat. I looked around in the cabinets and back in the icebox and there wasn't nothing there. So I told Cerese to wait there and I would see if I could find Tracie. I went out of the kitchen, in the front hallway, and tiptoed to the front room, where the door was shut. The music had stopped so I cracked open the door and peeked in. There were a bunch of people in there, laying around on the floor, and on Toomie. It was dark and I didn't see Tracie so I opened the door further.

"Well, what the hell is this? Sesame Street?" A voice called out from somewhere in the room and everybody laughed.

"Who are you? Come closer, I can't see that good." There was more laughing, and I didn't go in any further.

"Where's Tracie?" I asked.

"Upstairs, but I wouldn't go up there just now." And they all laughed some more.

I backed out and shut the door. Cerese had followed me and was standing in the front hallway looking scared so I led her through the kitchen, washer room and back down the stairs to the fruit cellar.

I knew there was no use going to find Tracie; she was probably taking a nap with Chuck, and if I woke them up, Chuck would beat me, and I didn't want Cerese to see all that.

Well, we'd just have to have some of the stuff in the green cans. Like I said, it wasn't bad and the thing was, you never knew exactly what you were going to have until you opened it up. So far we'd had beans and weenies, fruit, noodles, and some kind of meat stuff. One time I found some kind of candy and crackers, and boy, that was the best one of all.

"It's OK, we got food down here," I said, and I went digging through the boxes of green cans. I knew that the ones with an "M" had beanie weenies or something, and the "B" ones were where I found candy and crackers. There were some chipped bowls, a rusted can-opener, and spoons in the box, too, and I opened three "M" cans. Two had beanie weenies, and one had some kind of gloppy meat. The three "B" ones I opened had some hard candy, cheese and crackers, and some crumbly biscuits. I spooned meat and beanie weenies in the bowls, making sure I gave Antoe the most. I laid out the hard candy, cheese and crackers, and biscuits on the coffee table.

"C'mon and sit down," I said, and handed her a bowl. "This can be dessert." I pointed towards the candy and stuff on the table. Cerese took that bowl from me and raised it up to smell it and then shoved it towards me and when I wouldn't take it, she thumped it down on our table.

"It's cold. And it smells an' looks nasty. I ain't eating this." I looked at her, and I looked at the bowl. It might not look so great, but it wasn't *that* bad. "C'mon, try it." I took a big bite to prove that it wasn't gonna kill her.

"Nu uh." She was shaking her head.

Well, I was getting kinda mad. I don't know why she was acting like this; it wasn't like it was rotten or anything. I couldn't heat it up 'cause of those people up there.

"Me and Antoe eat it all the time, don't we Antoe?"

"Good." Antoe mumbled around a mouthful. He was about finished with his bowl and he looked over to where Cerese had put her bowl down.

"Reese don't want? Tonio eat."

She didn't say nothing so Antoe picked her bowl up and started on it. I ate another bite of mine but Cerese was just standing there with her arms crossed. I sighed and handed Antoe my bowl, too.

"You wanna go upstairs and see my room?" I asked her, hoping she'd get that weird look off her face.

"No, I wanna go home. I wanna go call Brady to come get me." She started to go back upstairs.

"Wait! You just got here, and he said you could stay till seven."

"I wanna go home!"

She was almost yelling, and I knew there was no other way but to go up to the kitchen and let her call Brady. So I went up with her, and showed her where the phone hung on the wall. She picked it up and started dialing. I could hear it ringing on the other end. It rang and rang and finally I heard somebody answer.

"Brady, come get me," Cerese said. "I don't like it here, it's got ghosts an' bones, and I'm hungry and I ain't eating no cold nasty food from no can and I wanna go home." She was crying now and I wanted to do something to make her feel better, but I didn't know what.

I could hear Brady saying something but I couldn't hear what it was, and then Cerese hung up the phone.

"I'm going outside to wait. Brady said to." She started towards the front room and I followed her. She had her hand on the front door when I heard a loud clomping down the stairs: Chuck. His fake leg always sounded real loud on the wood of the stairs, and it was how I knew it was him. He didn't have a shirt on and his hair was all wild and he looked like he was in a real bad mood. Hellshitdamn.

"Who the hell is this?" He asked in a loud voice.

"My friend Cerese."

"You got a nigger at my house?" He got down the stairs and started walking towards us.

"Tracie said I could." It ain't your damn house no way, I thought, but I didn't say it out loud 'cause he'd probably kill me if I did.

"She said you were having a friend over. She didn't say shit about it being a nigger."

I didn't know what to do. Cerese was crying and I knew she was scared. I was thinking Chuck was gonna beat me, or her, or both of us.

"We're gonna wait outside for her brother." I said and I grabbed Ceres's hand and pulled her out to the porch. I didn't see nothing of Brady yet, and I really didn't know what to say to Cerese, 'cause she was still crying.

"You wanna go swing till Brady gets here?"

She thought about it and then she nodded her head. Maybe if we could play some, she'd forget the bad stuff and still be my friend. I even let her get on the swing first and I started pushing her without her even asking me.

We were finally having fun, and Cerese was laughing when I saw a car coming up our driveway. It was old and sorta rusty and black, and it made an awful racket. I figured it was Brady. Cerese had said he liked to work on cars and was always fixing some old junky car up, driving it for a while, then selling it and getting another old junky one.

We didn't stop swinging and Brady pulled up and got out of his car. He was staring at Chuck's red, fancy car like he couldn't even believe it was there. Before I could warn him not to, he walked over to it and leaned down and peeked in the window.

Well, you should've seen Chuck shoot out of the house.

"Uh-oh." I stopped pushing Cerese and ran over to the car.

Brady wasn't paying no attention to anything but that car. He cupped his hands and peeked in the window and was walking around to the other side of it when Chuck got out there.

"Hey man, this your car? A '55 Vet? Wow, I ain't ever seen one before. This is some badass car! Do you fix it up? Man. I wanna get my hands on one of these someday!"

Brady was excited about the car and was still looking it over carefully, but Chuck wasn't saying a word. He realized Chuck was just staring at him, so he looked over to where me and Cerese were coming from and he looked back at Chuck and kinda shrugged and told Cerese to get in the car. I walked out to where the car was, and just watched them get in it and drive off. Cerese didn't even look at me when I waved at her.

"Get your ass in the house so we can have a talk about the kinds of "friends" you ask over." He was just standing there, like he was waiting for me to go in first. Well, if he thought I was gonna go in front of him, he was stupid. I just stood where I was.

"Did you hear what I said? I said get your ass in the house so we can have a talk about you bringing niggers home."

"You go to hell."

I didn't really mean to say that out loud, and when I did, Chuck's eyes bugged out like you wouldn't believe. If I hadn't been scared I was gonna die, I sure would've laughed. Well, he started towards me then, but from the way he was wobbling on the fake leg, I knew he was dog-ass drunk, so I waited till he was coming towards me, then I took off around the side of the house. The woods were back there, and sometimes me and Antoe'd go way out and play in them, so I hoped he'd think that's where I'd gone. But where I really went was to the very back of the house where there were some loose boards, and I pulled them back, and slid under the house.

This was my own special cave that not even Antoe knew about. It was all cool dirt and peacefulness under there. I would go hide for hours sometimes; it was the place I went when I felt like I couldn't handle anything else. Sometimes when Antoe was having a fit, or I'd been whipped, or Chuck had made me sit in his lap and rubbed his beard on my face and told me he loved me like his own daughter (yeah, right), or I just wanted to be all alone, this is where I came. I knew he'd look for me but then he'd go to sleep and forget about it by morning. If I had to, I'd sleep here. Even though it was real dark, I didn't get scared 'cause I kept a flashlight under there.

I heard him hollering and cussing, and I crawled way over to the front of the house where there were cracks so I could peek out, and I could see him walking out towards the woods. The ground was uneven and there were all kinds of sticks and stuff and he kept tripping and one time he pitched forward and had to grab hold of tree to keep from falling.

"I hope you break your stupid neck, you bastard," I whispered. He got out of my sight then, and it wasn't long before I heard the door slam like he went in the house. Then I heard the sound of people on the porch, and I heard voices, then the sound of car doors opening and shutting and cars leaving.

I stayed under there for a long, long time. I fell asleep too, and it was real quiet and kinda dark when I woke up. I wiggled my way out, and creeped around the house making sure I didn't hear anything. They were probably asleep by now. I wondered why Tracie hadn't come out to look for me. I made it around to the front of the house and I saw Chuck's ugly old car sitting there, and I was so mad I walked over to it, picked up a big, sharp rock and scratched a trail all along the side of the door. It didn't even show up, the car was that rusted and scratched already. I saw his bright, shiny, red car sitting there, and I put a little scratch there on the end of it. Not a real big one that would make him freak out, but one that I would always know was there and feel good about.

I tried the door next, even though I knew he always kept it locked, but what do you know, he must've forgot it today 'cause it opened! Well, I slid in that seat and shut the door quick as anything making sure to keep ducked down so nobody could see me from the house. If he came out the door and caught me, I'd be dead, but I wasn't gonna think about that.

The seats were all shiny black stuff, and smooth as could be. There wasn't a speck of dirt or trash anywhere in that car. I opened the ashtray and there was a little dried up piece of cigarette in there. I had seen how carefully he saved his cigarettes so I picked it up, rolled down the window, and threw it out.

Then, I pushed the button on the little door in front of the seat on the passenger's side and it swung open. I poked around in there and found a little book with papers that I took, and a big lighter that was clear with dice floating in the bottom of it. I took that, too. I was just about to get out with my loot, when I noticed that the carpet that was on the drivers' door was kinda loose. I pulled on it, and it came away and there was a little place there, like a little cave, and there was a bag stuffed down in the door, covered up by the carpet so nobody could see it. I pulled the bag out and threw it out the window on the ground beside the car and pushed the carpet back over the hole so it didn't look like anyone had bothered it. I rolled up the window and slid out of the car, grabbed the bag, and ducked down beside the car to wait and make sure it was safe.

I stayed there until I was sure nobody was outside, then I flew around the side of the house and back under it I went, fast as I could, carrying the bag with me.

I got under there, and opened it up to see what Chuck had hid. First, there was a big bag of balloons, only they were lumpy, like there was something inside. I squeezed one and it was soft. The top of the balloon were you put it in your mouth to blow up was all tied in a knot. I didn't know what it was, but I knew it must mean something to Chuck or else he wouldn't have hid it so good. I took them all out and counted them, and there were eighty-seven balloons.

I smelled one of them, and it didn't smell like anything but balloons. I really wanted to open one up, but

I could do that later, so I put them aside and saw that there was another bag, smaller, with a zipper in the top of it. I opened it up and it was full of money! Stacks and stacks of money! I'd never seen so much money in my life; I thought there might even be one million dollars in there.

I knew I should probably put it all back, 'cause I was going to get in more trouble than I'd ever been in before if they found out I took it. But I wasn't gonna. I thought maybe that this was enough money for me and Antoe to go somewhere else to live. We mostly lived by ourselves now anyway, and I was getting real tired of trying to keep out of Chuck's way. And here lately, Tracie wasn't much help either. She'd let him try to drown me in a muddy pond, and she didn't even care enough to keep people from eating my birthday cupcakes.

It was a nice thought, me and Antoe having a house all to ourselves. I could cook some, and Antoe could keep it clean, 'cause I would tell him he had to. I wasn't completely sure how we'd go about getting a house though, 'cause I was a kid and Antoe was...well, he was Antoe. But I knew I could figure something out, so I laid there and thought and thought and planned and planned till I fell asleep again.

SIX

I stayed under the house for a good long time. It was getting kinda cold and I was real, real tired. I wondered what time it was and I couldn't even guess. I dug a hole in the dirt under the house, even though nobody ever went under there, and I buried the bag of money and the bag of balloons. Then I crawled out and went around to the side door and listened to see if I could hear anybody, and I didn't, so I went in and went down to the fruit cellar. Well, wouldn't you know Antoe had locked the door? I didn't want to wake anybody up by banging on the door, so I went back up to the kitchen and tried to decide if I wanted to sleep upstairs in my room or if I should go back under the house.

I was real hungry, but the green cans were all down in the fruit cellar and I'd already looked and there wasn't nothing in the kitchen. All of a sudden, I heard someone on the stairs, and they didn't clump so I know it wasn't Chuck. Tracie stumbled in the kitchen rubbing her eyes. She saw the horse head and went over and fished around in it but didn't find anything.

"Shit. Damn."

Then she pulled her cigarettes out of her pocket, lit one and sat down at the table. "Hey, when'd you get home?"

"After school, like I always do."

"Did you get your cupcakes?" She picked up the lid of the white cupcake box and stared into it.

"Shit, y'all ate twenty-four cupcakes?" She asked, like she couldn't even believe it.

"The box was empty."

"Goddamn." She picked up the box and carried it with her to the front room. I followed her, and stood behind the coat rack full of old musty coats that was in the corner by the doorway, so I could watch and hear without them seeing me. She opened the door up with a *bam* and flipped on the lights.

"Who the hell ate the cupcakes? Goddammit, they were the kids! Now somebody better get their ass to the store and get some more!" I guess not all the people had left earlier.

She went on in the front room then, and I couldn't hear what she was saying, just a low mumble of people talking and laughing.

"What's all the yelling about?" I nearly jumped

out of my skin, and I was thankful I was buried up in those stinky old coats, 'cause I sure hadn't heard Chuck clumping down.

Tracie came out of the front room just as he was about to go in. I was still hidden in the coats.

"Those stoned bastards ate all of Girl's cupcakes. I got them for her, Antoe, and her little friend.

Tracie looked over and saw me standing by the coats, "Where's your little friend?"

"I'll tell you where she is," Chuck's voice sounded funny, like he could barely get his words out. "I sent that little nigger running home. Why'd you let her invite a nigger here?"

Tracie looked at him, then she looked at me, and she shrugged her shoulders.

"C'mon Girl, let's run to the store," she said. "We're gonna get you something for your birthday." I walked out from the coats then, and Chuck saw me.

"I'm gonna beat hell out of you if you don't stop running with damn niggers."

"Shut the hell up, you bastard!" I screamed at him before I even realized what I was doing.

I dropped my head, scrunched up my eyes, and braced myself for the fist I was sure was about to land upside my head, but it never came. I peeked up at him and he was just standing there looking at me like he was shocked. Then he started to laugh.

"Well, I be damn, maybe there's something to her, after all." And he laughed and laughed, and started to stumble towards me, lost his balance, and crashed face first on the floor. Tracie rolled him over on his back, and he was out cold. "Drunk bastard," was all she said, and then she went and picked up the keys to Chuck's old car. "C'mon if you wanna go with me."

I did, so I followed her outside, down the steps and hopped in the car. I thought about the money and the balloons buried under the house and I didn't feel one bit guilty. Tracie started the car up, lit a cigarette and we started driving towards Lakeside, which wasn't but a little ways up the highway, but was too long for me and Antoe to walk.

"Sorry they ate your cupcakes up. Did you find the hamburgers I got for y'all?"

"No, I found the sack, but they were all gone."

"Fuck. Stupid stoned bastards," she said. "Did you have anything to eat?"

I shook my head. "I opened up some green cans of stuff, but Cerese wouldn't eat it and Antoe ate it all."

"Girl. I'm sorry. I didn't know they were coming."

"That's alright." But it wasn't.

"I know I've been gone a lot, but I'm going to start being home more, OK? How're you doing in school? Don't they send letters home or stuff like that?"

Yeah, they sent a letter home every week, but I sure

didn't give them to her, 'cause most of them said something about me getting in trouble.

"Na, they don't send letters. But they're having parent's night some time, next week I think, and you could come to that."

"Parent's night, huh? Yeah, why not? Me and Chuck'll come."

Hellshitdamn. Like I wanted Chuck to be there. "Can Antoe come?"

"Maybe, yeah, we'll see."

She tossed out her cigarette, pulled another one from her pack and pushed the lighter on the dashboard in with her finger. When it popped out I pulled it out for her and held it to her cigarette and she puffed on it till it was lit. I held the lighter in my hand, liking the way the inside glowed less and less red till it went back to gray, but still stayed hot. I put it back in the hole it had come from and stared out the window.

We passed Perone's bait shop, it was all closed down for the night, and kept going around the curve, heading to Lakeside. I saw the big bright sign up ahead that was shaped like a giant bottle. It was dark out, so the sign was glowing and bright like a million flashlights all turned on at once. There were a lot of cars around and Tracie pulled in the driveway and parked but left the car running.

"I'll just be a second. You wait right here."

There were people coming in and leaving the place,

and most of them were carrying sacks and boxes. It was all open inside, and I could see Tracie towards the back, talking to a man. I saw her walk to the front and pay for whatever it was she bought, and then she was walking out of the store with a man carrying two big sacks for her. She opened the door on the back seat, and he set the sacks down, she was carrying a smaller sack and she tossed it in my lap when she opened the door. She told the man thanks, then got in and we took off.

I opened the sack and saw that there were honey buns and bags of potato chips in there.

"They didn't have cupcakes," was all Tracie said. I liked honey buns, and so did Antoe, but I was still disappointed over the cupcakes.

"Thanks."

I thought about the present I was supposed to get, but I guess she'd forgotten about it, or else those people stole it. When we got home, I got out of the car and followed Tracie inside. Chuck was still laying on his back in the hallway, and I didn't stop to see if Tracie tried to wake him up, but ran straight through the kitchen and down the steps. I tried the door and Antoe still had it locked, so I knocked on it and said, "It's me, Antoe, let me in." And I heard him getting up to unlock the door so I could go in. I locked it back, just in case, 'cause I didn't want to deal with nothing else.

I gave Antoe a honey bun and a bag of chips, and I

sat down to eat mine, too. Even though I was hungry, I only ate half and put the other half in my little box with the lock on it.

I was thirsty, but not thirsty enough to go back upstairs, so I fluffed up all of my quilts and laid down and turned off the light. Antoe was on his bed of quilts, right beside me, and pretty soon I heard him snoring. I was glad I didn't have school in the morning, 'cause I wasn't ready to see Cerese again. I wondered if she'd stop being my friend, and if she did, I couldn't blame her much. All in all, it had been a pretty bad day, especially when I thought about how excited I was that morning. But anyway, I was almost nine and nine sure had to be a little better than eight.

SEVEN

So on the morning of my ninth birthday, I got up early, same as I always did. I went tiptoeing into the kitchen to see was anybody else up, and if Chuck was still laying in the floor, but he wasn't. I wondered if he'd remember what I said to him last night and what he would do if he did. I opened the door to look outside and all the cars were gone, even Chuck's old one. I thought about the bags buried under the house, but I sure didn't think about putting them back in Chuck's car.

Then I went and looked in the front room and boy, was it a mess. There were bottles and cups all over the place, all laying on Toomie, and there were ashtrays piled up and overflowing and it stunk to high heaven. I left the door open to let it air out.

Tracie would more than likely sleep all day, so I could do what I wanted. I went back to the kitchen and it was a mess too. Worse than last night. There were broken bottles all over the place, and somebody had spilled something all over the floor, and it had mixed with the dirt already there, and now there was mud. I remembered how Cerese had looked around like she smelled something bad.

I went back down to the cellar and Antoe was fiddling with the broke radio.

"C'mon Antoe, you gotta help me."

"Do what?" He didn't like doing anything at all that wasn't his idea.

"We gotta clean the kitchen, it's nasty."

"Bad people out there."

"No, they all left. C'mon." He didn't move.

"I'll give you a honeybun if you help." Well, that got him moving so I opened my box and pulled out the half-eaten honeybun and gave it to him. He stuffed it in his mouth and followed me up the stairs.

"OK, you get a garbage sack out and hold it so I can fill it up."

He got a sack and held it for me and I went around the kitchen throwing paper, bottles, and emptying the ashtrays in it. It didn't take but a second to fill it up. I tied the top of it then and told him to take it out to the trash barrel. I got another sack and opened the icebox. There was the nasty spaghetti, and some milk I didn't know how long had been there. I raked that spaghetti in the trash sack and in the bottom of the bowl it was green. Then I put my shirt up over my nose while I poured the milk down the sink. It came out in stinky, white, clumps.

"All done!" Antoe came back in, and I handed him another sack before he could go back downstairs.

"Here, take this one to the front room and put the trash in it." He left with the bag and I pulled out more smelly stuff. There was a bag of rotted apples, some noodles that had green fuzz all over the top, and a bag of something brown I couldn't even begin to say what it was. When I finished digging everything out of there, the only things left were mustard, mayonnaise, and some cans of beer. I tried a can once, to see what it was like, and it was nasty. I was just fixing to go get Antoe and see if he wanted to walk to Perone's when I heard a car door slam out front. I ran to peek out the window in the front hallway and saw it was a shiny white car and a black lady was getting out of it and staring up at our house.

Hellshitdamn. I knew it had to be Cerese's mother, and I was betting she was mad. She was real tall and real dressed up. She was wearing a purple dress, and a purple hat, and the hat had little yellow flowers on it. The flowers on her hat were the exact same kind of yellow flowers that bloomed behind our house. She was carrying a yellow purse, and her shoes were yellow too. I'd never seen anyone so dressed up on a Saturday morning. She stood looking up at our house with the same kind of expression Cerese had when she saw it for the first time. She looked like she took a deep breath then, and started coming towards the front door. She walked up the steps carefully so she wouldn't step in a hole. Before she could knock on the door, I opened it and I must've scared her 'cause she jumped a little.

"Hi," I said, then, "Who are you?" Even though I knew, I wanted to make sure.

"You must be Girl."

"Yeah, how do you know?"

"I'm Cerese's mother." She looked at me real funny and I couldn't do anything but open up the door wider to let her walk in. So she did and looked around the front hallway and up the stairs where it was still pitch black. She turned to me and said, "I need...I need to see Tracie. Would you please go get her?"

"She's asleep, and I'll get in trouble if I wake her up. You could come back later, or you could just wait."

"No, I need you to get her now."

She sounded like somebody who was used to getting what she wanted, and if she didn't, she'd get real mad in a hurry. But still, I didn't want to go up those stairs.

"She don't like getting up early on Saturdays." I tried once more.

"I will go up those stairs myself if you don't go."

I bit my lip, then slowly made my way up the stairs. I got to the top and turned around to see what she was doing, and she was standing there, her purse over her shoulder, with her hands on her hips. Tracie's bedroom was all the way at the end of the hall, and when I got outside the door, I put my ear to it and listened. I couldn't hear anything but those fans whirring.

I cracked the door and smelled smoke and perfume, and I saw just one lump that was Tracie in the middle of the bed. I tiptoed to the edge of it, and all I could see were blonde hairs sticking up out of the covers.

"Tracie, there's a lady downstairs, and she won't go away until she talks to you."

She grunted and rolled over.

"She said she was gonna come up here if you don't come down."

If I kept bugging Tracie, she might get up and be *really* pissed off. If I went downstairs and told that lady I couldn't wake Tracie up...I didn't know what *she* might do. I decided to take my chances with the lady downstairs. Sometimes what you didn't know was a lot better than what you did.

I got down about the same time Antoe came dragging the full garbage bag from the front room. When he saw there was a strange lady there, he stopped dead in his tracks. I grabbed Antoe's hand and pulled him towards the lady.

"Antoe, remember my friend from last night? Cerese?

"Rese." He nodded.

"Well, this is her mother."

"Rese mother. Hi Rese Mother." He held out his hand. "Me Tonio."

"How are you Antonio? It's nice to see you."

Antoe nodded his head and puffed out his chest. "An-tone-eeoo. Yeah, An-tone-e-o. That's me." He liked it when people used his whole name.

"Is she coming?" Mrs. Miller hadn't forgotten.

"No. She's sleep. She said come back later."

Well, don't you know she took off up our stairs like she marched up them every single day? Antoe started dragging the trash towards the door to throw it away so I followed along behind her. She got to the top of the stairs and started down the hallway. She came to the first door and opened it, and it was the bedroom where me and Antoe camped sometimes. I was wondering if she'd look in every room on her way to Tracie's and sure enough, she did. I heard her make a noise in her throat when she looked in the bathroom. It was kinda messy in there; there were towels and dirty clothes were laying all over the floor. She got to Tracie's room and opened the door. I knew she knew I was behind her, but she didn't ever turn around to look at me. She walked in and left the door open and I stood right outside it, so I could hear what was going on. It was pitch black in there like it always was, and then Mrs. Miller found the light switch and the lights blazed on. I heard Tracie grunt again.

"I'm Rachel Miller and I need to talk to you." There wasn't a sound. Since the door opened out in the hallway and not in the bedroom, I got in the little space between the door and the wall where I could see what was happening in the room by peeking through the crack. This way, I was hidden behind the door so nobody could see me from the hallway or the bedroom. I could see the lump in the bed that was Tracie, and when Mrs. Miller spoke, all Tracie did was dig down a little deeper in the covers.

"We can do this the easy way, where you get up and speak to me, or we can do it the hard way, where I'll drag your behind out of that bed. It's up to you."

Mrs. Miller had crossed over to stand by the window, and she pulled up the shade to let the light come in. She turned around to stare at the bed where Tracie was and there wasn't any sign that she'd even heard her. I held my breath wondering if she was really gonna pull her out of bed. Mrs. Miller went back to the bed and walked over to it, then she reached down, grabbed a handful of cover and yanked. It came flying off the bed and Tracie was in a ball in the middle of it, naked, like she always was when she slept. Mrs. Miller made the same sound in her throat that she made when she saw our bathroom. Tracie sat up, her ninnies flopping everywhichway and rubbed her eyes. Mrs. Miller turned back to the window.

"I'd thank you to put on some clothes."

"Who the fuck are you?" She leaned way over the side of the bed and fished around till she found a tee shirt of Chuck's, and pulled it over her head. It came down just long enough to cover her behind. She lit a cigarette then, and stared at Mrs. Miller.

"I'm Rachel Miller, Cerese's mother. But, according to my daughter, you didn't actually meet her did you? I'm not sure who all she did meet, because she wouldn't say much about it. Which is why I'm here. I protect my children and I expect wherever they are, that someone's going be there to protect them, too."

"Nothing happened to her, did it?" Tracie got up and yanked on a pair of jeans then.

"That's what I don't know. Brady said she was hysterical when she got home but she wouldn't say why. If I find out someone touched my child, I will have the law out here so fast your head will swim."

"Are you threatening me?" Tracie sounded like she was getting mad now.

"Not at all. I'm just telling you that where there are children involved, specifically *my* child, you need to watch what goes on here. Although, I can assure you my child will not be back in this house, and you need to look after your own a little better."

"I do just fine."

"No, you don't, that child out there is as raggedy as a homeless girl, and Antonio is so filthy a week's worth of scrubbing probably wouldn't get him clean."

I looked down at my feet and saw that they were kinda black and the backs of my hands looked kinda rusty. I didn't like that this lady thought we were dirty. Cerese was always scrubbed shiny as a new penny.

I heard sounds and I peeked through the crack and saw Mrs. Miller had walked over to where Tracie was stubbing out her cigarette in the ashtray on the table by the bed.

"What I want to know is this: what would your mother say about how you were raising her and looking after Antonio?"

"What the hell are you talking about?"

"I knew your mother; I wonder what she'd say about the way you're living."

"That's none of your damn business."

"You don't remember me, do you?

"Should I?"

"Rosalinda was my child."

Tracie stared at her, and even though she'd just put out her cigarette, she picked up another one and lit it.

"I'd wondered, Cerese told me she was in class with a little girl named Girl, but then I knew for sure when I saw Antonio. Looks like somebody would have given that child a real name."

"After all this time you're gonna come here and question what we did? I don't remember you stepping up to do anything."

"And we both know why, don't we?"

There was quiet then, and I could see through the cracks that they were just staring at each other.

"I do the best I can."

"You need to do better."

They just looked at each other, and the lady started towards the door. I didn't want to be caught listening, so I ran down the hall and in my bedroom as quiet as I could. I could hear footsteps in the hallway, so I knew they were coming out, and I had gotten away just in time.

I heard them talking some more, but I couldn't hear what they were saying, then I heard them walking down the hallway. I peeked out and they were on the stairs heading down. I followed behind them then, wanting to know exactly what was going on. They got down the stairs and looked at each other again. The floor creaked under my feet and they both turned around and saw me. Tracie was about to say something when the front door slung open and Chuck came hopping in as fast as his one legged self could.

"What the hell?" He asked and there was a mean look on his face. Tracie got between him and the lady then, and said, "Shut up Chuck, she's just leaving."

"Well, ain't this something?" He looked up and saw me standing on the stairs. "I guess this is your doing?" He started to come up and before I could make a decision to run up or down, Tracie grabbed him.

"Stop it, it ain't her fault. She was just coming to talk to me."

"You a nigger lover too, now?"

"Shut up Chuck, don't show your ignorance!"

"What'd you say?"

"I said shut your damn mouth."

He grabbed her arm then, and twisted it behind her back and she hollered.

"Don't you ever, ever tell me to shut my damn mouth, or you can get your nigger loving ass right out of here!"

"It's my house, you sonofabitch!" She screamed at him, all the time trying to get her arm loose. When she said that, he yanked her around, drew back his fist, and hit her smack in the face. It looked like her nose exploded with blood and she fell down in a heap.

I couldn't move. I'd never seen him hit Tracie, it was worse than when he hit me with his belt. I wanted to go help her, but I was scared.

Chuck looked down at her and I thought he was gonna pick her up and knock her down again, but he didn't. He looked up and me and then looked at the lady and stomped back out the front door, which was still open. I heard the door slam on his car and then I heard the gravel exploding as he tore out of the driveway. I ran down the stairs to see if Tracie was OK, and the lady went over to help her up. There was blood all over her face and it was dripping down on her tee shirt.

"Run get me a towel." The lady told me, so I charged back up the stairs to find a wash rag that was sorta clean. I got one, wet it, wrung it out, and then took it back downstairs. They'd gone into the kitchen, and Tracie was sitting at the table and the lady was looking at her face. I handed her the wet rag, and she started to clean up Tracie.

"I don't think he broke it, but you're going to have a black eye, and your nose will be sore for a few days," she said. "If a man hits you once, he'll hit you again. You think that's a good thing for that child to see? Does he hit her too?"

Tracie didn't answer her, but took the rag away from her, stood up and walked over to the sink. She looked over at the horse skull that was still sitting on the table, and then turned around to face the lady.

"It's OK. He'll be sorry and make it up to me tonight. He always does."

"So he does this a lot?" Tracie didn't say anything, but I sure could've. I could've told this lady just how many times Chuck beat me, and for all I knew, he hit Tracie all the time too.

The lady, Mrs. Miller, stood there like she was waiting on Tracie to say something, and when she didn't, she turned around and walked out of the kitchen. I waited for the sound of the door opening, but then all of a sudden she was back in the kitchen.

"Why don't you let Girl come home with me? She could spend the night. I wouldn't say she's going to have much of a birthday otherwise."

"How do you know it's her birthday?"

"It's a hard day for me to forget, don't you think?"

Tracie didn't say anything for a second, then, "Chuck wouldn't like it. He wants her to go to church with us tomorrow."

"Church. You go to church?" The lady asked with her eyebrows raised way up.

"Yeah, Chuck's a preacher."

The lady just stared at her. "So you're not raising her Catholic?"

"No."

"Was she even baptized?"

"Yeah, Chuck did it."

"But not in the Church."

Tracie didn't say anything else.

"She can spend the night, and I'll have her back here in the morning, before it's time for church."

"No, it'd be better if you brought her home while we're gone. I'll tell Chuck she's staying at Bettes' house."

"Whatever you have to do."

"Girl," the lady turned to me then, "Would you like to come over to my house and see Cerese? And spend the night with her?'"

"Can Antoe come too?"

"Well..." She was thinking.

"Oh please," I begged, "He never gets to do anything fun or go anywhere."

"I guess so, if he wants to come." Mrs. Miller said, slowly, like she was still not sure.

"I'll go ask him." I galloped downstairs to get Antoe, and I knew he wouldn't like to, but I didn't want to be all by myself at someone's house, even though I knew Cerese. He was sitting on the floor carving something out of a new bar of soap.

"Hey Antoe, come on. We're gonna go with the lady, with Cerese's mother."

"Tonio stay here."

"No, you're gonna come with me, c'mon."

"No."

"Please Antoe." I stood in front of him and put my hands over his hands that were carving the bar of soap. "We're gonna go over there 'cause Chuck's being mean and he's gonna come home and beat you up if he finds you here." Well, I knew I shouldn't scare him like that, but I wanted him to go with me.

"Not like Chuck. Tonio go."

"OK, you get some clothes and put them in a bag, and I'll go get mine." I ran back up the stairs. Tracie was still sitting at the table, and Mrs. Miller hadn't moved from where she was standing.

"Is Antonio coming?" Mrs. Miller asked.

"Yeah, he's getting his clothes. I'll go get mine."

"Make sure you get some church clothes, we're going to go to church tonight."

I ran up the stairs and in my room, and wondered what I should wear to their church. I sure as hell wasn't wearing that ugly checked dress Chuck bought me, and anyway, it was still all wrinkled up from where he'd tried to drown me. I dug around on the floor where all my clothes were, and found one of my shirts and skirt. I found some underwear next, and put my black and white shoes on. I stuffed all my clothes in a paper sack that was in my room and ran back downstairs.

Antoe had come upstairs with his sack and he was showing Mrs. Miller what he'd carved. It was a lady, like the statue he had, and Mrs. Miller was making a fuss over it, and Antoe liked that.

"Well come on then, we need to get going so I can fix lunch. I bet you like to eat lunch don't you, Antonio?"

"What lunch taste like?" He asked.

Mrs. Miller laughed. "You'll like it, I promise."

We walked out then, Tracie following behind us, and Mrs. Miller turned around and said, "I'll bring them home tomorrow morning around eleven. Is that OK?"

"Yeah, we don't get home till late."

"Then they don't need to be here by themselves."

"They'll be fine, they always are."

Mrs. Miller looked like she didn't like this much. "Well, I'll bring them home later then." And she didn't say anything else. Tracie lit a cigarette and said, "Y'all be good." And she walked back in the house.

EIGHT

We got in Mrs. Miller's car, me in the front seat, and Antoe in the back, and she made us both put on our seat belts, which we never did. I looked around at her car, and I'd never been in one so big and clean. It had dark blue seats, and they were furry and soft like Toomie. I was so busy feeling the seats that I didn't really pay attention to the trip to her house. It wasn't long before we were pulling in a driveway where a little white house sat. It wasn't a very big house, but it was real pretty. You could see bright yellow curtains at the windows and there were two bikes propped up beside the shed that was out back. Mrs. Miller pulled the car under the garage and there was a big, black, shaggy dog jumping around and barking his head off. Antoe loved dogs of all kinds, and before the car came to a complete stop he was outside petting it. The dog just about wiggled himself inside out he was so happy with the attention.

"That's Boger. Antonio, you can stay out here and play with him. Girl, why don't you come inside with me and find Cerese?"

Antoe was happy to play with the dog and I followed Mrs. Miller up the steps and across the front porch. Their porch was real different than ours, it wasn't all falling down and the paint wasn't peeling off. We walked in the house and it was all open and bright as could be. There were pictures all over one side of the wall and they had a TV set much bigger than the one we had. It was really clean and smelled like lemons.

"Walk on back to Cerese's room. It's the first one past the bathroom. I'll call you all when lunch is ready." She disappeared into the kitchen and I walked down the hallway looking for Cerese. I was kinda worried that she'd be mad after last night. I found the bathroom and peeked in. There were white towels hanging on racks and there were no clothes laying all over the floor. Their bathtub wasn't big like ours was, but it was bright pink. I walked on in the room that was Cerese's and saw she was laying on the floor coloring.

"Hi," I said, walking in.

She jumped up and stared at me.

"Where'd you come from?"

"Your momma brought me over. And Antoe too."

"Oh," she said. We just looked at each other. Then,

"You wanna play?"

"OK."

She got out a big box of dolls; I'd never seen anything like them.

There were all different colors of brown, and they were all wearing beautiful, grown up lady clothes. Cerese wanted to play like the dolls were all going to a party, and she kept telling me to say this or say that, but I just wanted to hold them, stroke their hair, and look at them.

"You're not playing right!" She finally said, like she was mad. "Ain't you never played dolls before?"

"Excuse me? What was that?" Mrs. Miller was standing in the hallway.

"I'm sorry, Ma'am. I meant have you not ever played dolls before?" Cerese said.

"Go wash your hands, lunch is almost ready."

"Yes, ma'am." Cerese was quick to jump up, so I followed her. We went to the bathroom and I waited till she'd washed her hands and then I scrubbed mine.

"Does your mother ever hit you?" I asked.

"No. But she smacks Brady sometimes. Why?"

"Just wondering."

"Do you get whippings?

I didn't want to talk about all the whippings I got. "Are we gonna go to church tonight?" I asked instead.

"Yeah, we always go to church on Saturday night."

"I thought church was only on Sunday."

"No, it's on Saturday."

"I don't like church," I said, and she wheeled around and stared at me.

"Jesus gonna be mad with you if you say that."

I shrugged.

"C'mon," she called over her shoulder as she hopped down the hallway on one leg. It looked so funny, and it was the same thing I did when I was making fun of Chuck. We were both laughing when we got to the kitchen. Antoe was sitting quietly, and it looked like he had wet his hair and slicked it down. Brady came in then, and he stared at Antoe, then me, like the way we sometimes stared at bugs we'd catch.

"Brady." Mrs. Miller said his name, and he quickly sat down and looked down at this plate.

We all had to hold hands then, and Mrs. Miller said a blessing over the food. I looked around the table and I couldn't believe all the good things on it. Bettes cooked, but she'd only make one thing at a time, like soup or something in a pan, but never a whole bunch of stuff. There were fried pork-chops, green beans, mashed potatoes, corn-on-the-cob, and huge, white biscuits with brown bottoms. Mrs. Miller handed me a plate that was about to spill it was so full. I took it carefully and set it down and then looked over at Antoe, hoping he wasn't going to drop stuff or start eating with his hands, but he was quietly eating with a spoon. And he wasn't even shoveling it in like he normally did.

Nobody said much, 'cause everybody was busy eating that good food. Mrs. Miller gave Antoe seconds without him even asking. He grinned at her and she grinned back. Then she got up from the table and came back with a huge cake with pink icing and candles burning on top. Well, don't you know that it was for me? I couldn't believe it.

I got to blow out all ten candles, she said one was to grow on, and she cut me the biggest piece you ever saw and it had a big candy rose on it. She told Brady to go get the ice cream and she gave me a big scoop of that too. It was the first time I'd ever had ice cream *with* cake and I decided I'd like to eat it every single day for the rest of my life. It tasted like being happy felt.

After everybody got done, Mrs. Miller told me and Antoe we could go watch TV and Cerese and Brady would clean up the kitchen. I wondered if I oughta ask her if I could help, but I figured I better go with Antoe so I could keep an eye on him.

"Antoe, you better go to the bathroom," I whispered to him, knowing that if he wasn't reminded, he'd go in his pants. I didn't think Mrs. Miller would like that very much.

"Where bathroom?" He asked and I led him down the hall to it.

"Wipe good," I reminded him, "and make sure

you flush!"

I went back and turned the TV on and sat down to watch. It was a show where they were cooking, so I wasn't really that interested. I noticed there were a lot of pictures on the wall, of different people, so I got up to look at them. There was a bunch of black people, some looked real old. At the very top of the pictures was one of a black man with a mustache wearing a suit, and he was shaking hands with a woman. I looked closer and the woman was Mrs. Miller but she looked younger then.

Antoe came back then, and he walked around with me looking at the pictures. All of a sudden he stood stock still, and his mouth dropped open. He reached out towards one of the pictures and touched it carefully. I looked over to see what it was that had caught his attention. It was a short dumpy black girl. She had on a big yellow headband and she was wearing a bright yellow dress with big black circles all over it and she was grinning like anything at the camera.

"Girl!" Antoe shouted. "Girl look! It Rosie! It Rosie! Lookit Rosie!"

He was getting worked up and I sure did hope he wouldn't start tearing stuff up the way he sometimes did. Mrs. Miller came running out of the kitchen to see what was going on.

"Oh Lord, I forgot about the pictures."

"Lookit Rosie!" Antoe was still excited.

"I see, honey." Mrs. Miller said.

"Rosie pretty. Pretty, pretty Rosie. Where Rosie go?"

"Would you like to have this picture?" She took it off the wall carefully.

"Who is that?" I asked, but neither one of them answered me.

I had no idea who that woman was, and why Antoe knew her. I'd never seen Antoe get that excited over somebody's picture, and I wasn't sure I liked it.

"Tonio, picture. Look Girl! See Rosie?"

He brought it over to me and I glanced at it.

"You wanna go outside Antoe?"

But he didn't even act like he heard me, he just took that picture and went over and sat on the couch and kept right on grinning at it. Before I could bully him into putting it down and coming outside with me, Mrs. Miller told me to run get the clothes I was gonna wear to church.

I ran, got the sacks and took them back to the front room. She pulled them out and looked at them and made a different kind of noise in her throat.

"You can wear some of Cerese's clothes tonight. I have some old clothes of Mr. Miller's I think might fit Antonio. Mr. Miller was taller, but Antonio is wider. Come on with me."

She led me back down the hallway and started looking around in the closet and she pulled out a bright pink dress that had little green flowers scattered all over it. It had buttons going all the way down the front and when I looked closer, I saw that the buttons were little tiny strawberries.

"I think this might fit," she said, holding the pretty dress up to me. Cerese is taller than you are, and this used to be her favorite dress, but it's too short now. Do you like it?"

"Yeah, it's pretty!"

"Here, we say, yes, ma'am."

"Yes, Ma'am."

She kept rooting around in the closet and found a pair of shiny black shoes, then she pulled some socks and some underwear out of a drawer.

"Here, try these on and see if they fit. They're too tight for Cerese."

I flopped down on the floor to stick my feet in the shoes. They fit OK, but they were a little big and sorta flopped up and down on my feet when I walked.

"That's OK, we'll just stuff some tissue in the toes of them. You can keep those and take them home with you."

"Thank you, Ma'am."

"You'll need to take a bath in a little while. And you'll need to scrub good or I'll make you get back and scrub you myself, you hear me?"

Well, I sure did hear her, and I sure didn't want her scrubbing me.

"Yes, Ma'am."

I went back to the living room then, and Cerese was watching TV.

"You wanna go outside?" I asked.

"No, I wanna watch TV."

So I sat there and watched TV with her, although there wasn't anything good on. I was kinda getting sleepy when Mrs. Miller poked her head in the living room and told me to go take my bath, and she told Cerese to show me where the towels and things were.

Cerese took me down the hallway and into the bathroom and handed me a fluffy white towel, and a white wash rag. I put them down on the side of the sink and went to the bedroom to get the clothes Mrs. Miller had given me. I ran water in the tub then, and soaped my rag up and scrubbed myself all over. I didn't want Mrs. Miller doing it so I soaped up the rag a second time and scrubbed all over again. When I got up to let out the water, I saw it was real brown and dirty looking.

I dried off then, and put on the underwear and the pink dress, then the socks that had little pink bows on them, and the black shiny shoes. When I looked in the mirror, I thought I looked pretty good, except for my hair. It was all over the place and I didn't have any sort of brush. I went to show Cerese how I looked and almost ran into Brady going down the hall towards his bedroom. He acted like me and Antoe weren't even there, and he didn't say anything to me now. I knew he was mad about Cerese being at our house, and the way Chuck acted, but I wanted to tell him I didn't have nothing to do with that. I wanted to tell him, "I don't like him either."

Cerese was getting her clothes to go take her bath, and she grinned when she saw I was wearing her dress.

"That's the strawberry dress!"

"It's pretty," I said, smoothing the front of it down.

"Your hair's messed up," she told me, looking at me kinda the same way she'd looked around our kitchen.

"I don't have a brush."

"Momma'll fix it." And she ran off down the hallway to get Mrs. Miller and bring her back to the bedroom.

"Momma, Girl needs you to fix her hair."

And then she hopped off to take her bath. Mrs. Miller went to get a brush then, and she came back and told me to take a seat on the bed.

Hellshitdamn. She nearly snatched me bald, but when she was finished, she held up a mirror so I could see it and it looked nice. It was all braided in one long braid, like a horse's tail, down my back, and she'd tied the ends up with shiny pink and shiny green balls, like the ones Cerese always wore.

"Thank you!" I couldn't remember my hair ever looking so pretty.

She smiled at me then, and went off towards her bedroom. I went in the living room, and wouldn't you know Antoe was still sitting there staring at that stupid picture. I thought about going outside, but didn't want to get my new clothes dirty.

Mrs. Miller came to get Antoe then, and told him it was time for him to take a bath. I thought about telling her how you'd have to make sure he actually got in the water, 'cause sometimes he just wet his hair and washed his hands.

I was surprised Antoe went with her too. Normally he wouldn't go anywhere with anybody but me. I could make him go with people even if he didn't want to, but now he was acting like I wasn't even there. I kinda wished we were back at home playing outside.

Cerese came bouncing in the living room, and she was wearing a dress I'd never seen her wear. It was bright green and it had a big white bow at the neck and she had on socks with green bows and shiny black shoes just like the ones I was wearing. Her hair was braided too, only it was braided all over in about a million little braids and each braid had a shiny green ball on the end of it.

"How long does church last?" I asked, thinking that if it lasted as long as Chuck's, then we'd be there all night.

"Not long. But we have to be quiet and not talk or laugh, or Momma gets *real* mad." I nodded 'cause I sure didn't want to make Mrs. Miller mad. I had a feeling it might be kinda scary.

Mrs. Miller came out then, and Antoe was with her.

You could tell by the look on his face he thought he was dressed up. He had on a brown striped shirt that buttoned up, and for once it fit him without letting his fat belly hang out. He had on brown pants too, and they weren't too tight, and he had a pair of shiny brown shoes. He was even wearing a belt. His hair was slicked down and he was cleaner than I'd ever remember seeing him look. He carefully sat down on a chair, like he was afraid he'd mess something up by sitting down. Mrs. Miller went to get dressed then, and me and Cerese and Antoe just kept sitting there watching TV. Brady came out then, and Mrs. Miller and we all went to get in the car. Brady got in the front seat and me and Cerese and Antoe crawled in the back, with me being in the middle. I sure did hate the thought of going to church, if it was anything like going with Chuck. The only good part was he wasn't with us.

We drove for a long time and then turned down a windy driveway that had a little white building at the end of it. There was a huge white statue of a woman in the front, like the one Antoe had, only this one was way bigger. Mrs. Miller pulled into a parking place and turned off the car and we all got out.

The first thing I noticed was that all the people walking in the church were black. We walked up to the door and went inside. It was cool and dark and I saw these little bowls with water in them hanging on the wall. Mrs.

Miller and Brady and Cerese all dipped their fingers in the water and wiped it on their faces. I wondered why they did that and was I supposed to do it too, when I saw Antoe do the same thing. Before I could ask him why he did that, Mrs. Miller shooed us all towards a bench up at the front, and it was Brady, Cerese, Mrs. Miller, Antoe, then me. They pulled out these little benches that were up under the seats, and kneeled down on them. Antoe didn't even have to be told; he kneeled down quick as anything and bowed his head. I looked sideways at him, trying to get his attention, but he was ignoring me. I poked him and he shook his head at me and put his finger up to his lip, shushing me.

Hellshitdamn. Antoe didn't act like this. I never, ever remembered him telling me to be quiet before. Everyone got up from kneeling then, and I scooted all the way to the end of the bench. Pretty soon we stood up and they started singing and I saw three boys walking up the aisle and one was carrying a big cross and the other two had lit candles, and there was a man in a green dress, walking behind them.

The man got up front and he talked and talked, and then we sat down again, then stood up again, and kneeled down again, and there was some more singing in between. I wasn't paying much attention, 'cause I kept thinking how different it was from being at Chuck's church where everybody hollered and Chuck pounded on everything and shouted about hell and people were running and rolling around.

Then we all went down to the front, and Mrs. Miller waited and showed me to cross my arms in front of me and the man in the dress touched me on my forehead. The rest of them got a little cracker, even Antoe. I was about to say something, 'cause I wanted a cracker too, but I noticed that Cerese didn't get one either.

After that, it was pretty much over, and we stood up one last time and sang, and then we started to leave. Mrs. Miller was talking to people and I was just looking around when I noticed that Antoe had tears rolling down his face. He had stopped by a table and there were a bunch of beads on the table. He grabbed them up and really started to wail then. I didn't know what was going on, and I was going to him when he took off running towards the front of the church and crawled under the table that was up front and hid under the table cloth. I ran up there after him and looked under and he was rocking and hitting himself. Usually I knew what had set him off, but not this time. I was kinda glad though, 'cause he was acting like I was used to him acting.

"Antoe, don't do that." I pulled his hands away from his face so he wouldn't hit himself. "We gotta go now; Mrs. Miller's waiting on us." He was still crying.

"If you make Mrs. Miller mad, she's gonna take that picture away she gave you."

This stopped him in mid-wail.

"Take Rosie picture?"

"Yeah, she's gonna be pissed off and take it back if we don't go. Stop acting bad."

He crawled out then, and thankfully most of the people had already gone. We got back to the back of the church where Mrs. Miller was standing and she held out her hand.

"Antonio, let me have those." He put them behind his back.

"Ma'am? He's gonna get real upset again if you take them."

"Well, he can't keep them all, he can only keep one. Give them here Antonio, but you can have one."

Believe it or not, he gave them to her without saying a word. He gave her a smile and after they turned around, I reached out and snatched them up and stuffed them up under my dress and down my underwear. I still didn't have no idea what it was that set Antoe off.

We got in the car then and before Mrs. Miller started the car up, she turned around to look at us in the backseat.

"Does anyone want ice cream?" She asked.

"Me! I do!" Cerese shouted.

I didn't shout but I grinned and nodded my head.

"Tonio want."

"OK, then, we'll stop at the Dairy Queen and get some ice cream for Girl's birthday."

"She done had a cake." Brady spoke from the front seat, staring out the window.

"What did you say?" Mrs. Miller asked him.

"She's already had a cake."

"I don't recall asking for your permission, Mr. Miller. I'd appreciate you leaving that attitude wherever you picked it up."

He dropped his head and mumbled, "I'm sorry, Ma'am," and went back to staring out the window.

Hellshitdamn. Now he'd hate me worse than ever.

We drove to the Dairy Queen and the red sign out front was all lit up and there were cars everywhere in the parking lot. We all got out and went inside and stood in line. Mrs. Miller told us to look at the menu and decide what we wanted. As we were standing there looking at what all kinds of ice cream they had, I noticed all the people in the line were staring at us. I looked over at Antoe to make sure he didn't have his tallywacker out or anything and he didn't. So I couldn't figure out what it was. We all got to the front then, and Brady, Cerese, then me ordered, and I ordered for Antoe too, then Mrs. Miller ordered and she paid the lady at the counter. They told us we could sit down and they'd bring it to us so we went to sit at an empty table in the middle.

"I have to go to the bathroom," I whispered to Mrs. Miller.

"It's right up front, down that hallway," she pointed.

"Do you want me to go with you?"

"No," I said.

"No, what?" She asked.

"Oh, sorry, no ma'am." I never would remember to say that every time. I went down the hallway to the bathroom and had to wait 'cause there were two other people in front of me. A lady who'd been in line with us walked up behind me.

"Why're you with them niggers?" She asked me.

I looked at her.

"Are they kidnapping you?" Do you need me to call the police?" She asked me again, a little louder.

"We're having ice cream on account it's my birthday. And Bettes says anybody who uses that word is fucking stupid."

Well, you should've seen her eyes bug out of her head. The bathroom was empty by then so I sassed right on in there. I wondered what she meant by asking me if they'd kidnapped me. I went back out to the table only they weren't there anymore. Mrs. Miller had my ice cream and was holding the door open.

"Come on Girl, I think we'll just eat this in the car."

Well, she didn't know what kind of mess Antoe could make with ice-cream and there wasn't nothing that could be done about it. Brady looked mad, and Mrs. Miller's mouth was pinched up tight. Cerese was just skipping around happy to have her ice cream.

We got in the car then, and she drove down to where there was a big parking lot beside a store and parked and said, "Since the restaurant is so crowded, I thought we could just sit here and watch the cars go by."

I knew good and well that restaurant wasn't that crowded and nobody was interested in watching cars go by. I wondered what happened when I was in the bathroom. I thought about telling her what that woman had said, but I figured it wasn't a good idea. We ate the ice cream so fast I got a headache and nobody acted like they liked it much except for Cerese and Antoe.

Nobody talked on the way home, and when we got there, she told us all to go get ready for bed. I had a cot in Cerese's room, and she'd made Antoe a bed on the couch. He was quiet the rest of the night, just holding his picture and his beads. I hid the ones I had stuffed in my underwear down deep in my sack with the clothes I'd brought. I'd give them to him tomorrow when we got home, or maybe I'd just keep them for myself. They were real pretty.

I crawled in the cot and just laid there a long, long time and I heard Cerese snoring from the other bed. I wondered what it would be like to live in a house like this, with a momma who cooked and cleaned and washed clothes for you. I wondered if it'd be worth it to have to give up doing whatever we wanted. This was the first time I could ever remember being somewhere else at night, except for Bettes' house, and that didn't count. I wasn't sleepy at all, so I sat up on the cot and stared out the window at the darkness for a long, long time.

NINE

When I woke up, I was leaned up against the window where I'd been looking out. It was real early, and I didn't hear anybody up so I tiptoed down to the living room to see if Antoe was sleeping. He was, so I tiptoed back. Cerese was still sleeping, too, so I laid down and stayed quiet. I wondered how long it would be before Mrs. Miller took us home. I was real tired. It was Sunday, so that meant it had only been two days since Cerese had come home with me on the bus. It seemed a lot longer.

At least it was a different Sunday than it would normally be. Today we wouldn't be with Chuck, and I started thinking about what me and Antoe could do if we were at home. We would play outside 'cause I liked to roam around in the woods across the road. Sometimes we saw big snakes, and I was convinced that an alligator lived there. Mr. Perone had this huge, huge alligator in his store that was stuffed. He said he'd killed it on the lake out in front of our house a long time ago, before I was born. I'd make Antoe sit out by the water for hours, hoping to see one. I thought maybe I could find a baby one and make a pet out of it.

I got up and put on my clothes and I wondered if the Millers would sleep real late the way Tracie did. I heard someone stirring around in the hallway. I went to the door and peeked out and it was Antoe heading into the bathroom. I closed Cerese's door behind me and sat down in the hallway to wait on him. I was looking around the hallway and I couldn't believe how clean everything was. The floors were so shiny they looked like you could eat off them, there were pictures hanging on the walls, and little tables with clean white cloths draped over them. It smelled like lemons and the way it was right after it rained: fresh and new.

Antoe had been in there for a long time, so I got up and opened the door to see what he was doing, and would you believe he was washing his hands?

"Why're you washing your hands?"

"Tonio wash hands, Girl need wash hands too."

"I washed them yesterday. They don't need it again."

"Wash hands now." And he grabbed my hands and stuck them under the water and started to wash them for me. I pulled them away and dried them off.

"I wonder when we're gonna go home? Ain't you

ready to go home?"

"Tonio like it here. This where Rosie live. Girl see Rosie?"

And he went off to the living room to get his picture. I followed him and he had the picture and the beads on the couch, and he'd folded up his blanket and it was laying on the edge of the couch.

I picked up the picture and looked at it again.

"Who is this?"

"Rosie. Tonio love Rosie. Rosie went 'way. Rosie went 'way 'cause Girl came."

What did he mean by that? I didn't make that lady go away, I didn't even know her, and I bet I wouldn't like her.

I heard someone in the kitchen then, and I smelled cooking.

"Let's go eat."

We started towards the kitchen and Mrs. Miller was there fixing breakfast. She had on a pretty yellow dress and an apron. The apron was pink and it had little white flowers all over it. I thought about Tracie wearing something like that, and I couldn't even picture it. Not for the first time lately, I wondered if maybe we were real weird and the way everyone else did things was the right way.

"Good morning!" She said, smiling at us. I guess she wasn't mad anymore. "Are you all hungry?"

"Tonio hungry." I sat down across from Antoe. The table was set with plates and knives and forks and spoons, and there were napkins too. Not the paper kind like we had, but pretty cloth ones. They had big red roosters on them, and the roosters had bright green feathers.

"When are we gonna go home?" I asked her, I was kinda ready to leave this clean, lemon smelling place, even though it was nice, it was too different. And there were a lot of rules. Maybe we didn't have nice stuff, or maybe nobody cooked much of the time, but at least we could do whatever we wanted to. And that was something, wasn't it?

"Are you ready to leave? I thought you and Cerese might want to play for a while this afternoon and then I'd take you home around suppertime. Is that alright?"

I nodded.

"I hope you like bacon and eggs?" She was already bringing the food to the table to fill up our plates. She piled Antoe's plate high with the eggs and bacon, and then she brought over a pan of biscuits.

I didn't worry about talking, I just worried about eating. I didn't feel at home enough to talk to Antoe like we normally did, and I wasn't completely sure I wanted to talk to him anyway. Mrs. Miller wasn't eating; she'd gone back to the stove and was cooking more food. It was a good thing, too, 'cause Antoe ate every bite and he ate about six of those biscuits. I finished my plate and told her no thanks when she asked if I wanted more, and left them there in the kitchen.

I was sitting on the couch, wondering what to do, when she went down the hallway and I heard her waking up Cerese and Brady. I decided to go outside then, 'cause I wasn't much in the mood to talk to people. That was another good thing about home; there was nobody there to talk to you when you didn't feel like it.

I went around the side of the house exploring. I'd seen a pen that had chickens in it yesterday, and I wanted to check them out. There was a bunch of them in there all scratching and pecking and a rooster was walking around crowing and beating his wings. I wanted to get a closer look at them, and see maybe could I pet one, so I opened the door and climbed in the pen.

Well, as soon as I got in there and tried to pet one, they all started to run around like crazy, and the rooster came straight towards me like he was gonna jump on me. I ran to the back of the pen to get away from him and scared those other chickens so bad they started running and jumping and stirring up the biggest cloud of dirt you ever did see. I forgot to close the door, and don't you know over half of them went flying out that open door? But not the rooster that was chasing me, he managed to jump on the back of my legs and knock me down in the dirt. I got back to my feet quick as I could, and ran and jumped out of the pen and shut the door, but there were only three chickens left inside.

I looked around and Boger was chasing those

chickens all over the place. All of sudden there were two more dogs coming lickety-split and they tore into those poor chickens like you wouldn't believe. One big black and brown dog was grabbing them by the neck, then shaking his head back and forth, then tossing them up in the air. A little white dog would come from behind them and just gobble up their heads. All you could see was heaps of feathers and thick red blood. Those dogs looked like that was the most fun they'd ever had.

Just when I was wondering what to do, Brady came flying out of the house.

"Goddammit white girl, ain't you got no more sense than to let the chickens out? Git! Git outta here! Go on, Git!"

He'd picked up a big stick and was beating hell out of the dogs, but it was too late for the chickens. He turned around and looked at me.

"Why'n the hell did you let the fucking chickens out? Hell, I guess stupid runs in y'all's family."

"I didn't mean too, I just wanted to pet them and that big one started chasing me."

"Hell, I guess so, if you stupid enough to go in the pen with him. Momma gonna wring your white ass neck. Help me pick 'em up so she can get some good out of 'em."

He started to pick up the dead chickens.

"They're all bloody," I said.

"Well, no shit. Damn fool dogs done tore 'em up.

Just get outta my way."

He shoved me aside and picked up two more dead chickens by their feet. He was holding two in each hand and there were still three more on the ground. Even though I hated it, I picked up the last three by their feet. I felt bad 'cause I had 'caused them to die.

I followed Brady, carrying the dead chickens, and he went around the back of the house to where there was a big wooden table. He threw the chickens on the table then grabbed the ones I was carrying. Mrs. Miller walked out on the back porch to see what was going on.

"Brady, what on earth happened to my hens?" She was wiping her hands on a towel and she still had on her flowered apron from earlier.

"She let 'em out!"

I didn't know what to say and Mrs. Miller just looked at me.

"Well. Clean them, and I'll have to cook them so they won't ruin. I guess we'll be eating chicken and dumplings for a few days. We'll have fried chicken for supper."

She came out to the table where Brady had laid the chickens and was just looking at them. I wanted to say I was sorry, but I didn't think it would matter.

Brady started to pull the feathers off the chickens, and I looked away. Mrs. Miller just watched him for what seemed like forever, then she turned towards me, put her arm around my shoulder and walked me to the porch.

"Did you let those chickens out deliberately?" She asked.

"No Ma'am, I didn't mean too. I just wanted to pet them, and they started chasing me. I guess I forgot to shut the door."

"Well. Nothing can be done about it now. Those were my laying hens. That's where we got all those eggs for breakfast. Now we won't have eggs anymore."

I felt like crying.

"I'm sorry," I said. "I'll buy you some more if you'll tell me where to get them."

She kinda laughed then, so I didn't know if she was still mad or not, but she didn't say anything more and we went in the house.

"I think Cerese is outside riding her bike, why don't you go out there and find her?"

Glad to have a reason for leaving, I tore out of the house to find Cerese. I didn't see her, but I saw a big swing made out of an old tire. I got on it and used my feet to push off, and then I started to spin around. I was having a good time when Cerese came peddling up on her bike.

"Whatcha doing?" She asked.

"Swinging. You wanna swing?"

"Uh uh. I'm riding my bike. You can ride it too, only you can't scratch it up, 'cause I just got it last year."

Before I could say anything she went flying around

the side of the house towards the garage. Now the thing was, I'd never ridden a bike in my life, but I sure wasn't about to tell her that.

I followed her, and she was peddling like anything down the driveway. I stood there watching and she got to the end of the driveway, turned around and came flying back to where I was standing and put her brakes on hard so she skidded on the gravel. She laughed and got off and handed it to me. I could say I didn't feel like riding, but she was watching me so I took it from her. Tracie always said she'd be damned to hell and back if she couldn't do something, so I thought the exact same thing and hopped up on it.

I remembered how Cerese had straddled the long, skinny seat, and how she had her feet on the ground, so I did that. I remembered how she'd started the pedals going with her feet, so I did that too, and for a second it seemed like I had it, but then I felt myself falling sideways.

Before I could catch myself, I plowed up the gravel with my face. I got up and touched my nose and it felt all skinned. Pulling the bike up, even though my face hurt like hell, I was just about to hop back on when Cerese huffed over and snatched the bike away from me.

"You scratched it! Can't you ride a bike?"

"Not that one. Mine's different."

Cerese put her hands on her hips, wrinkled up her nose and drew in her lips.

"You're kinda weird, ain't you?"

I didn't say anything.

"Why's he like that?"

"Who?"

"Antonio."

I didn't say nothing.

"Like what he did at church last night. Momma was real, real mad. I heard her talking to Aunt Lolly last night.

"Who's Aunt Lolly?"

"She's Aunt Lolly. Why's he like that? He don't act like no grown-up. Is it 'cause he's afflicted?"

"I don't what afflicted is." People didn't bother you this much at home. The only thing Tracie ever wanted was me to find her cigarettes or fix her a glass of tea.

"I don't either, but I thought you might since he's your kin."

"He's not my kin. He's just Antoe."

"Uh uh," Cerese argued. "Momma told Aunt Lolly he was, I heard her say. Didn't you know that?

"Yeah," I said. "I'm gonna go swing some more." I was hoping she wouldn't want to come too, and she didn't. She got back on her bike and rode around the yard.

I got back on the swing and wondered what Cerese meant by saying Antoe was kin to me. I had wondered about it, I thought maybe he was my brother or something, but just like when I asked Tracie if she was my momma, she'd tell me to stop asking so many fucking questions. So I just figured it was something I'd learn when I was older.

The rest of the day was long, long, long. We didn't do much but eat some fried chicken for supper. It was good, but I couldn't really eat it for thinking about the way those poor chickens were all laid out bloody in the yard. And I was wondering about being some kind of kin to Tracie and Antoe. Kin how?

Finally, Mrs. Miller told us to get our stuff together, that she would drive us home. I went to Cerese's room to get my paper sack that had my clothes and the beads in it. I wondered if I was supposed to take Cerese's dress and shoes, but I didn't want to ask so I just stuffed them in the sack.

Cerese was standing there watching me. I just looked at her and said, "Well, bye."

"Bye," was all she said back.

Antoe was outside waiting by the car and Mrs. Miller was waiting in the living room with her purse and car keys.

"Ready?" I nodded and we went out and got in the car. I was thinking about the past day and what Cerese had told me. I started to ask Mrs. Miller about it, but I knew Cerese would probably get in big trouble and I didn't want that. Besides, Cerese was only seven so she probably didn't know what she was talking about.

"You're mighty quiet, Girl. Is everything all right?"

"Yeah...yes ma'am."

"Are you all going to parents' night next week?" she asked.

"I don't know. Maybe. I'll ask Tracie again. Are y'all going? When is it?"

"Of course. I always go to parents' night, and it's Thursday night."

"Tracie said she would but I'll have to remind her, she forgets a lot."

Mrs. Miller didn't say anything else and we were home in just a minute or two. Chuck's cars were both parked so I knew he was home. No other cars were there.

I had the door opened even before Mrs. Miller had stopped good, and I unhooked the seat belt and jumped out.

"C'mon, Antoe, thanks Mrs. Miller." And before she even had time to say anything, I'd slammed the doors and pointed Antoe towards the side so he'd know to go in that way. I just had a feeling. And I was right too, 'cause Chuck came out of the front door about the time we were half-way around the back and he looked crazier and madder than he usually did. He was going down the steps so fast he almost fell, I first thought he was after me, but he was heading straight towards Mrs. Miller's car.

Antoe had gone on ahead but I waited to see what Chuck was gonna do. He yanked open Mrs. Miller's door and leaned way in. I couldn't hear what he was saying, but I knew he was mad about something. All of a sudden Mrs. Miller tore out of the driveway with Chuck still hanging on her car and with the car door still open. He pitched forward flat on his face in the dirt. I didn't wait to see any more but ran as fast as I could around the side of the house through the back door and down to the cellar. Antoe hadn't locked it but he was down there. I grabbed the chain and the lock and put it in place. Then I stayed right by the door to see if I could hear anything.

After a while I heard the front door slam, and I heard Chuck yelling. I could hear Tracie too. They were hollering and carrying on something awful. I knew I should stay put, but I wanted to know what was happening so I took the lock off, and as quiet as I could, went up the steps to the washer room.

"...pure china white, and ten grand and it's gone!" I only heard the last part of what Chuck was yelling. I heard Tracie say something but she wasn't yelling, so I didn't know what it was.

"I'll kill him! I'm gonna go find him and string him up and that'll teach him..."

He must've been walking all over the place cause his voice would get loud then it'd fade away.

"...her fault! I'm gonna beat her ass and learn her not...a scratch on both of them!"

Then it sounded like he was in the kitchen, and don't you know he started crying? I mean really *wailing* just like Antoe. I kept listening at the door and he kept on crying then I heard him say, "What'm I gonna do? They're gonna kill me if I don't have it."

Well, I didn't wanna hear no more, 'cause I know he was mad about that money and those balloons and it made me feel kinda weird to hear him cry like that, but I didn't do nothing but go down to the fruit cellar and I wrapped the chain twice around the door knob and put the lock in place.

TEN

All next week something was going on. Chuck was meaner than a snake, more than usual, and every night when it got dark, men would come to our house. They weren't the ones who'd usually come either, these wouldn't come in the house and drink and smoke. These men would call Chuck outside, and if he wasn't there, they'd stand around for the longest time waiting on him. After they left, he'd come in the house and act crazy and him and Tracie would fight like everything. I didn't even bother going upstairs anymore, and neither did Antoe.

Tracie wandered around the house like she didn't know what she was doing, and you didn't ask her a thing or she'd yell and cuss, and I couldn't think when the last time Bettes had been over. Every day I wished like anything for Chuck to leave and not come back, but I guess wishing didn't work so good, cause he was there in the morning and when I got off the bus after school.

At school we were having to clean our room and hang up decorations and all kinds of things getting ready for parents' night. Since everything was so weird at home, I hadn't said anything else about it, even though I really did wanna go. It was Halloween and everybody was gonna dress up and go trick or treating around to all the rooms and there was gonna be all kinds of things to eat and drink, and there was gonna be a carnival set up in the parking lot. I didn't have a costume anyway.

Thursday afternoon when I got off the bus, Chuck's red car was gone but his old one was there. Since he never let anyone else drive the red one, I knew he wasn't home. It seemed like it had been forever since I'd gone in the front door. I busted through it like a tornado, and Tracie was standing right there in the front hall and she like to have jumped out of her skin.

"Goddammit, Girl! Do you have to knock the goddamn door off the hinges?"

"Sorry," I told her, and went right on through to the kitchen to see if there was anything to eat. I was starving since today had been brown bean day in the cafeteria, and brown beans were one thing I just didn't ever plan on eating no matter how hungry I got.

Tracie followed me in the kitchen and stood there watching while I made me a jelly sandwich. I'd rather had jelly *and* peanut butter but the peanut butter got eaten up a long time ago.

"So, tonight's parent night, huh?" She asked, and I was real surprised she knew about it, 'cause I'd only mentioned it the one time.

"Yeah, but you don't have to go."

"Oh, I don't? Well, what if I said I wanna go?"

I put down my half-eaten sandwich and stared at her.

"You wanna go?"

"Yeah, what time does it start?"

"I don't know, but I got a letter about it somewhere." I picked up my book satchel from where I'd thrown it down and started digging around to find that letter. There were tons of letters I'd gotten but I never gave them to Tracie 'cause I figured she didn't want to be bothered. Now, I couldn't tell which was which, so I just handed her all of them.

"Here, it's one of them." She just looked at me.

"I'll call," she said. I shrugged and stuffed the letters back in my book satchel.

"I don't have anything to dress up in."

"What?"

"It's Halloween, and we're supposed to dress up and go trick or treating around the rooms. I don't have nothing to wear."

"Bettes is making you a costume, she'll bring it over when she comes."

Antoe came up to the kitchen then, cause even though he couldn't tell time, he always knew when I got home, and I fixed him two jelly sandwiches. He sat down at the kitchen table to eat them.

"Is Antoe going?" I asked and Antoe looked up from his sandwiches.

"Tonio not go. Stay here."

"Bettes is gonna stay with him," Tracie said.

There was just one thing I was worried about: "Is Chuck taking us?"

"No, he may come later, but I'll drive his car," she said, and boy was I glad.

"What's my costume?" I asked hoping that it might be the Wonder Woman I'd asked her to make a long time ago.

"She didn't say, she just said she'd bring it."

"When?"

Tracie laughed. "After while. You got plenty of time, so go play." She pulled the chair over to the icebox and pulled the horse head down and took it to the kitchen table. She pulled out a little book and a little baggie of dried green grass and sat back down at the table.

"C'mon Antoe, let's go outside."

On the way out to the swing, I thought about how Antoe wouldn't get to go trick or treating, but then I realized he'd hate it anyway. I would give him half of my candy when I got home. We stayed outside doodling around at the swing till I saw Bettes' funny little car come chugging up the driveway. I jumped off the swing and took off running to see what my costume looked like. She was reaching in the backseat before I even got there. That's what I loved about Bettes: she just knew things and you didn't have to tell her or ask her or anything.

"Ta-dah!" She handed me something and I could tell it was red and blue so I just grabbed her and hugged her as she was getting out.

"Thanks, Bettes!"

"Don't thank me yet, you might not like it!"

"It's Wonder Woman! I love it!" I grabbed it from her and took off running to the house. I went in the front room to put it on. I yanked down my skirt and pulled off my tee shirt and grabbed the costume and wriggled in it. It looked like a bathing suit, only the bottom was blue with white stars and the top part of it was red with gold braid. It was beautiful.

I ran back to the kitchen to show Tracie. She was sitting at the table still, smoking a pink cigarette.

"Look! I'm Wonder Woman!" Bettes had made it in the kitchen and she had a sack that she handed to me. Tracie just laughed and laughed.

"Here's the rest of it!" I grabbed the sack and there was a headband, two gold bracelets, and white go-go boots, just like I'd always wanted.

I pulled the bracelets on and handed the headband to Bettes and she fixed it in my hair. Then I flopped down on the floor and yanked off my school shoes and unzipped the white boots and put my feet in them. I stood up and zipped them up.

"How do I look?"

"Beautiful!" Bettes said, "Just like a real super-hero!"

"Nobody's gonna mess with me tonight, I bet."

Bettes went over and took the pink cigarette from Tracie.

"Are we leaving now?" I asked, cause I knew when Bettes and Tracie got started smoking and talking sometimes they'd forget what they were fixing to do.

"In a minute, go show your costume to Antoe." So I tore out of the house to find Antoe, but he wasn't anywhere to be seen. I ran around the yard for a little while playing Wonder Woman, but I really needed Antoe to be a bad guy. I figured he'd gone back downstairs so I went around to the side door and I was in the washer room when I heard them talking.

"Did you know he was dealing?"

"No, I knew he always had money from somewhere, but I didn't ask."

"How long you gonna put up with that bullshit?"

"It's not that bad. Sometimes he treats me real good..."

Bettes snorted and asked, "Like when?" Tracie didn't answer and I heard Bettes sigh.

"His stuff's in my bedroom. I hope he doesn't give you problems, but if he does, they'll know what to do" Tracie said, and Bettes said something back but I couldn't hear her so I tried to get closer to the door and I knocked over the broom that was setting there and it sounded like somebody shot a gun it was so loud. It made me jump and I knew they'd heard it, too, so I went on to the kitchen.

"You ready?" Tracie asked and she got her purse and the car keys off the table and started towards the door.

"Have fun!" Bettes told me and I grabbed her around the middle and hugged her again for making me such a pretty costume.

"I will!" And then I followed Tracie out to the car. It took us a long time to get to the school 'cause Tracie was driving real slow and she never drove slow. I kept thinking that we should talk some but I didn't know what to say. Seemed like there was a time when Tracie was always talking about something stupid or singing or laughing and it used to be so much fun.

When we got to the school, I could see there was all kinds of stuff set up in the parking lot where the buses usually were. Tracie found a parking place and I asked her if I could run ahead.

"Yeah, go on. I'm gonna sit here for a while anyway. I'll come get you when it's time to go."

"Ain't you coming in?"

"In a little bit. Go have fun."

There were games and stuff to play and I was glad

I had some money. Earlier in the week when they were sleeping upstairs, I'd found Chuck's billfold laying on the table and I'd swiped a twenty dollar bill from him. The only bad thing was he thought Tracie'd took it and they had a big fight about it.

First of all, I bought a bag of fudge from Mrs. Perone. Even though they didn't have kids, she always helped out doing stuff around the school.

"Hey there, Miss Girl. Where's Antonio tonight?" She asked me as she was giving me my change back.

"He's home with Bettes and Tracie's sitting in the car. She's gonna come in later."

I took my change and shoved it down in the top of my boot since I didn't have a bag or pockets. I wandered around eating my fudge and just looking at everything. I saw there was some kind of spook house where you went in and got scared, and I saw that Brady was there with a bunch of other big kids. I waved at him but he acted like he didn't see me. There was also a place where you could pick up little plastic ducks and win a prize, and there was a cakewalk, and all kinds of different food for sale. I finished my fudge and got me a hot dog next and paid to pick up a duck and won a necklace that had a real whistle dangling from it. I put it on and was thinking about trying another duck when I heard a loud car screeching its tires in the parking lot.

It was Chuck in his red car. He pulled up beside

where Tracie was still sitting in his other car. Dale, Richie, and Tiny were with him and they got out, too. I saw him lean in the window and say something to Tracie. Well, I decided right quick to go on inside and do my trick-or-treating first. When I went inside the school, some lady handed me a trick-or-treat sack and told me I could go in every room. So I started way down at the end, which is where the sixth graders' classes were and got behind a group of grownups and kids and followed them in. I walked around looking at all the stuff they had out to show what all they'd been doing and when I was leaving, the teacher dropped some candy in my bag. Then we went on to another classroom and just kept working our way down the hallway.

I was thinking that my sack was getting pretty full when I heard yelling and hollering coming from outside. The grown-ups that I'd been following around from room to room ran to look out the windows that faced the parking lot and as soon as they did, the men took off outside in a hurry and the women followed them dragging their kids. I went over to look out and there was a huge crowd of men around where they'd had the spook house. All the women and kids were standing up on the sidewalks.

I heard a siren squealing then, and I saw flashes of blue and red lights so I figured it was the police getting there. I went to the next room and nobody was in there, so I just helped myself to a handful of candy. It was the same thing all the way down: nobody was in the class-rooms but their candy was so I just took a handful from each. Well, I took two handfuls, 'cause I wanted to make sure I had enough to give Antoe half. When I got to the end of the hall where my classroom was, I opened the big double doors we used to go outside for recess, and even though it was dark, I went out and got on a swing. There were lights out there so it wasn't like I couldn't see anything. The parking lot where something was hap-pening was on the other side of the building, and I could hear the people hollering and carrying on. It went on for a long time and then I heard a siren start up again, or maybe it was a different one, and I could tell it was leaving 'cause the sound got quieter. The people were beginning to settle down and pretty soon I couldn't hear much noise at all.

I was sitting there in the swing eating some candy when the back doors opened. I couldn't tell who it was so I stood up and made sure I had a good hold on my sack in case I had to run. I could tell it was a kid, then all of a sudden I saw who it was: Tiny. Well, even though he hadn't been so bad that day at the church, I wasn't com-pletely sure I trusted him so I started to walk towards the doors.

"Hey," he said.

"Hey."

"You leaving?"

Yeah, I was gonna go find Tracie."

"She ain't here."

"How do you know?"

"On account of what happened. She probably went down to the jailhouse to get Chuck."

"Chuck's went to jail?" That was better than winning a big prize in the duck pick!

"Didn't you see what happened?" He walked over and sat down in the swing I'd just left.

"Nu-uh, I was inside, but I heard people hollering."

"Him n'Richie n'Dale beat up a nigger."

"That's a bad word."

"So? I heard you cuss before. Them's bad words too."

"Saying that's a lot worse n' cuss words. Cuss words are just words somebody decided was bad." That's what Bettes told me once.

"Well, anyway they beat him up and they had to take him away to the hospital and they took all my brothers to jail."

There wasn't anything for me to say really, 'cause I was real glad but I didn't wanna say that to Tiny. Just then the lights went off in the school. I ran to the door but somebody'd locked it already.

"That's OK, we can walk around," Tiny said. I was kinda glad he was there 'cause we had to walk all the way down by the cafeteria and up the other side and it was dark as all get out. And don't you know when we got around there, most all of the cars were gone? I didn't see Tracie nowhere, so I guess Tiny was telling the truth and she had gone to get Chuck at the jail. I didn't know how I was gonna get home. Then I saw the Perone's were still there; Mrs. Perone was putting stuff in boxes and Mr. Perone was loading them in the back of his truck. I ran over to them.

"Girl! Where on earth did you come from?" Mrs. Perone stopped what she was doing to stare at me.

"I was around back swinging. Tracie's not here is she?" I asked.

"No...I 'spect she hadda leave..." She was looking around then. "Have you been here this entire time?"

"Yeah, I went trick-or-treating then I went out back to the playground and just sat on the swings for a while."

"Well, c'mon, we'll take you home." She put her arm around my shoulder and led me towards their truck. I looked around, but I didn't see Tiny nowhere. Mr. Perone finished putting the stuff in the back of the truck and he opened the door and Mrs. Perone got in then I crawled in behind her.

"How's my buddy, Antonio? Mr. Perone asked and I noticed he had his Sunday teeth in.

"He's good. He's home with Bettes. I brought him candy." I held up my bag and shook it.

"You made a mighty good haul, didn't you?" Mrs. Perone asked.

"Yeah, do you know where Tracie went? Did Chuck really go to jail? I heard sirens and everything." Mrs. Perone glanced up at Mr. Perone.

"Oh, it was just some boys fightin.' Tracie knew we'd bring you home."

Mr. Perone started tell a story about another alligator that had come up to their back yard and before I knew it, we were at my driveway. I threw open the door and hopped out as soon as we stopped.

"Thanks for the ride!"

"Is somebody here?" Mrs. Perone caught the door before it shut and she was looking worried. I looked around then and I didn't see Bettes' car there but all the lights in the house were on.

"Yeah, see all the lights? Bettes is in there with Antoe." I told them.

"Well, OK, then." Mrs. Perone still looked worried but she let me shut the door and I ran to the house and turned around to wave at them. They sat there for a second more then Mr. Perone backed the car up and they took off. I watched them go and grabbed the doorknob. It came open without me even turning it. When I pushed it open, I stood there looking around, and boy, was I shocked.

Everything was wrecked. All the stuff on the shelves and tables was in the middle of the floor, and all the coats were off the rack laying everywhere, and they were all ripped up. I walked into the front room and it was more of the same. Somebody had cut open poor Toomie and his insides were all flopping out and pieces of him were all over the floor. The little flower vases and boxes that were on the shelves were in the floor, broke, and the TV was busted up in a million pieces. I walked in the kitchen and it was an even bigger mess. The horse head was in the floor smashed to bits, all the drawers and cabinets were open and everything that'd been in them was thrown all over. There was broken glass everywhere. I was glad I was wearing my Wonder Woman boots. I went through to the washer room and saw that somebody had torn up the washing machine and the dryer. There were pieces of it laying all over. The side door was sitting wide open.

"Bettes?" I called and the sound of my voice made me jump. "Antoe?" I didn't hear a sound. I went down to the fruit cellar and the door was open. All those old jars of stuff had been smashed and it stunk to high heaven. My secret box was smashed too, and my stuff was laying on top of it. The green cans with food were all over but they weren't opened, and I didn't know if any of them were missing. I gathered up everything, and I saw Antoe's beads and the lady statue, his wood pieces, soap, and his pocket knife were on top of the quilts that were piled up in a wad. That made me stop and think. Antoe was real careful about his stuff, and he never, ever, went anywhere without the knife Mr. Perone had given him in his pocket.

I left the fruit cellar and when upstairs. The thing that got me was all the lights were blazing just as bright as anything. I didn't even know there were lights in the upstairs hallway. I stopped about half-way up and for the first time, I wondered if maybe somebody was still here. I'd sorta thought maybe Antoe had a fit and wrecked everything 'cause he sure could tear stuff up when he got worked up. But I knew he'd never, ever break the jars in our cellar. And he wouldn't have left his stuff thrown around.

"Bettes? Antoe?" My voice was way too loud again. I listened just as hard as I could and I didn't hear anything. So I went on up. Even though the lights weren't ever on up there, and it was weird to see them, it also made me feel a little bit better about being by myself.

The upstairs was just like downstairs. I went in my room first and all my clothes were in a pile and all the stuff in my dresser had been pulled out and my dresser was out in the hallway broken. I looked around and started to pick some of my clothes up, but then I didn't know what for, so I dropped them again. I looked in the camping bedroom and it was the same. The seat on the commode had been ripped off and was laying in the bathtub. Somebody'd even smashed the bathtub up. It wasn't completely broken, but there were big chunks knocked out of it and the faucet had been torn off the wall.

Tracie's bedroom was the worst so far. The mattress had been ripped apart like Toomie, only all of the insides had been pulled out and the room was covered in mattress guts. All of their clothes were thrown all over the place, and all the stuff Tracie had in the bottom of the closet was rooted out to the middle of the room. I kept kicking stuff out of my way so I could get over to the closet. I saw the big metal box that I'd always wondered what was in it, but that Tracie kept locked, laying there broke. I picked it up and nothing was left in it. There was a bunch of papers crumpled up beside it. I bent down and picked them up along with a huge, old bag of Tracie's and just stuffed the papers inside. There was a little medal laying there that I picked up, too. It was purple ribbon with a heart, and I put it in the bag.

I also picked up one of her long floaty shirts I'd always liked. I took it back to my bedroom and tried to figure out what I was gonna do. I knew nobody was here right now, but I wasn't sure they wouldn't come back. I thought about going to Bettes house 'cause maybe she'd had to go home to get something and decided to stay there but it was a long way to walk. The fruit cellar was ruined so I couldn't go there; the only place I would feel safe was under the house where I'd buried those balloons and that money.

In my bedroom I picked up a pair of my blue jeans

that were in the corner and I pulled them up over my Wonder Woman costume I still had on, and grabbed the old green sweater of Tracie's. I also grabbed the quilt that I kept on my bed. I got the bag with the papers in it and took that and the quilt back downstairs. I ran back down to the fruit cellar and grabbed those beads and the knife and Antoe's statue. I knew he'd want them when I found him.

Now that I'd been all over the house and everything was wrecked, I was starting to feel real creepy so I ran down the stairs and out the back door and around behind the house to the place where I crawled under. I dragged the bag and quilt behind me and scooted over to where I buried the stuff and grabbed the flashlight I kept under there, but I didn't turn it on. I rolled myself up in my quilt like a papoose, which is what little Indian babies were called, and after I was all covered and couldn't see what might be under there, I felt better. There were snakes around sometimes, but really, people were a lot worse than snakes. Snakes would generally leave you alone if you didn't bother them.

I laid there and tried to make some kind of sense about what had happened and where Antoe and Bettes were. I wondered if maybe somebody had got them. But then I remembered Bettes always carried something in her knitting bag that I wasn't ever supposed to touch. Then I went back to earlier in the night: Did Chuck really go to jail? And why? And who was it they beat up? There was so much to think about that my head was hurting and I didn't think I'd ever be able to go to sleep but I did.

ELEVEN

The sun peeking through the wooden slats at the front of the house was what woke me up. I had to lay there and remember where I was and what had happened. I fought my way out of the quilt I'd stayed wrapped up in all night and once I got my head out, I looked around. No snakes or anything, and the mound was still there where I'd buried the balloons and money. I had the bag I'd taken from Tracie's bedroom and I thought it might be a good idea to dig up the bags and keep them with me. I mean, it wasn't so unusual for everybody to go somewhere and leave me and Antoe there, but normally nobody took Antoe anywhere. And if they did, it sure wasn't overnight. I didn't really want to go back in the house that was wrecked, but I couldn't stay here all day. I guessed I wouldn't be going to school.

I dug up the balloons and the money, and I put

them in the bag. I rolled the quilt up and dragged it to the opening. Instead of taking it with me, I left it and the bag right underneath the house so I could come back and get it later on. After I made sure it was safe.

I crawled the rest of the way out from under the house and went around to the back door and it was still open where I'd left it last night. I went in and was kinda shocked all over again at the way everything was broken. I went downstairs to the fruit cellar and found my little gold and brown book that didn't have words and got that. I didn't see any more of my stuff and it smelled so bad I had to get out of there. I went in the kitchen and looked around.

I wished somebody would come get me and tell me what had happened. I missed Antoe, though I was glad he wasn't there to see everything wrecked 'cause it'd upset him something awful. I made up my mind that I was just gonna walk to Bettes' house. I went back out the back door and around the house to go get my bag. I'd have to leave the quilt there. I put the long strap of it around my neck and I shoved my little book I'd picked up down in it. It was kinda heavy but I might need all that stuff, 'specially Antoe's. I got to the end of the driveway and took off in the direction of the Perone's store. I knew Bettes lived down the first dirt road past their store, and it was a road that ended when you got to her house. I'd never walked there, but it didn't take too long in the car.

I was about half-way to the Perone's when I saw Bettes' car coming down the road. Even though it was a long way off, there wasn't another car that was painted with big flowers all over like hers. I got off on the side of the road and waited till she pulled up beside me.

"What the hell are you doing, Girl?" She asked me as she pulled off the road and jumped out of her car.

"Going to your house," I said.

"Where's Tracie?" She asked.

"I don't know, where's Antoe?" I asked.

"What do you mean, you don't know?"

"She never came home last night. Is Antoe at your house? Where've you been?"

"Get in." She told me and started to get back in her car so I did, too.

"She said she was gonna go to parents' night. She didn't go?"

"Yeah, but she didn't get out, and somebody said Chuck went to jail and then she was gone when I went back around there and the Perone's gave me a ride. Who wrecked our house?"

"What? What do you mean?"

"Our house is all wrecked. Everything is broke." Bettes looked at me and didn't say anything just took off so fast her little car was screaming like it was being murdered and I was scared it was gonna blow up. She turned into our driveway so fast it slung me up beside her but she kept right on going and screeched to a halt and jumped out of the car and tore up to the house faster than I'd ever seen Bettes move. I followed her. She was standing inside the front room just looking around with her hands up on her cheeks, rubbing.

"Son of a bitch. Was it like this last night? Was somebody here?"

"I came in and it was like this. Nobody was here but I slept under the house," I said.

"Oh my God." She grabbed me and hugged me and you know, I was kinda glad but she didn't let me go and was about to smother me.

"Ow, Bettes, I can't breathe."

She let me go then and walked through to the kitchen. She kept whispering, "Goddammit," over and over again. Then she picked up the phone and started dialing. I didn't know who she was calling but I was wondering where Antoe was and why she hadn't answered me. She slammed the phone down. "Goddammit!" Then she picked it back up and dialed another number.

"Is Antoe at your house?" I asked her, but she'd stretched the cord out into the front hall and I heard her talking in a low voice. She came back to the kitchen and hung the phone up and said "Goddammit" one more time.

"C'mon." And so I followed her back out to the car. She tore out of the driveway just like she'd tore in it and when we got on the highway we went back and forth across it and I thought we were gonna end up in the ditch, but we didn't.

When we got to her house she just turned the car off and sat there.

"Are we getting out?" I asked her but she was staring into space and had lit a cigarette so I got out and took my bag and went in the house. Antoe wasn't in the living room, so I went back to the bedroom we stayed in when we slept at Bettes. He wasn't there either, and he wasn't in the bathroom or in her bedroom.

I came back and checked in the kitchen. Nothing. I figured he was outside somewhere 'cause Bettes had a great big yard and there were all kinds of places to hide. One of our favorite things to do was play with all the little men with red hats that sat around in her flowers. We'd gather them all up and play games with them. Antoe liked the one that was stretched out sleeping best. He said the eyes on the others scared him 'cause they looked mean.

I walked all the way around the yard, even back out behind the woodpile, but Antoe wasn't nowhere to be seen. I was getting mad now. Bettes had better tell me where he was. I saw she wasn't in her car anymore so I went in the house to find her. Normally, I loved it at Bettes' house. There were all kinds of stuff, little shells and boxes and stuff that set around all over. She never cared if I looked in all of them and took whatever I wanted, but today I wasn't interested in the boxes. I went back to the bedroom where I knew she was. She didn't have a regular bed, just mattresses piled up in a corner and about a million quilts and stuff on top. I loved to sleep on her floor bed. She was sitting in it cross-legged and she was braiding her hair.

"Bettes, where's Antoe?"

She kept on braiding her hair.

"Is he alright? Why won't you tell me!"

"Girl...I took him—

We heard the front door open then and Bettes jumped up like she was shot and ran down the hallway to the kitchen so I followed her. Tracie had come in, and she was still wearing the clothes she had on yesterday. She looked worse than the back roads of hell. There was black streaks all down her face, her long blonde hair looked like a bird's nest on top, and she was standing right there in the door like she didn't have the strength to walk another step. Bettes just went to her and grabbed her and hugged her tight. Tracie sorta fell against Bettes and started crying like all get out. Bettes led her in the kitchen so I followed and stood in the doorway watching while she wet a paper towel and started to clean Tracie's face. They weren't saying anything so I just stood in the doorway, peeling off the brown paint chips that were hanging on the sides of the doorway. The paint chips looked like bird shit.

"Where'd he go?" I asked peeling off a particular-ly big strip. It kinda reminded me of peeling off a scab, 'cept it didn't hurt.

"Where's Antoe?"

"Shhh, Girl, not now." Bettes said, trying to get the black streaks off Tracie's cheeks.

"Goddammit!" I stomped my foot as hard as I could. "I wanna know where he is NOW!" I screamed so loud it made me dizzy and felt like my head was gonna explode.

They both turned to stare at me; the wet towel dangling from Bettes' hand. I never screamed out loud, ever, only at Chuck in my mind.

"You're not being fair! ' Cause I don't know if he's killed or what!"

I thought maybe Tracie would get up to hit me even though she never had. But she didn't. She just breathed real hard, once, and turned to look at me.

"Girl, he had to go away. It was for his own good. He'll be much happier there."

"Happier where?" He was happy here! With me."

"I couldn't take care of him anymore. He's going to where they can take care of him better. He'll be fine."

"You lie! He won't be fine, he'll miss me! And you didn't take care of him anyway, I did! I hate your guts!" I was so mad at her I wanted to pick up something and hit her as hard as I could and make her bleed like Chuck did that time.

"I can't deal with this." She got up from the kitchen table and went down the hallway towards Bettes' bedroom.

"Girl..." Bettes was looking at me. Sorta begging like.

"YOU took him! I hate you, too!" And I ran outside because I didn't wanna look at either one of them a second longer. I ran out and flopped down in the flower bed where all the little men were from the last time me and Antoe played with them. I couldn't stand them anymore so I just started kicking them as hard as I could, everywhichaway. They went flying in all directions and some of the paint chipped off them and some of them even cracked but I didn't give a damn. I kicked those little men all over the yard until I didn't have any breath left then I just fell down in a heap and cried like I don't ever remember crying in my life.

When I finally stopped, I knew one reason I never cried was 'cause it made you feel real, real bad. My head hurt and my nose was stopped up and I just felt tired. I got up and went back in the house.

My stuff was by the door where I'd dropped it when I came in. I picked it up and took it in the bedroom that was mine when I stayed there and sat down on the bed to think. I knew Tracie and Bettes would probably stay in her bedroom for the rest of the day, then when it got dark they'd come out and wanna talk. But that wasn't gonna happen. I wasn't gonna be there. 'Cause all of a sudden it came to me what I was gonna do. I was gonna leave. I was gonna find Antoe myself, 'cause I knew he was scared as he could be. I didn't have no idea where he was but I'd figure it out. The first thing to do was get as far away from them as I could.

I dumped out the bag I took from our house, and it was full. I put all the papers back in the bottom, then the bag of money, then those balloons, then the shirt of Tracie's. I put all of Antoe's stuff on the bed, along with my sack of Halloween candy that was still in there, 'cause I knew I didn't have room for all of it. I dug down in my candy sack and pulled out a Milk Way bar and a Snickers bar and unwrapped them and popped them in my mouth. I sat there looking at the candy wishing I had room for it. I put the bag in a dresser drawer that was empty, and if I ever came back, maybe it'd still be there.

Then I walked down to the end of the hall and listened outside Bettes' bedroom. It was quiet and I figured they were probably asleep and would stay asleep until it got dark outside. I ran in the living room and looked at the clock. It said it was twelve-thirty, so I had a few hours.

TWELVE

I had never been without Antoe, never. He wasn't much help but I always knew I could count on him just to *be* there. Even though I didn't know where he was, my goal for now was just to get away. Then when I got far enough, I could think about what to do.

I went in the kitchen to see if there was some food I could stuff in my bag. The only thing I found was a package of cheese. It made me sad cause it was the kind Antoe loved; the little slices that were all wrapped up. I put the cheese in the top of my bag. There wasn't any way I could take water, so I got a big plastic cup out of the cabinet. I dug around in the junk drawer and found a flashlight and found two pairs of Bettes' socks. I went back to the bedroom that was mine and looked in all the drawers and I found a pair of cut-off shorts I'd left there one time so I got those and put them in my bag.

I was still wearing my wonder woman costume with Tracie's old sweater and my jeans and the white boots. I wished I'd thought to grab my tenny shoes 'cause they were better for walking. I thought about grabbing the blanket Bettes kept over her couch, she called it an African, but I didn't want to carry too much stuff.

I went out the front door and let it bang behind me. They wouldn't hear it and even if they did, they'd just think I was going outside, which I was, but they didn't know that I wouldn't be coming back. I walked around to the back of the house where the woodpile was. Right behind the woodpile was a trail that went back in the woods. Me and Antoe'd gone down that trail a bunch of times and it came out beside a creek. I knew that the creek went on and on. One day we'd followed it for a long time, till Antoe got tired, and it was all thick woods. I knew they wouldn't think to look in the woods, they'd think I walked down the highway back towards home.

Since I wanted to get as far away as I could before they figured out I was gone, I took off running. I came to the creek in no time and just followed along beside it, running like hell.

I got to the place where there was a log laying all the way across the water, and on the other side it looked like there was less bushes and briars, so I carefully made my way down to the log, and instead of walking over it, I sat down on it and scooched my way across. I didn't even get my feet a little bit wet, either.

When I got to the other side, I started to run again, but not as fast as before. I ran until I lost my breath, then I'd stop for a little while, then take off again. When I'd stop, I'd look around to make sure there were no animals around that might eat me. Normally, I wasn't worried about that, but it was a lot more woods and stuff than what I was used too. Besides, when I'd stop, I could hear sounds of something moving around, crunching leaves and branches.

The woods were getting a lot thicker, so I had to slow down. Even though I was being careful, my sweater kept getting caught on briars and my arms were getting scratched up something awful. Every time I'd get my sleeves loose, it seemed like another bunch would grab my legs. I was betting I was a bloody mess under my clothes.

When I came to a place that was cleared off some, I sat down and pulled out the package of cheese and ate five slices. I was pretty thirsty too, so I pulled out the plastic cup and dipped up some out of the creek. It didn't look too dirty but I really didn't care. It tasted like fish smelled. But not so bad that I didn't have a second cupful. Which was a big mistake 'cause then I had to pee. Bad. And here was a problem: I still had that stupid costume on with my blue jeans over it so that meant I was gonna have to take everything off just to pee. Not for the first time did I wish I was a boy like Antoe and could just flop out my tallywacker and go to town.

I pulled my jeans off then my sweater, then the Wonder Woman costume and that meant I was in the middle of the woods wearing nothing but a pair of white go-go boots. I found a place that didn't have many briars and squatted and tried real hard not to pee on my feet, but I did anyway. I put the costume back on, then my pants, my shirt, and my sweater. I was hoping that would last me for a while 'cause that was just too much trouble. If Antoe had to do that every time he had to pee, he'd just pee in his pants *all* the time instead of some of the time.

I started off again, and I had no idea where I was or how much time had passed. The thing that was beginning to worry me a little bit was that it was gonna be getting dark soon and I didn't know how I was gonna find my way in the dark.

I was still following beside the creek 'cause I figured it would come out somewhere. Plus, there was less briars close to it than out in the woods. Sometimes the creek got really skinny so I kept crossing back and forth whenever I could. I was back on the side I'd crossed to in the beginning and I stayed there since it was clearer.

I walked and walked and walked. I was tireder than I'd ever been in my whole life but the sun was going down and spending the night in the woods was something I didn't even want to think about. The creek was real wide now, almost like a pond. I saw up ahead that the trees looked like they were getting thinner and pretty soon, I came out to a clearing. But what I saw made me want to sit down and cry some more. The creek ended and it was huge. And there were all these trees in the water and the same kind of moss like we had at home, only that moss didn't scare me and this did.

I walked beside the creek (which wasn't a creek anymore but a pond) for a long time and it was getting darker and darker. Just when I was about to give up and start looking for a tree to climb and spend the night, another tree caught my attention; a dead one that had fallen across the water. It didn't go all the way across but it went far enough that I thought I could make it. The bottom of it was sticking up on the other side of the water and all the roots of it were up in the air. The top part was almost to the other side where I was, but not quite. If I could figure out a way to get to the thickest part of the tree, I could scooch across like I'd done on the other one.

There were stumps sticking up all in the water around the tree and after looking at them for a while, I figured my best bet would be to use the stumps to get me to the part of the tree that would hold me up, and get across just as quick as I could. The only thing I was worried about was my bag of stuff. I had to keep it from falling in the water even if I did. Since it had a long strap, I doubled it and put it over my head. Now the bag part was right up under my neck and it didn't feel so good but at least it wouldn't get wet unless I fell in, and I didn't wanna think about that.

I found a stump that was big enough to stand on right up close to the bank. I nearly slipped in once, 'cause the bank had mud that was slimy and those stupid Wonder Woman boots were slick on the bottom. I caught myself and got on the stump. It was pretty easy; I just pretended that I was playing in our yard and there wasn't no water to fall in. The only thing was, those stumps were black and slicky and wet, and some of them were real little and pointy and I could barely stand on them. So I had to jump quick.

I got to one that was pretty close to the bigger part of the dead tree and I jumped. I made it and grabbed hold of that tree for all I was worth, but my feet and legs sloshed right down in the water and it was cold as all get out! My bag was dry and that was what mattered. I scooched along that tree quick as I could and when I got to the end, I climbed up over the roots and was on the ground in a big muddy hole. I unhooked my bag from over my head and put it back across my body. I sat down on the first clear place I could find to rest a little bit.

It was dark now, and even though I'd been dreading it, it wasn't so bad. I could hear all those frogs singing like they did at home. Up ahead of me I could tell the woods were ending, and I could see lights like from a house. I would have to be careful around a house 'cause I didn't want anybody to see me, but I thought maybe I could find me a place to sleep where there were people close by and it wouldn't be as scary.

I could see the house real good now. It was a big wooden one with the paint peeling off kinda like ours. It had a big back porch with a screen that went all the way across the whole house and there was a light on in it. I could see a woman moving around out there so I made sure I was hid good. Pretty soon she turned the light off. There was a clump of bushes closer to the house, so when she turned off that light, I ran and got behind the bushes so I could see what was going on better.

The woman, she looked kinda old like Mrs. Per-one was, walking around in a room on the other side of the porch. Then that light went off too. I went up to the side of the porch, hoping they didn't have any dogs. I got to the corner of it and nothing happened so I went on around to the side. There was a truck parked there, so I ran over and peeked in the back of it. There were piles of sacks that had F-E-R-T-I-L-I-Z-E-R written on it but I didn't know what that was. There were tools and other junk in there, too. Well, I knew right then that was where I was sleeping tonight, so I climbed up on the tire and hopped in. I got up next to the cab and moved all the sacks, laid down, then pulled them over the top of me so nobody could see me. Those sacks were scratchy and smelled like cow shit and dead fish but I didn't even care 'cause I was that tired and sleepy. I was glad too, 'cause it meant I went to sleep without thinking about all the bad things that'd happened and I didn't even miss Antoe. But I sure did wish I'd grabbed that African like I almost did.

THIRTEEN

When I heard something slam, I nearly jumped out of my skin. I laid there as still as I could and wondered what it was. I heard a man say, "I'll be home around eight." Then I heard the truck door slam and the motor start up. I hadn't even thought about somebody driving the truck off while I was in the back, but there wasn't nothing I could do now 'cause we were moving.

Hellshitdamn. For all I knew we were heading back the way I'd come! The back of that truck was rough as hell when we started off but then it sorta changed. It was like humming with your whole body. Even though the wind was whistling overhead, it was warm up against the cab of the truck and the humming feeling made me sleepy again but I didn't go to sleep.

I was so mad at Tracie and Bettes. Especially Bettes. It didn't really surprise me that Tracie'd sent Antoe away, but I couldn't even believe that Bettes had helped do it. She'd always been the one I could talk to and she wouldn't lie to me the way grownups lied to kids. I wanted to believe Tracie made her do it, but I didn't really think Bettes would ever do something she really didn't want to do.

I was hungry so I dug the package of cheese back out of my bag and ate the rest of it. My legs were stiff and felt like they'd gone to sleep 'cause they were all tingly. I moved them around to try to get the feeling back in them. All the stuff about Bettes and Tracie kept going 'round and 'round in my head and I didn't even notice when the noise stopped. I heard the truck door open and shut and I heard the man walk around to the side of the truck closest to my head. I waited till it was quiet then I peeked up from under the bags. We were at a gas station and the man was at the side of the truck, filling up his tank. I waited till I heard him put the cap back on the tank and I raised up. I saw he was walking towards the store. I didn't waste no time but looked around real quick and jumped over the side of the truck near the gas pumps. I ran around behind them and made sure I had everything and then I walked right into that store. All that cheese I ate was about to make me die of thirst and the creek water I drank had been a long, long time ago.

The store was kinda like the Perone's store, but it was a lot bigger. When I pushed the front door open I heard little bells jangling that told them somebody had come in. I went to the back where the cold drinks were kept and got me a grape drink and an orange one. I looked around a little bit and got me a big bag of potato chips and a Three Musketeers and a Sky bar. I pulled up my blue jeans leg and fished around in the top of my boot and pulled out the wet money I had left over from the carnival. That sure did seem like it was long time ago.

The man whose truck I'd ridden in was right in front of me and I got tickled when I thought about how surprised he'd be if he knew he'd given me a ride. He was wearing overalls like Mr. Perone wore and he had on a hat. He looked pretty old, too. He paid for his gas and walked out of the store and got in his truck. The lady at the cash register was young and she kinda looked me up and down before she rang up my drinks, candy, and potato chips.

"That'll be a dollar twenty five," she said, so I handed her two dollars and she gave me three quarters back.

"Could you open these?" I asked her and she looked at me again and grabbed a bottle opener from under the counter and popped the caps off the bottles. I grabbed the candy and bag of chips and stuffed them in my bag and carried a drink in each hand. I pushed the door open with my elbow and went outside. I walked over to where there was a bench in the front of the store and sat down and took a swallow of that grape drink. It was so good I finished off the whole bottle and started on the orange one. I didn't know where in the Sam Hill I was, or what I was gonna do next, so I just sat there thinking. Pretty soon it was getting real busy out at the gas pumps so I wanted to get away. I didn't know if Tracie had realized I was gone yet or not but I couldn't take no chances of somebody looking for me, especially since I didn't know how far away I was. I put my empty drink bottles in a box with other empty ones and walked to the end of the store parking lot.

There was a highway that ran beside the store, and there was a bunch of cars going by. I looked up one way, then the other way, and went to the left because it was sorta going downhill and I was still tired from yesterday. I got the Three Musketeers out and ate it as I walked down a hill, then back up another big hill, then back down another little one. There were a lot more cars here than at home. I didn't like it much, but it was better than walking through the woods. When I got to the bottom of the little hill, there was a little narrow dirt road that looked like it could be somebody's driveway, but I couldn't see a house. There was some kind of big white statue setting in the middle of the road but it was too far away to tell what it was. So I headed up to check it out.

The closer I got to it, the bigger it looked. At first it was scary looking, but then I realized it was the same exact lady statue as the one Antoe had, and the one outside of the church I went to with Mrs. Miller. Only this one was big, way bigger than me or even Antoe. I walked up to it and looked at it, then I sat down for a minute. It had snakes on the bottom, and the lady's feet were on top of the snakes. I thought about how Antoe would like to see it, and I made up my mind that when I found him, I'd bring him back to look at it.

And that reminded me of something I was trying not to think about: How was I gonna find him? I didn't even know where Tracie'd sent him, and I sure as hell didn't know where I was. There wasn't any way I could ask anybody, either. I was beginning to think maybe I should've planned this running away thing a little better. My best bet was to maybe find a place I could spend the night.

I really could've stayed there by the lady statue all day and been OK, but I knew I had to keep going. So I looked at her one more time, then I looked both ways on the road. I wasn't sure what was up ahead, but I knew the highway was behind me, so I kept going forward. There were still trees on one side of the road, but on the other side was now a fence, and on the other side of the fence was a big, big pond. There were cows there, and I could see the gravel road kept going up another hill, then it curved around and I saw it ended way up and at the end of it was a huge, huge house. Our house was big; it was tons bigger than Bettes' house or Cerese's house.

But this one, this one was about three times bigger than ours. It looked like the pictures I'd seen of castles.

I was about to turn around and go back towards highway 'cause it was one of those things where you just knew people who lived in a castle probably wouldn't help a dirty little kid, and they'd probably call the police or worse, when I saw a green painted house up ahead of me. It was setting off in the woods and it was low and kinda flat on top. I got off the road and headed up through the woods so that I could get a better look at it. I thought maybe I could come up with some kind of story that might let me get a drink of water from the people that lived there, if they were nice. And maybe use their bathroom. Those two cold drinks weren't the best thing I could've done, 'cause now I was thirstier than ever and had to pee real bad again.

It wasn't too hard walking through the trees, they were kinda little and there wasn't a lot of briars and stuff to grab me. I got to the edge of the woods and I could see the side of the green house. It didn't have any windows on the side I was looking at, so I decided to go closer for a better look.

I got up to the side of the house and waited there to see if I could hear anything. I didn't, so I decided to walk around to the front of the house, planning on telling them I was staying with my grandma down the road, and I was out walking and really needed to use a bathroom. I just couldn't face taking all my clothes off in the woods again just to pee. Plus, somebody might see me.

The front of the house had a little porch on it, and a big window with no curtains in front. There was a screen door, and a big door behind it. I walked up and knocked on the screen door and I didn't hear a thing. I opened the screen door then and knocked on the big door. Nothing. I knocked louder. Still nothing. I went to the big open window in front and peeked in. There wasn't nobody in there. There was some chairs and little tables in what looked like the living room, but no people. I went back and tried the doorknob and it opened. I pushed the door open and stepped inside. It smelled dusty. I let the screen door close behind me but I kept the big door open in case I needed to run.

Straight ahead was a wall and a doorway, and through the doorway I could see a kitchen, with an icebox and a stove, and there was a little white table setting in the corner. The living room was off to the side. It had one ugly gold couch and three fat chairs, and there was a scratched up coffee table there, like the one we had at home. I walked through the living room down a hallway and there was a little bathroom that had a big bathtub like ours, only this one didn't have animal feet. The next door was a big bedroom that had three little beds in it. There was rugs on the floor and little tables and on one of those tables was a statue of a man with his heart outside and he was pointing to it. It looked just like the picture I'd found in our house and I remembered seeing that same man when I went to church with the Millers. The beds all had quilts on them, and they looked like the ones me and Antoe had down in the fruit cellar. On the other side of the hallway was another bedroom, but this one was little, and it only had one bed in it. None of the closets had clothes or anything in them, and the drawers in the chests were all empty, too.

I went back to check out the kitchen and I opened the icebox and nothing was in there. I went to the sink and turned the faucet on. It gushed out brown, nasty looking water at first, then it got clean, and I got out the cup from my bag, filled it up, and drank and drank and drank. I thought I wasn't ever gonna get enough water.

I had to pee so bad I was gonna take my chances on somebody coming in and finding me. I went in the bathroom and stripped off all my clothes and peed and peed and peed. I pulled my jeans back up and instead of putting on my Wonder Woman costume I dug out the shirt I'd picked up on Tracie's bedroom floor. It was way too big and hung down past my knees but my costume was filthy dirty. I wished again I'd thought to get my old tenny shoes 'cause those boots had rubbed blisters on my feet and they'd all busted and they hurt something bad. I sat on the side of the bathtub and washed my feet and the cool water felt good. I looked around and there was a towel hanging there and I got it and dried off my feet and put the boots back on. The blisters felt a little better for a minute or two, then they started to hurt worse but there wasn't much I could do.

I wondered about the house and why it was empty. It wasn't like it was falling down or anything, and there was furniture in there, but you could just tell nobody was living there by the way it smelled. I took my Wonder Woman costume and folded it up and put it on the ugly couch in the living room and sat down. I dug around in my bag and found those beads I'd swiped from the Mrs. Miller's church. I'd picked them up from the wrecked house and thought they'd be pretty against the shirt. I put on all three pairs of them. I still hadn't figured out how to find where I was or how I was gonna find Antoe, but I was thinking maybe I could stay in this house for a day or two. I'd have to be real careful though, and make sure I was hid good at night in case somebody came. But I really couldn't think about that right now, right now there was all kinds of places that needed to be explored.

FOURTEEN

Before I left the house, I pulled out my sack of potato chips, opened them up, and folded the top of the sack down to where the chips were. I put my bag back across my body and made sure I shut the door real good behind me. All I was leaving was my Wonder Woman costume and I didn't care if anybody found it or not.

The road in front of the house went down to the castle, even though I knew it probably wasn't a *real* castle. Instead of going that way, I saw a little trail that led down to the big pond, or maybe it was a lake like we lived beside. All those ducks were out there swimming around and I wanted to get a closer look at them.

There was a bridge up ahead but it wasn't like any bridge I'd ever been on; it was narrow and wiggly like a snake. I walked up on it and it started swinging back and forth. At first, it was kinda scary 'cause I thought I was gonna fall in the water, but then I started jumping up and down on it and it was fun. It reminded me of those carnival rides.

When I got to the end, I thought about going back and doing it again, but then I saw something else. It was a graveyard, only it didn't look like the ones I'd seen at home. Those had big tall tombstones that were covered in moss and stuff and they looked real, real old. This graveyard had all the tombstones on the ground, flat, and they were real white and looked clean. The whole place was up off the ground and it had some kind of concrete wall all the way around it. I had to hop up on the concrete just to get myself up there.

They didn't have flowers or anything, just those flat, clean tombstones. I read some of the names and they all had Brother something-or-other. I did find a few that said Father, but none said mother or sister. I wondered what kind of graveyard this was to only have men in it.

After I covered every inch of it, looking for some ladies that were maybe buried there, (there weren't any) I hopped down on the other side. The castle was pretty close up ahead, and there were some trees and bushes there so I hid behind them to watch. Some men were out in front of the castle and they had on dresses like the ones at Mrs. Miller's church. Brown dresses. They were throwing stuff on the ground and all the ducks were running like all get out so I guess they were feeding them.

Then I heard some bells ringing and they threw what they were holding down to the ducks and went inside the castle. I waited a little bit but none of them came back out so I went closer.

There was another big statue in the driveway, only this one was a man holding a sheep on his shoulders. The ducks must've thought I was there to feed them too, 'cause they all came running towards me. They made me think about those poor chickens I'd 'caused to die. I shook out the rest of my potato chips for the ducks and they just dived right in. I folded the empty sack and shoved it in my bag.

I walked all the way up to the front door but there weren't any windows I could look in. Then I walked around to the side and the ducks kept following me. I wasn't worried about the men catching me out there, 'cause I knew I could outrun them since they were wearing those long dresses. I knew you couldn't run nearly as good in a dress as you could in pants.

At the side of the house was a little open porch, and there was a lot of junky stuff setting there, sorta like what was around our house. There was a huge metal washtub up on some boxes; I peeked in it and it was filled with all these round white crackers. I wondered if that's what the men were feeding the ducks, and since they were all around my feet quacking like crazy, I threw them a handful and they gobbled them down. So I gave them another handful. I left the ducks and walked around to the back and there was what used to be a garden but it was all dead and brown now. There was an old rusted lawnmower and some garden tools under the trees.

I kept on going around the castle hoping to see in a window, but all the windows had thick curtains over them. When I got to the last one, it was wide open and there wasn't even a screen covering it. I went up to it and stood on my tiptoes but I wasn't tall enough to see in. I looked around and found an old piece of wood and dragged it over to stand on.

I got the wood to be still then I climbed up on it and held on to the window ledge. I couldn't see anything at first, 'cause it was so dark in there, but then my eyes could just make out a bed and a little chest for clothes and that was it. There weren't any clothes on the floor or anything. There was a statue of a woman on the chest but it wasn't like the white lady statue. This one was painted and she was holding a big bunch of roses. Everything was real clean and neat and I was thinking about climbing in the window to get a better look when I heard a man's voice behind me.

"Hey there, what are you doing?"

It scared me so bad I let go of the window ledge and when I did that, the piece of wood rolled out from under my feet and I went flying sideways, bonking my head on the window ledge on the way down. I knew I should run like hell, but hitting my head kinda made me dizzy so I just laid there and felt the man's hands picking me off the ground.

"Are you OK?"

I couldn't say anything; I tried to nod but it hurt too bad so I just squeezed my eyes shut to stop the tears that were leaking out.

"Here, come over here and sit down." The man half walked me, half carried me back around the side of the castle and set me down in one of the old rusted chairs I'd seen earlier. My head was still hurting, but not as bad. I got a good look at the man and it was one of the ones I'd seen wearing a brown dress.

"Why're you wearing a dress?" I blurted out, then wished I'd kept my mouth shut, but he laughed.

"It's called a habit. Do you know what that means?"

"Something bad?" I asked and he laughed.

"No, it's not a bad habit. I'm a Carmelite Brother."

What's that?"

"It means I live here and serve God."

"Oh. Is that like a preacher?"

"Well, it's something like that I guess."

"Chuck's a preacher. And he's full of shit."

The man looked shocked like grownups always did, then he laughed again. "Who is Chuck?"

"He's...just... you live here?

"Yes, along with the rest. What's your name? "

"Teresa." I lied to him for two reasons. One, I didn't wanna tell anybody my real name, and two, I didn't wanna get into the whole you've-got-weird-name thing. Plus, I really liked the name Teresa.

"That's a great name," he said. "In fact, that's the name of our patron saint. St. Teresa. Although, you don't look or sound much like a saint." He laughed again. He was young, and he had nice teeth, and he didn't have hair growing all over his face.

"Why were you peeking in my window?" I hoped he'd forgot about finding me trying to climb in.

"I just wanted to see what it was like on the inside. I've never seen a real live castle before."

"This is a monastery. Do you know what that is?"

"A church?"

He reached out and touched the beads around my neck and smiled. "Those are pretty."

"Yeah," I said, stepping back away from him.

"OK, Teresa, if your head is feeling better, I have to go now, can you find your way home?" He held his hand out to me to go back towards the front of the castle; I didn't take it but I followed beside him.

"Do you live around here?" He asked me.

"Uh, yeah, down the road. Can I come back and visit sometime? Like tomorrow?"

He smiled. "I think that would be OK. Come back after lunch and we'll feed the ducks."

"I fed them today; I gave them some of those white crackers in the tub."

He threw his head back and laughed and laughed. "That's good, I'll see you tomorrow, Teresa."

And then he went inside and I went down the driveway back towards the path and the bridge, but I didn't go that way. Instead, I followed the long driveway all the way back down to the white lady. When I got to the white lady I cut back up through the woods again, and back to the house. I wondered if it belonged to the men in the castle.

Even though I probably shouldn't, I knew I was gonna go back and visit that man tomorrow. I really did wanna see the inside that castle.

FIFTEEN

Back in the little green house, I thought about how hungry I was. I remembered the Sky Bar that was still in my bag and got it out. I ate it part by part, trying to decide which part I like best, and decided it was the vanilla. I thought I might better go back to that store and get me some more food, 'cause that candy bar was the last of it. I dug down in the bottom of my bag and got out the bag of money to make sure it was still there and to get some to put in my pocket. There was no way I was gonna pull it out in front of everybody.

I left the house for the second time that day and went through the woods till I got to the driveway and walked down towards the highway. I didn't pass the white lady statue because I went through the woods too far. I'd look at her on the way back.

I headed back in the same direction I'd come from

earlier. It was no time till I got to the store and now there were three old men sitting out front on the bench. They were all wearing overalls and hats. One of them was spitting in a rusted coffee can and one was smoking a big, fat, brown stinky cigarette, and one was carving on a piece of wood, just like Antoe. They said, "Hey little girl," and I just smiled at them and went in the door. The bells jangled again when I went in and there was a different woman standing at the counter. This one was older and had short brown hair that was real big and she wore black glasses.

"Hey there little girl, what can I help you with today?"

"I'm just here to get some stuff...for my granny," I said, 'cause sometimes when people asked questions like that, they'd get all weird when a little kid came in by herself.

"Aren't you just the biggest little thang? And so sweet to help your granny, let me know if you need some help."

I was already looking over the shelves so I didn't bother to answer. Most of the stuff needed cooking and I didn't wanna cook in the green house, so I got a package of bologna, a loaf of bread and a box of Hostess Twinkies. I took it and laid it on the counter, then I went back to grab two bags of potato chips and two bottles of Coke.

I took it all to the counter where the rest of my stuff was and pulled a twenty dollar bill out of my pocket. The lady started punching numbers on her cash register.

"This is for my Granddaddy's lunch. He likes bologna sandwiches and potato chips. And he likes Coke and Twinkies, too. He gets up every morning and makes his lunch and puts it in a brown paper sack."

"Who's your granddaddy?" Hellshitdamn. Now this woman wanted to ask me questions and she wouldn't have if I had just kept my damn mouth shut.

"You wouldn't know him; we're just passing through, they just sent me to get stuff. They're visiting our other relatives. They let me out and are gonna pick me up."

"That'll be four dollars and fifty seven cents." She told me, looking at me kinda funny. I handed her a twenty, she gave me change and I grabbed the sack from her and said, "Thank you ma'am," and tore out of there before she could ask any more questions.

I walked to the edge of the parking lot, which was just black gravel, and looked back and she was watching me from the front door. I knew she was checking to see which direction I was going but I couldn't help it. I made sure to stay on the edge of the road so I'd be out of sight as soon as I passed by a couple of trees. I peeked over my shoulder a couple of times but nobody was following me. I got back to the road that led to my house. It was funny how I already thought of it as "mine." I passed by the lady statue and headed up through the woods. Before I went to the front door, I looked around real good to make sure nobody was around. I opened the wooden door and left it open while I checked the house right quick to make sure nobody was there. After I made sure it was OK, I went back and shut the big door. Then I took my groceries to the kitchen and opened the up the bologna and bread and made me two sandwiches. I got the Cokes out but I hadn't thought about not having a bottle opener.

"Hellshitdamn." I jumped a little 'cause my voice sounded real loud in that quiet house. I looked through all the drawers and there were some silverware, but nothing like a bottle opener. Then I remembered something I'd seen Chuck do: He would put his beer bottle under one of the drawer handles and pop the cap off pretty as you please. I tried it with my Coke bottle and it worked! I took my Coke and sandwiches to the couch in the living room.

After I finished eating, I saw it was getting dark outside so I turned on the little lamp that set on a table by the couch. The thing that was real nice was how quiet it all was. Nobody was screaming and hollering, there wasn't a bunch of scary people around, and I wasn't having to hold my breath cause I was scared I was gonna get a whipping. I thought about how it'd be if me and Antoe could live in the little green house, just the two of us. I wouldn't go to school no more so I could take care of him and we'd be just fine with the money I'd found till

I'd be old enough to get me a job.

Then I started to wonder about that money. I knew it was Chuck's and I figured it was the reason he'd been in a real bad mood lately. I wondered if he was still in jail. I finished my Coke and took the bottle to the kitchen.

I was tired so I went back to the bedroom that was at the back of the house and sat down on the bed. It was real squishy and soft so I laid back on it. I almost fell asleep but the sounds the house made woke me back up. Seemed like there was an awful lot of creaking and there were bushes that were brushing against the outside windows. There was no way I was gonna sleep up here for anybody to find me, so I took the quilts off the bed and dragged them under it and made a nest to sleep in. It wasn't as comfortable but I'd be safer if somebody came. I put my bag under there first, then I went in the bathroom and got a wash rag and washed my face real good 'cause I really couldn't remember the last time I took a bath. I was just hanging the wash rag up on the rack when I heard the squeak of the front door opening.

Well, I ran out of there as quick and as quiet as I could and slid back under the bed where the quilts were and sorta rolled myself up in them. My heart was beating a hundred million miles a minute 'cause I couldn't even imagine how I was gonna get out of this. I heard footsteps coming back towards the bedroom and I didn't even dare breath.

"Teresa? Teresa?" I heard a man's voice calling. "I know you're here somewhere, won't you come out so we can talk?" It sounded like the one I'd met earlier.

Hellshitdamn. He must've seen the lights shining in the house. But he hadn't seen me yet, so maybe if I kept quiet he'd go away.

"OK, Teresa, I'm going to sit here on this bed and wait until you come out. I can wait all night long."

Well, he sat on the bed and it sagged down with him. Since it was already real low, I felt like he was gonna squash me, so I freaked out, 'cause I hated nothing worse than when Antoe would sit on me; he thought it was funny, but I didn't. This felt the exact same.

"Get off me!" I shrieked and started tunneling my way out of the blankets I was wrapped up in, and then started crawling out from under the bed.

The man stood up then, and it didn't feel like I was being squashed anymore, so I thought maybe I could stay under there, but he reached under the bed and grabbed me by one of my legs and hauled me out from under on the bed of blankets. If things'd been different, I would've loved skating across those smooth wood floors on those blankets.

When I came to a stop on my blanket raft I was right up against the wall, and I just stayed put and looked up at this man. He was probably pissed off at me, and I figured I was probably about to get beat. I looked around the room quick to see if there was any way to escape.

He sat there on the bed and looked at me. "Now. Suppose you and I talk about why you're here?"

I didn't say anything, just watched him to see which way he was gonna move.

He stood up and I made myself as small as I could get, but then he just came over to me and held out his hand.

"Come on, let's go to the living room and talk, OK?" I didn't move. He kneeled down beside me.

"I'm not going to hurt you." He spoke real soft.

"I just want to know why you're here, OK?"

"Is this your house?" I asked.

"Well, not mine exactly, but it belongs to the Monastery."

"Why don't people live here?"

"They stay here sometimes."

"Oh."

"Are you from around here?" He asked and I shook my head and he waited.

"Did you run away from somewhere? Or are you visiting someone?"

"Yeah. I'm visiting my Granny. Down the road."

"Don't you think she's looking for you since it's getting dark out? Want me to take you home?" He just kept sitting there looking at me.

"What's your name?" I blurted out.

"Joseph. But I'm called Brother Joseph."

"Why?"

"Because we're all brothers in Christ. Now, your grandmother?"

Hellshitdamn. He knew good and well I didn't have no grandmother around here and he was just waiting to see what I was gonna say.

"I ain't visiting my granny."

"Did you run away?" He asked me then, not looking at me, but looking in the kitchen where I had left my bread and bologna.

"Is that yours?" He asked.

"Yeah, I went down to the store. You can have a sandwich if you're hungry."

He smiled and said no thanks he wasn't hungry and then he looked at me like he was waiting.

"Did you see the lights? Is that how you knew I was here?"

He nodded. "That, and I saw you coming up through the woods with sacks." He stood up.

"Why don't you get your stuff and let's go up to the house?"

"The castle?" I asked.

"Yes." He smiled and held out his hand to help me up. I didn't really wanna go with him cause I knew he wasn't finished asking questions, but I sure did wanna see the inside of the castle. I didn't say anything but let him help me up and went and got my food and put it

248 / RHONDA G. WILLIAMS

back in the sack. I had a feeling I wouldn't be coming back to get it. He was waiting for me at the front door, and he took the sack from me and held the door open so I could go through it, when I remembered my bag.

"Oh, I gotta get something." I ran back to the bedroom and my bag was laying in the middle of the blankets where he'd pulled me. I looked at the window and thought for a minute about pushing out the screen and running, but Brother Joseph looked like he could run pretty fast, 'specially since he wasn't wearing a dress, so I went back to where he was waiting for me.

He shut the door behind us and we walked up the hill towards the castle, neither one of us saying a word. I was too busy trying to figure out what I was gonna tell him and getting my stories straight, but I wasn't sure why he wasn't talking. I didn't mind one bit.

He followed me across the swinging bridge and neither one of us made it jump. I headed up towards the castle past the graveyard (I thought about asking him why there weren't girls in there) and up the driveway. When we got up close I looked around at him, not sure which way to go. He went ahead of me then and opened up the front door and held it open for me.

There was a big hallway sorta like in our house. Off to one side of the hallway was a room that had little fancy chairs in it. I'd never seen chairs like these; they were real little and they had flowers all over them. The other side of the hallway had a big double door that was closed. I really wanted to go in those rooms and look around and I was so busy trying to look at everything that I wasn't watching where I was going and walked into the back of him when he stopped.

"Ooops!" He grabbed me before I fell down.

"C'mon, let's go in here and meet everybody." I wasn't sure I wanted to meet everybody but I didn't have much choice. He led me in a big kitchen where there were six men sitting there at the table and they were playing a game laid out on the table.

"Hey, Brother Joseph, where'd you go?" One of them, who had a white beard like Santa Claus, asked.

"I found our squatter." He put his arm around my shoulder and pulled me forward closer to the men.

"This is Teresa. Teresa, this is Brother Andy, Brother Michael, Brother Paul, Brother David, Brother Christopher, and Brother David Paul, but we call him Brother DP. Sit here with them while I go find Father Bonaventure, OK? Then we'll figure out what to do with you."

"Hey there Teresa, I'm Brother DP, do you know how to play Monopoly?" I shook my head.

"Well, you can still help me watch Brother Andy, he cheats! They all laughed. I was busy looking around the kitchen. It was real clean and it smelled good, like somebody had cooked something.

"Teresa, do you want something to drink?" The one

who had a white beard asked me.

"Yeah, but I've got a Coke here." I ran over to the sack of food Brother Joseph had set down and pulled out my Coke. "Do y'all have an opener?" I asked. If they didn't, I was gonna show them how to do it on the drawer handles.

One of them got up to get a bottle opener and he got out a glass and put ice in it and brought it over and opened my Coke and poured it up.

"Thank you," I said.

"So. Where are you from, Teresa?" Another of them asked me, but I had no idea which one it was.

"Hush, Brother Michael, she'll tell us if she wants us to know."

"Do y'all have wives?" I asked, and you should've heard them laugh.

"No, we're not married."

"Oh." I thought for a minute. "Then who cooks for y'all?"

Brother DP, I think it was, said, "We all take turns, but I'm the best, Brother Joseph can't even boil water! Can you cook?"

"Yeah, some things. I can make real good mayonnaise sandwiches. That's what me and Antoe eat mostly. Bettes is a real good cook."

"Who's Bettes?" One of them asked.

"She's my friend." But then I shut up. I knew what

they were doing, they were trying to act real nice and get me to tell them where I was from and they were gonna call Tracie and I wasn't about to go home just yet so I figured I'd ask them some questions myself.

"What town is this?"

"East End. Do you live here?" The one who looked the youngest, Brother David I think, asked.

"No," I said.

"How old are you, six? Seven?"

"I'm nine."

"That's pretty old." The Santa Claus one said.

"What grade are you in? Third? Fourth?" The one who asked me wore black glasses.

"First. Only I ain't supposed to be in the first, but they won't let me move up to third 'cause this is my first year going to school."

Before any of them could say anything else, Brother Joseph came back with another man. He was real, real tall, and real, real big. Mr. Pat was the tallest man I'd ever seen and Antoe was the fattest, but this man wasn't like either of them. He wasn't fat like Antoe, he was just *big*. Like a giant. He would've made Mr. Pat look real little. And he had a black beard sorta like Chuck had, only his wasn't all long and wild. He didn't look mean but sometimes that'd fool you.

"Teresa, this is Father Bonaventure." Brother Joseph held out his hand for me to come over to them but

I stayed put.

Father Bonaventure squatted down and he was still taller than me.

"Teresa, it's nice to meet you. Won't you come with me and let's have a little talk?" He held out his hands to me.

I looked up at Brother Joseph. I didn't want to go without him and he must've known that 'cause he took my hand and led me closer to the giant.

"C'mon, we're just going to talk, OK?'

I let him lead me down a long hallway, past a lot of doors that were shut and I sure did wanna look around. We got to the end of the hall and the giant opened the door and there was a room with bookcases filled up with books and a big, big desk, kinda like Mrs. Huitt's desk at school, but a lot bigger.

"That's a big desk!" I blurted out.

"It is, but then again, I'm a big man!" The giant laughed. One thing I'd noticed, all these men here sure did like to laugh and they all seemed real nice and friendly. I was sorta working on a plan; since they all seemed real nice, maybe they'd take me to where Antoe was. Maybe. And after we found him, maybe, just maybe, they'd let us live in that green house. Antoe could help them out around the castle, cleaning and stuff, and I could, too.

I sat down in one of the chairs on the other side of the desk, and Brother Joseph sat next to me. The giant sat behind the desk.

"Now. Suppose you tell us where you're from."

I looked at him. See, I kinda wanted to tell him 'cause he might help me, but I still wasn't sure.

"Don't you think they're worried about you?"

"No. I mean, maybe, but they probably only just noticed I was gone."

"Do they treat you badly? Is that why you left?"

"No. They sent Antoe away and I'm trying to find him, only I don't have no idea where he is." Hellshitdamn. I was disgracing myself by crying and I wasn't even *trying to*!

"Who's Antoe?"

"He's...he's..." How did I tell somebody who Antoe was?

"Do you know the name of your town?" He asked me when I never finished answering his other question.

"Lakeside."

The giant looked real surprised.

"That's a pretty long way from here." He looked at Brother Joseph. "Did someone drive you?" "Yeah, only he didn't know it. See, I fell asleep in the back of a truck and spent the night there. A man got in it and drove to that little store up the highway and I jumped out and came here."

The men looked at each other some more. I had stopped bawling and I was mad as hell I'd told them the name of my town.

"I know I have to go back home, but I just wanna see Antoe, please?"

"Where is he?" Giant asked me.

"I don't know; Bettes took him somewhere."

"Do you know your phone number?" Brother Joseph asked me then.

"Yeah, (I'd learned it after Brady thought I was stupid for not knowing it) but there ain't gonna be nobody there."

"Why?"

"Cause our house got wrecked and Chuck went to jail and Tracie's staying with Bettes, only I don't know her phone number."

"What's Bettes' last name?" The giant asked me.

"Her name is Bettes Jamison," I said, "but I don't know her phone number."

The giant, Father somebody, was fiddling around with a pen on his desk. "OK, well, we'll sort it all out, but for now, I think you could probably do with a bath, don't you think?"

"Yeah, but I ain't got no more clothes."

"Well, we'll find something for you to wear tonight and we'll get your clothes washed, OK?" I nodded.

"Brother Joseph, why don't you take her to the bathroom and show her where everything is, and then we'll get a bedroom ready for her and then we'll take her home in the morning."

"I can stay here tonight?" I asked.

Brother Joseph smiled. "Yes, would you like that?"

"Yeah, I ain't ever stayed in a castle before! They both laughed. Brother Joseph held out his hand and said, "C'mon then."

He took me down the hallway and showed me a little bedroom. It looked exactly like the one I'd looked in the window at, the one Brother Joseph said was his.

"You can stay here tonight. I'll make up the bed for you. But before you get in those clean sheets, I think you need to do some serious scrubbing!" He took me down the hallway a little further and we came to a real little bathroom. There wasn't nothing in there but a commode and a bathtub and sink. He showed me where there were some washrags and towels in a cabinet and he left and then came back and handed me a white tee shirt. "You can sleep in this tonight and tomorrow we'll find something, OK?"

"OK," then, "Brother Joseph?"

"Yes?"

"My name ain't Teresa. It's Girl. I know that sounds like a stupid, made up name, but it ain't. If you call somebody and tell them you got Teresa, they won't know who the hell you're talking about."

He looked at me funny, nodded, and then shut the door behind him.

I took a real good bath and washed my hair and

was even real careful to get all the soap out. I got out of the tub and let the water out and it was so dirty and brown it looked like a mud hole. I guess I was dirtier than I thought I was. I put on the tee shirt and it hung down to my ankles, which was a good thing, since I didn't have any underwear but what I was wearing. I happened to remember that old pair of cut off shorts I had stuffed in my bag so I pulled them out and put them on. You couldn't see them but it made me feel better. Then I gathered up my dirty clothes and the towel and wash rag and went out to the hallway. I didn't see nobody around so I went down to the little bedroom and shut the door. I laid all my dirty clothes on top of the little dresser that was there and took my bag over to the bed. I didn't wanna take no chances with somebody getting it. There was a knock on the door then Brother Joseph stuck his head in.

"You look much cleaner!" Do you feel better?"

"Yeah," I said.

He came over and sat on the bed.

"So your name is...Girl?" He asked.

I nodded. "Girl Brown. I just told you Teresa cause sometimes that's what I call myself when I get tired of people making fun of my name. I wish it really *was* my name, 'cause I'd like a real one."

"Tomorrow I'm going to have to take you home, OK?"

"Did you talk to somebody?" I asked.

"No, no one answered."

"Could we please find Antoe?" Before you take me home, I mean?"

He looked at me. "I don't know where he is, do you?"

"No, but Bettes'll tell you if you talk to her. She was the one who took him somewhere."

He sighed. "I can't promise anything, but we'll see."

"OK." I said.

"Goodnight...Teresa Girl." He turned the lights off and was closing the door.

"Brother Joseph?"

"Yes?"

"Maybe me and Antoe could live here? Or in the green house? I could help out with cleaning and stuff and Antoe can do most anything as long as you tell him what to do. He's real big and strong."

He didn't say anything but just stood there in the light of the hallway and kinda smiled and waved.

I felt good 'cause he hadn't said no outright. Maybe he'd think about it and ask the giant, cause he kinda acted like the giant was his boss, or maybe his daddy or something. Maybe they were all real brothers and that's why they called each other that.

I wasn't the least bit sleepy and I laid there listening to the old house sounds and I could hear people walking around for a while then it was real, real quiet.

And if you think I stayed there in that bed and slept when there was a real live castle to explore, well, you'd be wrong. I snuck out as quiet as I could and I looked that house over from one end to the other.

Now I understood why Cerese was worried about our house being haunted with ghosts, 'cause I wasn't sure but what ghosts weren't all around here. Ghosts really didn't bother me too much; they were just dead people. I was more worried about living ones.

I didn't go upstairs because the stairs creaked real bad and I wasn't sure where all those men were sleeping. But I went downstairs and checked out that little room with the fancy chairs. There were shelves with books and stuff, and there was the same man with his heart out, and the same lady with roses I'd seen in Brother Joseph's room. Next, I went down the hallway past the kitchen, down a steep staircase that went way down to a room like our fruit cellar, only this one was huge. They had a TV in there and everything. Next, I went back up and looked around the kitchen. The table they had in there had twenty chairs, I counted them, and there were about a million cabinets. I looked in their icebox and they didn't have much more in it than we did. I wondered if they were poor.

I went back down the hallway and I won't lie, I thought about sneaking out of that front door and just running again. But the thing about running away was it was real tiring. Plus, I hadn't figured out a plan yet, and I was learning it was better if you had a plan before you did something. I opened up those big double doors and they squeaked bad so I had to do it real slow. When I got them open I saw that it looked like the inside of a church like the one Mrs. Miller took me to. It had that same table up front and benches lined up on either side. There was a big statue of the same man on the cross up front. I sat down on one of those benches and just thought.

I didn't know if they'd get Bettes on the phone tomorrow or not, and I didn't know if she'd tell them where she'd taken Antoe, but I knew if they took me back home, I was gonna figure it out and just run away again. I didn't even wanna think about what Chuck might do when I got back. I guess it would all depend on if he was still in jail or not. I hoped he was. I'd a lot rather blame all that'd happened on Chuck. It was easy to be mad at him.

What I didn't understand was this: Tracie was always hollering at him, calling him a goddamn drunk bastard, and then he'd hit her in the face and yelled at her in front of Mrs. Miller. Why did she keep on letting him stay at our house? I know Bettes always told her to kick his ass out but she wouldn't. I just knew that he was behind sending Antoe away. If she'd get rid of Chuck, maybe things could go back to the way they were before he got there. Thinking about all this stuff was making my head hurt like crazy and I jumped up to get away from it. There was still rooms I hadn't looked in yet.

SIXTEEN

I roamed around till I started hearing sounds of people getting up so I hopped back to the bedroom I was staying in and jumped under the covers. I heard someone open the door and look in but I played like I was asleep. I must've gone to sleep too, 'cause the sun was way up when the door opened again.

"Wake up, sleepy head." It was Brother Joseph. "You missed breakfast and now you're going to miss lunch if you don't get up. You don't want to miss lunch either, Brother DP's cooking and he's the best cook we've got!"

"It's late?" I asked rubbing my eyes, trying to wake up. I *never* slept late. But even after I crawled in bed last night I couldn't sleep; I had too much on my mind.

"It's eleven."

"Did you talk to Bettes?"

He shook his head. "Not yet. Do you have any idea

when they might be home?"

I shrugged. "If she's there, she'll get up about three o'clock. Or she'll get home about then." He nodded. "Here, I got your clothes washed for you. Looks like they've taken a beating." He handed me my blue jeans, the shirt of Tracie's, and my underwear. I got out of the bed and took them from him.

"Can I wear this shirt?" I asked, 'cause I liked the feel of that soft, big, tee shirt.

"Yes, if you want. Get dressed and let's go see how lunch is coming." He shut the door behind him and I got up and put on my underwear, jeans, my beaded necklaces, and those boots. I was wishing I'd asked for some socks and then I remembered I'd put some in my bag. I dug around in the top of my bag and found them, took off the boots, put on the socks, then put the boots back on. They sure did feel better with all those blisters. I wished I'd thought about the socks earlier.

I went out in the hallway and Brother Joseph was waiting for me. He held out his hand and I took it and we went together down the hallway towards the kitchen. I wanted to ask him what that room that looked like a church was, but I didn't want him to know I'd roamed all over their house last night.

When we got to the kitchen, Brother DP was there, wearing an apron, and it made me laugh 'cause the only person I'd ever seen wearing an apron was Mrs. Miller.

"Are you laughing at my apron?" He asked.

"Yeah, I didn't know men wore aprons."

"It keeps my clothes clean because I'm messy! Are you hungry?"

I nodded.

"Well, good, because we're having fried chicken, mashed potatoes, corn on the cob, and green beans. Does that sound good?"

"Yeah, Mrs. Miller made fried chicken for me and Antoe only I couldn't eat it 'cause I thought about those poor chickens I'd caused to die."

"How did you do that?" Brother DP asked.

"I let them out of their pen and the dogs got 'em. But I didn't mean to."

"I see. Who's Antoe?"

"Can I do that?" He'd dumped the potatoes in a bowl and added some milk and butter and now he was mashing them up with a masher. It looked like fun.

"OK, come over here so you can reach." He took the bowl and the masher over to the table and I got in one of the chairs on my knees so I'd be tall enough and took the masher from him.

"Like this?" I asked making sure I was doing it right; it was harder than it looked.

"That's perfect. Make sure you mash them until they're fluffy or Father Bonaventure will complain!" He laughed so I knew he was joking.

Well, I mashed hell out of those potatoes and helped Brother DP set the table, eleven people were gonna be eating.

"Do we have enough food?" I asked 'cause I'd never seen that many people eating in one place before, except for that time at Chuck's church.

"Oh, yes, we'll have more than enough."

And he started to put all that food in big dishes and set it all on the table.

"You can ring the bell." He told me and showed me this bell on the side of the wall that had a string you pulled. I wasn't tall enough so he held me up and I rang that bell and boy, was it loud! It wasn't no time till all those men came into the kitchen and all sat down at that big table. I wondered where I was supposed to sit and Brother Joseph came in and led me over to sit beside him and the giant sat on the other side of me, at the head of the table.

When we were all sitting, the giant looked around at everybody and bowed his head and said "Bless us, O Lord, and these Thy gifts, which we are about to receive from Thy bounty, through Christ our Lord" and then they all said "Amen" together.

Well, that was about the best food I'd ever ate in my life. And there was so much I even had seconds of everything. After everybody had eaten all they wanted, the giant looked around and bowed his head again and said, "We give Thee thanks for all Thy benefits, O Almighty God, who lives and reigns world without end. Amen. May the souls of the faithful departed, through the mercy of God, rest in peace," and then everybody said, "Amen," again and I did, too.

All those men got up and started cleaning up the kitchen. I helped them, doing whatever they told me to, 'cause I wanted them to see what a big help I could be. One of them, the one I still thought of as Santa Claus, even started singing. We were about finished when I realized Brother Joseph and the giant had left a little while ago. I bet they were trying to call Bettes. I hoped she didn't answer her phone; I really wanted to spend one more night in the castle.

"There, that's all done!" Brother DP looked around that kitchen and everything was so clean it shined. I couldn't believe all that mess had been cleaned up that quick. That's one of the reasons Tracie didn't cook, 'cause she said she couldn't deal with the fucking mess.

"Girl, could you come here?" It was Brother Joseph, he'd come back in the kitchen and was standing by the door so I went over to him. He led me down the hall to the bedroom I stayed in and shut the door behind him.

"I finally reached Ms. Jamison and she was overjoyed you're OK. I told her I'd bring you home this evening."

"Who?" I asked.

"Bettes," he said.

"Oh."

"You don't want to go home?"

"I gotta find Antoe."

He didn't say anything for a second. "She told me she'd taken him to the State hospital."

"Why? He wasn't sick."

"Noooo...but it's not that kind of hospital...was... did...Antoe? That's what you call him? He's...special..."

"Yeah, Cerese, that's my friend, she said he was weird and afflicted, only Bettes said that was a stupid goddamn word."

He looked shocked then he laughed. "Yeah, it kinda is. But anyway, the State Hospital is for people like... Antoe. He's living there now, and he's going to be able to work and really, I think he'll be happier."

"Well, I don't! He ain't gonna be happy 'cause he don't like being around strangers, and he misses me! If you take me home, that's fine, but I'll just run away again, 'cause I wanna see him and make sure he's OK."

I turned my back on him and started to make up the bed that I hadn't made up earlier. I never made up my bed but I knew in this clean, neat place making a bed was expected.

"I can't take you there, can you understand that?"

"No."

He sighed and then he looked at his wrist watch.

"You just want to see him? Make sure he's OK?"

He asked.

"Yeah."

He sighed again. "OK, listen. It's not that far from here, we'll run by there for just *a minute*. No longer. I'm not even sure you'll be able to see him. But we can't stay, you can see him, see he's OK, then I have to take you home, OK? Is that a deal?"

"Yeah, it's a deal." And I held my hand out to him and when he took it, I just grabbed him and hugged him around the middle.

"One more thing," I looked up at him, "Don't say anything about it to anyone here."

I nodded. "Will you get in trouble?"

"Not too much...maybe," he said. "Now get your stuff and go tell the others bye then meet me out front by the van."

Well, I grabbed up my bag and threw on my sweater and tore out of there to find the rest of the brothers. Some were coming down the hallway towards the bedrooms.

"I'm going home now, I wanted to tell y'all bye and thank you for letting me stay here."

"You're welcome, it was nice to meet you, Girl." Santa Claus said and all of them shook my hand.

I went in the kitchen and Brother DP and two more were still there.

"I'm going now, thank you for letting me stay here and mash the potatoes. And thank you for dinner, it was good!" I hugged Brother DP around the middle.

"You're very welcome, come back and visit us again," he said.

"Could I really? Come back and visit someday?"

"Sure! Only, next time make sure they know where you are!" He winked and I grinned and went to the front hallway and out the front door. I saw the van in the driveway, Brother Joseph was in it already, it was pale blue in spots and rusted red in others. I wasn't sure it would make it too far. I opened the door and climbed in.

"Ready?" He asked and cranked it up. That old blue van made a worse noise than Bettes' car did. He backed up and we left. I turned around and there were some of them out front waving. I leaned out the window to wave at them and then we passed by the little green house and the white lady statue then down to the end of the driveway and we turned out on the highway. I was going to get Antoe.

SEVENTEEN

For quite a while we drove and Brother Joseph didn't say a word, so I didn't either. I wondered if he'd get in bad trouble. Probably so 'cause he didn't know this, but I wasn't leaving without Antoe. I was thinking up a plan where we could hide and get away. I hated to do that to him, but it couldn't be helped.

"So…I expect they'll be glad to see you at home."

"I guess."

"Ms. Jamison said…your…Tracie? Was really upset."

"Yeah."

"And…your step-father?"

"Chuck ain't my step-father. He'll be mad as hell."

"Does he get mad a lot?"

"All the time. Bettes says it's 'cause he's batshit crazy. He ain't got but one leg and that has something to do with it. He was someplace they were fighting and got it shot off."

"He was in Vietnam?"

"I think so."

"Does he whip you?"

"With a belt," I said.

"I see." Brother Joseph's voice was quiet. I looked over at him and you could tell he was grabbing the steering wheel real hard and looking straight ahead.

"What do you do to get your...to get whippings?"

"Sass him. Sometimes he gets mad at something Antoe does...and he grabs me instead."

"Chuck doesn't whip Antonio?" he asked.

"No, he hit him once and Tracie didn't like it. They went upstairs and screamed at each other for a long time. He usually only hits me when he's been drinking the brown stuff."

He didn't say any more and pretty soon we started to see more and more cars, kinda like it was in Greenville. He turned in a big parking lot and found a space and turned the van off. We were right in front of a huge grey building. It looked like a big jail 'cause there were even bars on the windows.

"This is where Antoe is?" I asked.

He nodded. "Now, I've got to check to make sure you can see him, and we can only stay a little bit, just so you can see he's fine, OK?" I nodded. He got out of the van and reached in the backseat and pulled out a brown dress and started putting it on, over his jeans and tee shirt. He had a belt he put on next and then he pulled out a big beaded necklace, just like the ones I was wearing, only this one was way, way bigger and he put it on the side of his belt so it hung there.

"Why're you putting on your dress? And where'd you get them beads? Antoe would like them, could we get him some?"

He just smiled and finished putting everything on, and then he held out his hand. "Let's go." I grabbed my bag then and jumped out.

"You can leave that here, it'll be OK." But I acted like I didn't hear him and put the strap over my head. I wondered if it would make him mad, that I had ignored what he told me to do, but he didn't say anything, just held out his hand for me to take. So I did.

We walked all the way through that big parking lot and the closer we got to the building, the bigger it looked. I couldn't imagine how Antoe was living there. There wasn't any trees or anything in that parking lot and I bet he was sad all the time. Well, he wouldn't be sad for long.

We went through big doors in the front and then down a long hallway. It smelled funny in there. It looked like that hallway kept going and going but there was a big desk right in the middle. Ladies in white dresses and hats were behind it and I knew they were the same ones who'd given me my shot last summer. Nurses. I didn't like those nurses.

"You stay right here, I'm going to ask them where he is and if you can see him." Brother Joseph left me by some orange chairs that were in a little room before you got to the big desk with the nurses. I sat down on the edge of one and just waited. He went up to one of those ladies and was talking to her. I knew they were talking about me, 'cause every now and then the lady would look over at me. I didn't like it either, so I got off the orange chair and started to walk over to where they were when all hell broke loose.

There was this man, a big fat man with a bald head, and he came running down the hall where Brother Joseph was standing with the lady. The man was screaming at the top of his lungs and he wasn't wearing any clothes. He came tearing around the corner and there were all kinds of men chasing after him. When he got in front of the desk where the nurses were, he stopped and grabbed hold of his tallywacker and shook it at them and then went tearing off down the other direction, still screaming at the top of his lungs. All those men were chasing him and they all disappeared around a corner. They must've tackled him then, 'cause there was a thud and screaming like you never heard before. Antoe was a pretty good screamer, but he couldn't come close to the noise this man was making.

I saw Brother Joseph take off down the hallway, too, like he was gonna help out the men. It was kinda funny watching him run, 'cause his skirt was flapping around his feet like bird wings. I didn't watch him long though, 'cause I knew this was my chance to find Antoe. I took off running down the opposite hallway.

The screaming man must've still been causing trouble 'cause I kept meeting all these people going past me running as fast as they could and nobody paid me no attention. One man did say, "Hey, what're you doing here?" But I just kept running.

I got to the end of that hallway and there was a door. I opened it and saw stairs that went up and stairs that went down. I just took the ones that were going down 'cause I was too tired to run up them. When I got down to the bottom, there was another door, and I pushed it open and there were all these baskets full of clothes and washers and dryers all lined up, one beside each other, against the walls. I knew Antoe wasn't down there, but I thought maybe if I found him, we could come down there and hide in some of those baskets until I could figure something out. So I ran back up the stairs, to where I'd come in, and kept going up. When I got to another door I pushed it open and there was another hallway. I ran down it without thinking, and there were people sitting outside doors on the floor, and they didn't even look up when I ran by. There were doors all along the hallway, and some were open and I saw men sitting in chairs and some were laying in bed. Pretty soon I got to the end of that hallway and it was a big open room with more people sitting around. There wasn't any door out of this room either, and I wanted to cry when I thought about having to go all the way back. I stopped for just a second to catch my breath and I happened to look way in the back and there was Antoe sitting by himself looking at a book. I walked over to him, 'cause Antoe didn't like it if you ran up and scared him, and said, "hey, Antoe," just like we were back at home. He looked up from his book and got a huge grin on his face.

"Girl. Hey, Girl!" He got up then, and came to me and put his arms around me and hugged me so hard he liked to have smothered me just like he always did.

"Ow, Antoe, you hurt," I said, just like I always did, then I laughed 'cause I was so relieved I found him. I sat down beside him and he showed me the book he was looking at. It was about the monkey called Curious George. "Girl read?"

"Antoe, can we go outside?" I didn't know if he got to go out or not, but I wasn't real surprised when he shook his head.

"Tonio no go outside, be trouble." And he reached over and patted me on the leg.

"Antoe you gotta come with me 'cause they're gonna come get you and take you back to Chuck and he's gonna beat you up." Chuck scared Antoe worse than anybody.

Well, he looked around and then started to shake his head. "No, Chuck not come here. Tonio OK here."

I jumped up and grabbed his hand to pull him. "No, we gotta go Antoe! We're gonna go back and live in this little green house. Just me and you. Won't you like that?" I was getting desperate to get him to stand up so we could leave; we were running out of time. I thought sure telling him that Chuck was coming would do it.

He looked at me and took his hand back from me. "Tonio have job. Work every day. In kitchen. Clean dishes get paid!" He looked so excited and happy I wanted to sit right down and bawl 'cause one, I'd never seen him look that happy about something that didn't have anything to do with me, and two, I knew he wasn't going to leave.

"What about carving? Don't you miss carving your wood?" I knew they probably wouldn't let him have his knife in there.

"Tonio carve. Mark help Tonio."

"Who's Mark?"

"Tonio friend. Mark good friend."

I didn't know what to do. Antoe could be like a stubborn mule, I knew this. And if he ever made up his mind to do something or not do something, there just wasn't anything or anybody that was gonna change it. I hadn't even thought about what to do if he didn't wanna leave. I didn't think that was even possible.

"There Mark!" Antoe looked up towards the door and grinned. I saw a man walking back towards where we were sitting. He was wearing dark blue clothes like the ones who chased the naked man. I pulled on Antoe's hand one last time, hoping to get him to come with me but he just pulled me up with him to go meet Mark.

"Hey, Tony, who's this?" He asked when he got there.

"This Girl. Girl, this Tonio friend, Mark."

"It's nice to meet you, Girl. I bet you're the one they're looking for, aren't you?"

I just looked at him and he looked at me.

"OK, I'm just gonna call down to the front. Wait right here."

"Antoe, don't you wanna go with me? I found us a house we can live in." Well, not really, but I figured we could work that out later.

"Tonio stay here. Like. Nice here." And he went back to looking at that stupid damn book. "Girl read?"

Before I could answer I looked up and saw Brother Joseph coming in the room. He looked relieved when he saw me.

"There you are!" He put his hand on my shoulder like he was afraid I was gonna run again. "And this must be Antoe?" He asked looking at him.

"Tonio." Antoe stood up and held out his hand for Brother Joseph to shake. I'd never seen him do that to anybody.

"Tonio. Nice to meet you, I'm Brother Joseph."

"Brother Joe. Nice meet." He shook his hand like he was pumping water or something.

"Well, Girl, you can sit here and visit for a little bit, then we have to go, OK?"

I looked away from him. I was mad as hell and I wasn't even sure who I was mad at: him, Antoe, Bettes, Tracie or just all of them together.

"That's OK, I'm ready," I said and he looked surprised.

"You can visit for a little longer," he said.

"No, I'm ready to go." And I stood up.

"Well...OK, then. Tell Antoe...Tonio, bye."

"Bye Antoe," I said, and he looked up and grinned for a second before putting his nose back in Curious George. Brother Joseph held out his hand but I acted like I didn't see it. He sighed like he was real tired. There wasn't much I could do but follow him back the way I'd come, past all the hallways, the nurses, and right back out those big front doors.

EIGHTEEN

Brother Joseph tried to talk some on the way back to the van, but I ignored him. He sighed some more but I didn't care. I was madder than I'd ever been in my life 'cause tears were just leaking out and rolling down my face and I couldn't make them stop. When Brother Joseph went to digging around in his dress pocket for the keys to the van, I just did it: I took off running like hell.

"Girl! Girl, come back! Girl. Girl? Girl! Oh, SHIT!" I heard him hollering and knew he was coming after me but I never looked back. I dodged in and out of those cars in that parking like you wouldn't believe. I knew he wouldn't catch me, especially not wearing that dress. I could hear him hollering my name but it was sounding further and further away.

The parking lot was big, way bigger than any I'd ever seen before and when I got to the end of it, it started off in another direction, so I kept going. When I got to the end of that part there was a street with cars going up and down it. I looked behind me for a second and didn't see anything of Brother Joseph so I watched till the cars stopped coming and ran across into another parking lot that was even bigger than the first one.

I hadn't ever seen so many cars in one place in my life. Seemed like there were hundreds of them, blue, black, green, red, white, and they were all clean and shiny. Not like the ones Chuck or Bettes had, and no trucks like Mr. Perone had. I kept on going across the lot and I could see where way up ahead of me it started to get narrow and there were trees along the side of it. Those trees sure looked good to me 'cause I think they were the first ones I'd seen since we got to this place. I ran along where the trees were and wouldn't you know it, there was another street. Only this one had a lot more cars going up and down. There were four rows of them and they were whizzing by fast as anything. I waited and they kept coming. Finally, I just couldn't stand it anymore. It was clear in the row right beside me so I jumped. When I got to the second row I had to wait, and then I jumped again. I didn't have any choice but to just keep running and hope they didn't hit me. I heard the most awful horn blowing and brakes squealing you ever heard in your life and voices were yelling at me. 'Cause I just knew somebody was coming after me I never looked back and kept running and wouldn't you know I found *another* parking lot.

"Hellshitdamn!" It just seemed silly to have this many places for cars to park.

It felt like my side was on fire it was hurting so bad and I was breathing hard, like Antoe did whenever he tried to run. At the end of this parking lot was a building and it was the hugest thing I'd ever seen in my life. It looked like about a million of our houses could fit inside of it. It was so big it scared me and I didn't even want to cross by it so I turned and started running down the other way, 'cause I wanted to get as far from that big thing as I could.

I saw a grass covered hill up ahead of me and I headed up towards it. The hill wasn't that big but since I was already tired it seemed like it took me forever to get to the top of it. When I got there finally, the first thing I saw was a statue of a man dressed in blue and he had on a weird hat with horns coming out the side. The man was huge, almost as big as that building, but not quite. There was a big sign in front of him that had War and M-e-m-o-r-i-a-l A-m-u-s-e-m-e-n-t Park. I ran up behind him and the sign and threw myself on the ground to catch my breath.

As I was catching my breath I saw a bunch of people heading into what looked like a carnival. Bettes took me and Antoe to the carnival last year, a real one, and

we both loved it. I knocked over bottles and won a gold-
fish, rode the merry-go-round, and the bumper cars,
and I wanted to ride the Ferris wheel but Antoe was too
scared and Bettes said she only wanted to be high on
the ground

The best thing about that carnival though, was the
cotton candy we got to eat. I couldn't believe how good
it was and we ate so much we got sick on the way home.
But I didn't care; I would've eaten it all over again even
knowing it'd make me sick. It was that good.

I hadn't figured out a plan yet so I might as well go
into this place and see maybe if they had some cotton
candy. I hadn't eaten since Brother DP's chicken, and it
was getting dark now and I was starving. I didn't really think Brother Joseph had followed me, he'd probably
gone back to get the van and was driving around looking for me. At least here there weren't any streets.

I went to the front of the carnival and saw it had a
fence all around it and people were going in through a
gate in front. I waited till there was a big group going
in and followed right behind them. People got all crazy acting if they saw a kid by herself. I didn't wanna do
anything to get attention. When I got inside I just stood
there looking around. It was a lot better than the carnival
last year. This one had all kinds of booths with games,
there were bumper cars, little pink and blue whales that
were floating on water you could ride in, and great big

animal statues everywhere. I just walked around looking at everything.

I came to a place that was all dark had SPOOK HOUSE on the outside, but I wasn't interested in that. I was interested in checking out the big doll that was in a huge glass box. She was shaking and laughing and her mouth was open. Every time some little kid came up there, he'd start crying at the top of his lungs. I just stayed there watching the doll. It said her name was Sally and she kinda reminded me of Bettes, especially the way she'd shake all over when she laughed.

I saw some kids walking up and they were all carrying sticks of cotton candy, so I left and went in the direction they'd come from. I smelled it before I saw it. There was a little stand and one man was in there waiting on people.

"I want a great big cotton candy!" I said.

He just grunted and picked up a long white stick and stuck it down in a bowl thing and it was like magic 'cause there wasn't anything in the bowl but all of a sudden pink strings of cotton candy started sticking to the white stick. The man kept twirling the stick around and around the bowl and the wad of pink cotton candy kept on getting bigger and bigger. Just when I thought the stick was gonna break in two from the weight of it, the man handed it to me.

"That'll be fifty cents." He looked at me then for the

first time, and I saw he was wearing a patch over his eye, like a pirate. I was trying to dig the money out of my pocket without dropping my cotton candy and I finally pulled out a twenty. I handed it the man and he grunted again and turned around and got my change and handed it back to me all wadded up in a ball. I took it from him and jammed it down in my pocket and took the biggest bite of my cotton candy I could manage. It was in my mouth for a second then it wasn't. So I took another bite, and then another, and before I knew it, the entire thing was gone. My face was sticky now, and it felt like it may be in my hair too, but I didn't really care. I was trying to decide if I wanted to go back and get another when I saw the most wonderful thing ever.

It was a merry-go-round, but it wasn't like the one I'd ridden with Antoe. That one was tiny and the horses went up and down and that was all. This one was huge, and it moved around like it was on water. The horses were sparkly and had jewels on them. Well, I knew I had to ride this merry-go-round. I got in line and gave the man a dollar and told him I wanted to ride it that many times. He gave me ten tickets and I ran and jumped up on the merry-go-round and started walking around trying to pick out a good horse. I finally decided on a black one with blue jewels and climbed on.

Well, that was the best ride ever. It didn't go up and down, but it felt like we were flying. When it was finished I hopped off the black horse and went to get on a white one. The man came around and took a ticket from me and then it started again. This time was even better. When the second ride finished I jumped off again and walked around the whole thing, looking at all the horses. There were benches too, and they had birds on them, so I decided I was going to just ride around on the bench. I sat down and waited for the man to take my ticket again but I didn't see him. I turned around and was looking back to see where he was when someone sat down beside me. I jerked around to see Brother Joseph.

Hellshitdamn. I knew there wasn't any way I could run again, 'cause I was way too tired and besides that, he had put his arm around my shoulder and I knew he wasn't gonna let go this time.

"Hey there," he said. He didn't sound all that mad, I peeked up at him and he didn't look it either, if anything, he looked tired and relieved.

"Hey." I wasn't sure what else to say. The ride started then, and we begin to go around in circles and sitting on the bench made it seem like we were on a boat on the water the way it went up and down.

"You've got something all over your face." He pulled a snow white handkerchief out of his pocket and tried to wipe my face, but that cotton candy was so sticky it wouldn't come off.

"Yeah, I had me some cotton candy." I told him and

he smiled.

"You know you've taken at least ten years off my life, don't you?" And he sorta laughed.

"I'm sorry."

"Why'd you run like that? Do you really not want to go home?" He asked.

"Antoe wouldn't come with me. He didn't even act like he was glad to see me."

"Girl...he was...he just doesn't show emotions like some people. He likes it there; I found out he has a job and is doing really well. Aren't you happy for him?"

"No. He was supposed to come with me and we were gonna live in the little green house." I looked up at him.

"I was gonna ask."

He smiled. "Maybe you can live somewhere with him when you get older, have you thought about that?"

I shrugged and the ride came to an end.

"Are you gonna be in trouble for being late bringing the van back?" I asked him as we were getting off.

He made a face and said, "Yeah, probably," then he laughed. "It won't be the first time."

He took my hand and I let him this time. We walked back towards the front where I'd come in and we were passing the cotton candy stand.

"Could I get one more cotton candy? Please? I got money."

"Well...OK, I guess. Are you sure you won't get sick?"

I didn't even bother to answer, but dug a dollar out of my pocket where I'd put it earlier and was at the stand before Brother Joseph even realized it. I heard him laugh.

"I want two cotton candies." I told the man working there. He didn't say anything but started to roll it up on a stick. When he finished it he handed it to me.

"You're going to eat two?" Brother Joseph asked when he came up behind me.

"This is yours." I handed it to him and turned around to pay the man and get mine. I laid my dollar on the counter and the man handed me the other cotton candy stick.

"Thank you. I haven't eaten cotton candy in forever."

"I wish I could eat it every day!" We went out of the front gates, both of us eating our cotton candy. I was eating mine faster than Brother Joseph and I could tell it was getting all over my face again.

The blue van was parked way down the hill, the one I'd run up just a little while ago. When we got to it, he opened the door for me and I hopped in. I took my bag off and put it in the floor board of the van. This was the first time I'd taken it off since this morning. He opened his door and got in and started the truck up. We didn't say anything while we were leaving; I was too busy watching all the cars everywhere. Pretty soon we got out on a highway that didn't have so many cars. I was getting sleepy, too. Just as I was about to fall asleep Brother Joseph cleared his throat and asked "Has Chuck... has he ever..." He stopped then and I was about half-asleep. "Huh?"

"Has Chuck ever done anything...to you...besides whipping?"

"Like what?"

He didn't say anything for a second, then, "Like... touch you?"

"Like sex and stuff?" I asked him and he looked shocked.

"Yeah...like that."

"No, he don't ever do stuff like that. Bettes asked me about that, too, and made me promise I'd tell her if he ever did."

"Oh. Well...good."

I was still sleepy and could feel myself nodding off again when he asked "Does Tracie know about him whipping you?"

"Yeah, she hollers at him, but sometimes he hits her, too. One day, when Mrs. Miller came to our house, he smashed her in the face and made her bleed."

"You said he was in jail now."

"Yeah, he beat up somebody, some kid. His brothers helped him."

He was quiet then and I soon fell back asleep. What woke me up was the sound of the van being turned off and the door slamming. I raised up from where I'd slid down in the seat and saw we were parked in front of the store where Tracie sometimes went to get beer. Brother Joseph had walked in the store and was talking to a man in there. He was still wearing his dress and I could see how everybody in there was staring at him. After a few minutes he left the store and came back out to the truck.

"What'd you stop for?" I asked.

"I was making sure I knew the way to Ms. Jamison's house." He told me.

"Oh. I could've told you how to get there. It's just down the road."

He smiled. "I didn't want to wake you up; you've had a rough few days."

"I'm OK."

"You're taking me to Bettes' house? Not ours?" I asked.

He nodded. "She said that would be best. Until we can figure out what's going on with...Chuck."

We passed the Perone's store and it was dark 'cause they didn't open on Sunday. "It's the next road on my side," I said.

He came to the road and turned down it. We bumped over the rough road that led to Bettes' house and pulled up in her little driveway. There were lights on all over the house and as soon as we came to a stop she was out the front door and running to meet the van. She yanked open the door and grabbed me before I could say a word.

"Oh my God, Girl, I'm so glad to see you!" She was squeezing me and squeezing me and she had my head buried in her shoulder.

"You're choking me, Bettes!" I said and she pulled back and looked at me and laughed like she always did and I did, too.

"Well, come on then, and you too...Father?" She looked over at Brother Joseph. He smiled and held out his hand to her.

"Brother. Brother Joseph. And thank you, but I better be getting back. This old van might not make it as it is." But he got out and came over to where I was standing and kneeled down in front of me.

"I'm so glad I got to meet you, Girl." He told me and I threw my arms around his neck and hugged him tight.

"Here, I want you to have my address and phone number and I want you to let me know how things are going, OK?" And he looked at me real careful and I knew what he was talking about. I took the piece of paper from him and he got up and went back to the other side of his van.

He got in it to start it and when he tried to it made a rrrwwwaarrrr noise and clicked. He tried it again and it did the same. He sat there for a minute then got out and raised the hood and looked under it with a flashlight he'd gotten from inside the van. He poked around under there for a few minutes then looked up at me and Bettes standing there beside the steps.

"I don't suppose you know of a mechanic who'll be open on a Sunday night?" He asked, making a face.

"No, there's one in Lakeside, but he's closed on Sundays. What's wrong?" Bettes walked out to where he was and I sat down on the top step.

"Well, I'm not an expert by any means, but it looks and sounds like the alternator is shot."

"Well, you're not going anywhere tonight. Come on in and you can have the couch."

Brother Joseph just stood there for a minute like he wasn't sure what he was gonna do. Then he put the hood down and smiled.

"Well, I need to use your phone if it's no trouble."

"Shit, it's not trouble, if it was, I wouldn't have said it!" Bettes laughed. "C'mon in. Are y'all hungry? I bet y'all are." She went inside and I waited on Brother Joseph and took his hand and led him to where the phone was. I knew he was probably calling the castle and I didn't wanna listen in so I went out to the kitchen where Bettes was banging around.

She had gotten out a package of bacon and was throwing it in a skillet. She turned the burner on then turned around and grabbed me again.

"You scared the shit out of us, Girl, you know that, don't you? I thought somebody had grabbed you and you weren't ever coming back."

"Who'd you think grabbed me?" I asked. "Those men who wrecked our house?"

"Maybe. Where'd you go? And why?" She turned around and picked up a tomato and started to cut it up.

"I went to find Antoe. I did, too."

"I heard. Hand me the bread." I got the loaf of bread out of the bread box and handed it to her. "And the mayonnaise," she said.

I opened her icebox and found the mayonnaise and set it on the counter beside her. The bacon was popping and spitting and wiggling in the pan and Bettes flipped it over and started laying out slices of bread and slapping on mayonnaise and tomato slices.

"How was he?" She asked, not looking at me.

"He's OK." I didn't tell her he was happy there and didn't wanna leave with me.

"Do you still hate me?" She asked, still not looking at me.

"I never did, I was just real mad at you."

"Are you still?"

"A little. If you hadn't took him in your car, he wouldn't be gone now."

She kept on making the sandwiches and I went back to see if Brother Joseph was still talking on the phone. He was hanging it up.

"Are they mad at you?" I asked.

"Nooo, not mad so much...but disappointed." He

had taken off his dress and the belt and beads and was folding it up carefully and laying it over the arm of the couch.

"You can sleep here tonight," I said, flopping down on the couch. "It's real comfortable; I've slept here lots of times."

"Could you show me where I can wash my hands?" He asked and I took him down the hallway to the bathroom.

Bettes came out of the kitchen and looked around for us as he was coming back down the hallway.

"Hey, you like bacon and tomato sandwiches?" She asked, even though it was too late if he didn't 'cause she'd already made them.

"That's great, thanks," He said. He went in the kitchen and took the plate from her.. Bettes poured him a big glass of tea, and then handed me a plate with two sandwiches.

"Hey Girl, why don't you take this and see what's on TV," she said. I knew she wanted to talk to him when I wasn't around. I didn't feel like watching TV so I took my plate back down to the bedroom that was mine. It was only a few days ago that I'd left it and everything was just like it was. All of Antoe's stuff was still on the bed, and I checked the drawer and got out my Halloween candy to eat after my sandwiches. I put them down on the chest and took off my bag. I wanted to check that all my stuff was still there since I hadn't looked at it since I'd left. I shook it out on the bed and the bag of balloons and money came out and then all those papers.

I sat down on the bed to look at them and forgot all about the sandwiches. There were three or four letters in envelopes that were stuffed with papers about Tracie. It said something about her being arrested for possession of something and one said something about batteries and there were some about Chuck. One had a word in it I didn't know: P-A-T-E-R-N-I-T-Y and there was a couple that was just a million tiny words that I wasn't even gonna try to read. The last one I opened was all folded up and at the top it had Birth C-E-R-T-I-F-I-C-A-T-E on the top. I was about to put it with all the rest when I saw my name was on it. It had GIRL BROWN printed at the top, then under that it had FATHER and Antonio Brown and then it said MOTHER and it had Rosalinda Miller.

Well. I had to read that two times and there was some kind of weird roaring in my ears that made it seem like I was underwater or something. I just sat there and tried to make my brain work. This paper was about me. It said my name and it said that Antoe and Rosalinda Miller were my momma and daddy. Rosalinda Miller. Rosie. She was the black lady in the picture that Antoe'd had a fit over. She was my mother. The black lady. Antoe. He couldn't be my daddy, could he? People said he was afflicted. Afflicted people couldn't be daddies, could they?

I put the papers all together and went and picked up my sandwiches. I took them back to the living room and sat down on the couch and took a bite of one and sat there holding it. Bettes and Brother Joseph came out of the kitchen and Brother Joseph sat on the couch beside me.

"Is there anything good on TV?" He asked and I went to turn it on.

Bettes perched on the side of a chair and you could just see she wanted a cigarette and she wanted to go somewhere. Bettes wasn't much for staying in one place unless she was sleeping.

"Hey, if y'all are gonna watch TV, then I gotta run over to see someone right quick. If I'm not back before y'all go to bed, I'll take you to Rodney's place first thing in the morning, 'Kay?" She said to Brother Joseph and then she whooshed back towards her bedroom where I knew she'd put on makeup and change clothes.

"OK," he said, but she'd already gone. He looked over at me and said, "Well, you can't say we haven't had adventures today!" And he laughed.

"Yeah, do you like Bettes?" I asked 'cause I wanted him too.

"Yes, she seems really nice."

"She is. I wish I could live with her."

"More than living with Tracie?" He asked, and I nodded.

"Yeah, Tracie used to be lots of fun, but since Chuck's been there she's not been and now Antoe's gone..." That was something I'd tried not to think about:

how was I gonna make it just me by myself with Tracie and Chuck?

I heard Bettes coming back and she had on a different dress and her purse and she was out the door. "See y'all in a little bit!" But I knew "a little bit" could mean anything from an hour to a week.

Me and Brother Joseph were just sitting there and I jumped up. "Can I show you something?" And before he could say yes or no I galloped back to my bedroom and got those papers. I came back and flopped beside him.

"I found these on the floor when I was in the house right after the men wrecked it. I forgot I had them. But look."

I handed them to him and he went through them one by one. As slow as he was going, I could tell he was reading them all so even though I wished he would hurry up so he could tell me exactly what they were, especially the one that said Antoe was my daddy, I waited.

He took forever, and every now and then he'd look up from the papers and look over at me. When he had gone back over the one about me again, he laid it down and just sat there.

"Could you tell me about those?" I asked.

He cleared his throat which is what grownups did when they were trying to figure out how to answer your questions.

"Well, I think it's mostly for grownups. I shouldn't

really tell you if you don't know what they're about."

That made me mad. "I'm not stupid," I said. "I know most of them are about stuff Tracie done and Chuck too but I don't much care about those, I wanna know if that one's saying Antoe is my daddy and how that could be."

"You read them?" He asked.

"Yeah, only some words I don't know yet."

"Yes, that's your birth certificate."

"What's that exactly?"

"It's a record of your birth, when you were born."

"And it says Antoe is my daddy? And Rosie is my mother?" I asked him, even though I knew that's what it said, I wanted to double-check.

"Yes. Do you know who Rosie is?" He asked.

"Yeah. Well, not really, but I know she was Mrs. Miller's kid and when Antoe saw her picture over their house he liked to had a fit."

"Who's Mrs. Miller?" He asked.

"She's Cerese's mother. My friend. Only now that would make her..." I stopped to think.

"Your grandmother." He said looking at me and I looked back at him.

Hellshitdamn. I had a grandmother! But then I stopped to think. Did she know I was her granddaughter? And if she did, why didn't she tell me? I was getting real tired of everybody keeping stuff from me when it seemed like I had a right to know.

"Does she...know?" He asked me.

"Yeah, cause she knew Antoe. From before." That was the first time I realized that was the reason Antoe didn't say a word about going with her that day. He knew her and she knew him. Before I was born. So there wasn't nothing else to say about that.

Brother Joseph picked up the heart medal with the purple ribbon and was turning it over in his hands. "Where'd this come from?" He asked.

"Tracie's bedroom." I was real tired all of a sudden and just wanted to go to bed.

"I'm gonna go to bed now. Will you be here in the morning?" I asked him.

"Well, I'm hoping to be on the road pretty early, but I'll wake you up, OK?"

I nodded. "Good night, then. And I went off to the bedroom.

I took off my boots and jeans and just left the tee shirt on Brother Joseph had given me to sleep in. I put all the stuff back in my bag and I held the bag of balloons for a minute, wondering again what they were. I guess I could ask Brother Joseph about them too, but something told me they were bad and that all hell would break loose if I did. I pulled back the covers and laid down and just tried to think about breathing.

NINETEEN

I didn't hear another sound until the next morning when somebody was clanging around. I jumped up and went to see what Bettes was doing. Only it wasn't Bettes, it was Tracie, and she was looking for something in the kitchen. She was pulling out pots and pans and making a godawful racket. I stood there in the doorway watching her until she finally turned around.

"There you are." She said to me and kept right on scratching under the sink.

"You know Chuck's probably gonna whip your ass for this shit," she said.

"Why's he mad? He ain't my goddamn daddy."

Well, that made her straighten up and look at me. I knew she wasn't gonna do nothing, she never did, so I just went to the living room, turned the TV on and sat on the couch.

She followed me halfway there and stood there looking at me.

"Where'd this attitude come from?"

"Why didn't you tell me Antoe was my daddy? Seemed like you might've told me that."

I looked at her and she stared at me. "Who told you that?"

I shrugged. "Is it true?" I asked.

She turned around and walked back to the kitchen and I followed her. She sat down at the table and was rubbing her head.

"Girl, I can't deal with this right now. I just can't."

"Is that why you sent him away? So I wouldn't find out?"

"No, I...goddammit. I can't deal with this now. I came to get you so get your shit and let's go and don't say nothing else about it. Especially not to Chuck." And she stood up and went to the door. "Get your clothes or whatever you have and let's go."

"But I wanna see Brother Joseph before he leaves," I said.

"I can't help it. I gotta go take care of something." I didn't move and she got impatient. "Get your stuff." She went out the door to where Chuck's old car was sitting in the driveway beside Brother Joseph's van.

I went to the bedroom and put on my pants and grabbed my boots (I didn't bother putting them on) and stuffed all those papers back in my bag and went out to the car and got in. She started it up and pulled out of Bettes' driveway.

"So where'd you go?" She asked me but I kept staring out the window. If she wasn't gonna answer me, I wasn't gonna answer her.

"Huh? Where'd you go?" I didn't say nothing.

"Whatever, Girl. I'm doing the best I can if you wanna act like a damn spoiled brat then that's fine."

"You need to do better," I said, and she just sighed.

We got to our house and I jumped out and was half way up the steps before she'd even turned the motor off. I saw that somebody'd cleaned up all the mess in the front hall and the front room, too. Toomie had big pieces of silver colored tape all over him where he'd been cut open. He looked like hell.

I hadn't eaten Bettes' bacon sandwiches last night so I went to the kitchen to see if there was anything. The icebox was still empty, just some beer and mustard. There was bread in the breadbox and I got two pieces out and saw that there was mayonnaise setting there beside the sink. I was making me a sandwich when Tracie came in there.

"Don't eat that, it's been setting out for God knows how long," she said. I looked at her and then looked at the sandwich I was holding.

"Eat it then and get sick! See if I care!" She stomped

off and I heard her going upstairs. I threw the sandwich away 'cause I didn't really wanna get sick, and fixed me another one, only this time with mustard. I took it upstairs to see if my bedroom had been cleaned up. I saw that some of the torn up stuff was out of the hallway, but the room we camped in was still wrecked and so was my bedroom. I shut the door and cleared a space off my bed and sat there eating my mustard sandwich. I wondered exactly what day it was, and from what I could figure out, it was Monday. I guess I'd have to go back to school tomorrow, so I thought maybe I'd better clean up in here and see if I could find some clean clothes to wear.

While I was digging around the piles of clothes, I heard her coming back down the hallway. She stopped at my bedroom door and watched what I was doing.

"We'll talk when I get back, tonight, OK?

"OK?" I looked up at her and said, "OK."

"Hey, what if I bring you some cupcakes? Would you like that?" She asked.

She was trying, so I smiled at her and she smiled back and was gone. I turned back to the clothes and began to sort them into piles: one dirty and one clean. Sometimes it was hard to figure out what was clean and what wasn't. I found that ugly ass dress Chuck'd bought for me, still wadded up and muddy in the corner. I shook it out and it was a wrinkled mess. I found my other favorite blue jeans, and the white dress I'd worn the first day of school and all my skirts, underwear, tee shirts, and socks. Everything went to the dirty pile. Tracie probably wouldn't be doing any washing today so if I didn't wanna go to school in dirty clothes (dirtier than usual), I was gonna have to do it. I'd done it before; it wasn't that hard.

I grabbed the sheets that were all wadded up on my bed and used them to make a sack. When I finished loading all the clothes up in the sheet, it looked like the bag Santa Claus carried, only I knew he wasn't really real. I thought about the brother who looked like him and wished I could've stayed there with all of them. My bag was still on the bed and I thought about the money in it. I had to hide it real good 'cause I didn't know if Chuck or Tracie came in my room when I was gone. I dumped everything out but the bag of money; it got stuck in the bottom. So I rolled the bag up around the moneybag and looked around for someplace to stash it. I crawled under my bed and there was a piece of wood in the floor that was kinda loose. I pulled it up and there was a little space below it and I stuffed the bag down in it and put the piece of wood back on top. There! Nobody, even if they were looking, would be able to tell that bag was there. I crawled out and picked up the Santa bag and headed down the stairs to the washer room.

When I got down there, I remembered whoever messed up our house had messed up the washer and dryer too. And guess what? It was still messed up.

"Hellshitdamn!" I didn't have any clean clothes and we didn't have a washer and dryer. There was a bucket setting there so I took it to the kitchen and filled it up with water and put in some washing powder. I figured I could wash some stuff in the bucket and take it outside and hang it on the clothesline we never used.

I started off dumping in my underwear and socks 'cause those were the smallest things. I swished the water around like the washing machine did and then wrung them out. I laid the wrung out stuff on the washing machine and put in a pair of blue jeans. I dumped in some more washing powder 'cause they were real dirty looking and swished them around. I was just about to take them out when I heard the front door slam then a slapping merry-go-round sound. Chuck was back.

My first thought was maybe if I stayed real quiet he wouldn't know I was here. I wasn't sure what he would do but I didn't wanna find out. I heard him in the front hallway, and then I heard him come in the kitchen. I jumped in the doorway that went down to the fruit cellar and was half way down the steps when he came in the washer room.

"Well, well if it ain't the prodigal daughter. They killed the fatted calf for the prodigal son, what you think we oughta kill for you?"

I froze on the steps. I didn't think he'd try to come

down them, he never had before.

"You know you're gonna get it, don't you?" He walked closer to the doorway and I went down another couple of steps and opened up the door to the fruit cellar.

"What are you doing down there?" He asked.

"I was gonna clean the fruit cellar," I said, holding on to the door ready to jump through and slam it shut if he started down.

"Yeah? Well, you clean good then, but it ain't gonna get you out of what's coming to you." He stood in the doorway for a second or two then he turned around and left the washer room. I waited there at the bottom of the steps, listening to his footsteps going through the kitchen and clumping up the stairs. Then I breathed.

I left the door open to the fruit cellar 'cause it stunk to high heaven in there. Nobody had cleaned those smashed jars up and I didn't feel like doing it now. The main thing now was to figure out how to keep out of Chuck's way till he forgot why he was mad at me.

I went back up the stairs and got the blue jeans out of the water and started trying to wring the water out of them but it was a whole lot harder than the underwear and socks. I twisted them one way then the other and then did it again. I finally had them where they weren't dripping and I gathered up the wet socks and the underwear and took them outside to hang on the clothesline.

The clothesline was behind our house and I don't

think Tracie ever used it. I'd hang Antoe's stuff there sometimes when I had to hose him down after he shit his pants but Tracie said it was too much work. There were some clothespins in a bag up by the house so I got them and hung it all up to dry.

When I got back to the washer room, I saw that the bucket of water was dirty so I took it to the kitchen to pour it down the sink and get some fresh. I figured I could wash some shirts and some of those skirts and that would get me through the rest of the week for school. Maybe by then the washer and dryer would get fixed, but probably not.

I filled the bucket too full. I couldn't get it out of the sink, so I tipped it over to pour some of it out when I heard Chuck coming back down the stairs. Hard. And fast. As fast as his one leg would let him. I heaved the bucket up out of the sink and tried to run with it to the washer room and I should've just left the damn thing there 'cause it sloshed out all over the floor and 'cause I was hurrying, I went sprawling across the floor. Before I could get up he came charging in the kitchen looking more wild-eyed than I'd ever seen him look. In his hand was the sack that I'd left out on my bed. The one with all the balloons. Hellshitdamn.

"You little BITCH!" He screamed at me and faster than I could get my legs under me, he grabbed me by my shirt and yanked me up.

"What the hell? What. The. Hell?" He was in my face and he had my shirt scrunched up and was holding me up in the air with one hand while he shook the sack of balloons in my face with the other.

"Ow, you're hurting me!" He was choking me with my shirt and then he shook me and dropped me and I hit the floor with a thump. Just as I jumped up to get away, he drew back his fist and it felt like my head exploded with colors just like the fireworks they set off over the lake: red, orange, white, and blue. I landed up against the wall and the back of my head hit something. Hard. I couldn't even begin to get up before he was standing back over me.

"Do you know what you've done? Do you? You stole this outta my car, didn't you? Didn't you?" He wasn't screaming now, he was almost whispering and that was a lot scarier than him screaming. He grabbed my arm and yanked me up by it and I heard and felt something go POP and it was a kind of pain like I'd never felt before. It hurt worse than when I'd fell off the swing last year.

"Where's the money?" He got right down in my face and gritted his teeth.

"I found those balloons in the yard; I didn't get them out of your car." Something from either my head, or my nose, or both, was bleeding. I could feel hot wetness on my face and I looked down and there was red all over the white tee shirt I was still wearing.

"You're lying!" He shook me again and it hurt so bad I couldn't help but cry some. "Tell the truth and you'll be better off."

"I'm telling the truth! Those balloons were laying in the yard when I got home the night...parents' night at school. I picked them up! I didn't know they were yours!" I was lying and I knew it, but I also knew if Chuck hit me again I was probably gonna die.

He let go my arm then and shoved me and I went flying backwards and bonged my head against the broken washer machine. He stood over me for a second or two and I thought he was gonna pick me up and hit me again, but all of a sudden he stomped back in the kitchen. I lay there and made myself just breathe.

TWENTY

I must've passed out for a little bit, cause I woke back up and I was still laying on the floor. I sat up then, and my head was spinning. I tried to move my arm and it hurt like crazy so I didn't try again. I pulled myself up with the other one and stood there swaying a little. It took me a little bit to remember exactly what happened. I listened to see if I could hear anything in the kitchen before I went out there. It was all quiet, so I went out there, trying to walk light so my head would stop feeling so crazy.

Chuck was sitting at the table. Hellshitdamn. I just walked over to the sink and got me a paper towel from the roll that was setting there and wet it. My face felt stiff and sticky so I took that wet towel and wiped it carefully. My nose was real sore so I didn't wipe it much.

"Fix me a sandwich," Chuck said, and it made me jump.

I turned around too fast and it made my head hurt worse and it made me a little bit dizzy so I grabbed hold of the sink to keep from falling.

"Quit putting on, you ain't hurt none. Fix me a sandwich or I'm gonna give you something to put on about." He was sitting there at the table. He'd taken his leg off and the empty pants leg was pinned up and he had his cane to help him walk.

I knew there wasn't anything in the icebox so I asked him, "Out of what?"

"Out of what?" He mocked me. "Outta the stuff in that sack, whatta you mean, outta what?" I cut my eyes over to him and saw he was fixing to give himself a shot in the arm.

He looked up and saw me watching him so I bent down and got a sack off the floor and put it on the cabinet. There was a package of bologna and a package of cheese and a loaf of bread in there. I'd made sandwiches for him before and I knew he liked two pieces of everything and a lot of mayonnaise.

And I knew without asking that he wanted two of them. I laid the bread out and put on the bologna and the cheese but when I got the knife out to spread the mayonnaise, I remembered what Tracie had said about it and I wondered whether or not I oughta say something.

"I ain't got all day." And he reached out with that stupid cane and wacked me. Hard. On my side. Well.

That made up my mind right then. I was gonna use that mayonnaise and I hoped he got as sick as that dog of Mr. Perone's after he ate rat poison.

I spread it on both sides of the bread, thick, and I put both of the sandwiches on a plate and took it over to where he was sitting. He was drinking out of the bottle and the needle was laying there on the table. I went back to the washer room to sit down and rest 'cause I wasn't feeling all that good. I sat beside the washing machine and leaned my head up against it 'cause it was hurting bad and the cool metal of the washing machine felt good.

After a little bit, I heard Chuck get up and it sounded like he was stumbling some. I heard him go out in the hallway and from the sounds it seemed like he stopped there. Then I heard him go on towards the living room. I fell asleep sitting there leaned up against the washing machine.

"Hey!" I snapped up when I heard him call me from the kitchen. I got up to see what he wanted. He was standing in the doorway, kinda swaying a little, and he held out the plate where the sandwiches had been.

"Fix me another one."

Even though I wanted to scream and cuss at him, I knew he wasn't drunk enough. So I took the plate and fixed him another sandwich, using even more mayonnaise on this one. I put it on the plate and tried to hand it to him but he had already turned around and was hopping back towards the living room. I followed him in there and he flopped down on Toomie and grunted and moved around and I set the sandwich plate on the table beside him. As soon as I set it down he reached out, quicker than a snake, and grabbed me by the wrist. It was the arm that he'd hurt so I hollered.

"Anybody asks what happened to you, what you gonna say?" He asked.

I looked at him and he tightened his hold on my wrist.

"You tell 'em you fell down those steps, you hear me? That's what you tell 'em." I nodded and he let go and picked up the sandwich. He had a new bottle of brown stuff beside him. Good. I hoped he'd pass out soon.

I picked up the jar of mayonnaise from the counter and took it outside. I didn't want Tracie to know I'd given it to him in case he did get sick. We had a big rusted barrel where we burned stuff sometimes, but I knew that jar wouldn't burn. So I took it around behind the house and ran out to the edge of the woods and slung it as hard as I could. Nobody would find it out there.

I stopped by to check on my clothes hanging on the line, but they weren't dry yet. Well, the shirts almost were but those blue jeans were still sopping wet. About the time I got back in the house I heard a godawful crash. He must've dropped something and I heard it shatter all over the place and he was cussing to beat the band.

"Goddammit. Girl...Girl?

"GIRL! Get your ass in here and help me or you're gonna be sorry." His voice was funny, all slurry sounding.

I waited. It sounded like he was walking, or trying to anyway, then I heard another crash and it sounded like he'd knocked over something big.

"Girl? Girl, help me, please." He wasn't yelling now, he was begging. And then I heard him start puking. It was a nasty sounding noise, puking and coughing and it sounded like he was still trying to call me but couldn't 'cause there was puke all in his mouth.

"Gross." I listened some more and kept hearing the puking noises mixed with coughing and choking sounds. I stayed there in the hallway listening to it for a long time. Then all the sounds stopped. I wanted to go lay down on account of my head hurting but there was one more thing I needed to do first.

I went upstairs and down the hallway to Tracie's bedroom. The door was open and all those fans were going ninety to nothing. I turned on the light and looked around till I saw it: Chuck's fake leg was propped up in the corner. I picked it up and it was real light and felt like plastic. It didn't look real up close. I carried it downstairs and out the back door. I went over to the hole that led under the house and I crawled under it and took that leg with me. I wasn't ever gonna tell what happened to it either. Without it, he couldn't run at all and I was just real tired of him hitting me. I took it way under there and pushed it behind one of the big blocks the house sat on. I crawled out then and on my way back to the kitchen, I pulled my underwear, socks and tee shirts off the clothesline. The blue jeans still weren't dry.

When I got back in the house, I went to the living room to see if I could see what he was doing. Peeking in the door all I could see was that the table that used to have our TV on it was turned over and so were two of the little tables that set beside Toomie. I saw Chuck's arm sticking out on the other side of Toomie. I tiptoed over to it 'cause I knew he wouldn't be able to get up too fast. I looked over and saw that Chuck was laying on his back with puke all over him. But something wasn't right. His eyes were wide open. They looked just like that deer looked out in the highway after it got run over by a truck. I'd run out there to try and help the poor deer and it was just laying there and its eyes were wide open but they weren't looking at nothing. Tracie told me it was dead. And now Chuck looked just like the deer.

I wasn't sorry he was dead (if he really was) but I was worried. What if they were able to prove that I killed him with that mayonnaise? Tracie was gonna be mad. At least I'd thrown the jar out in the woods but now I was thinking I better go get it and bury it or throw it in the creek. I was just about to get up to go get it when I heard a car.

I got up to look out but by the time I made it to the front window, the door was opening and I saw it was Bettes. And right behind her was Brother Joseph. Well, I was real glad I'd get to see him one more time.

"Girl, I brought..."Bettes started saying something then she got a look at me. I guess I looked pretty bad.

"Oh my God, Girl! Girl, what happened?" And she knelt down and put her hands on either side of my face. "Oh my God."

"What happened?" Brother Joseph was right behind her and he stopped real quick like he saw something that scared him.

"Dear God. Are you alright?" Before I could answer him he picked me up and carried me to the kitchen and sat me down in a chair.

"Girl, what happened? Did you fall? Who did this?" Bettes was right behind us.

"Chuck did."

"Motherfucker. Where is he?" Bettes spit it out.

"He's in the front room. He looks like that dead deer."

"What?" And she took off running.

Brother Joseph got a paper towel and wet it and started wiping my face off.

"Ow!" I said when he was wiping my nose.

"I'm sorry; it looks like you've got a broken nose. We're going to have to take you to the hospital. Does anything else hurt?"

"My arm," I said, "and my head feels kinda funny." He carefully felt around my head and there was a place on the back of it where I hit it on the washing machine, or the wall, that was real, real sore and I jerked away from him.

"Does that hurt?"

"Yeah," I said.

Bettes came back in the kitchen then and stood looking at him. He looked at her. "He's dead," she said. "Girl, what happened? Do you know? Why did he hit you?"

"He came downstairs and was mad 'cause he found those balloons I had."

"What balloons?" Bettes asked.

"I don't know, I found them in the yard the night of parents' night." I was gonna stick to my story.

"What kind of balloons?" She asked.

"They were just balloons that had stuff in them. There was a bunch and I just picked them up and put them in my bag and I left them out on my bed and he found them and thought I stole them out of his car."

Bettes was looking at the table and she saw the shot laying there Chuck had give himself.

"What's this?" She picked it up.

"He was giving himself a shot," I said.

"Sonofabitch." She whispered, then she asked, "Where are those balloons?"

"I don't know. He left, then he came back. I think I

fell asleep in the washer room." I told her. My head was feeling real fuzzy now and I felt like I was gonna be sick and before I could say a word, it came up and I was sick all down the front of Brother Joseph.

"She's probably got a concussion; I've got to get her to the hospital." He didn't even seem to care he was covered in puke and he picked me up and Bettes handed him her keys.

"Here, take the car and I'll deal with him." He carried me outside then and down to the car and sat me down carefully in the seat.

"Hey, you're going to be fine," he said, "only you can't go to sleep right now, OK?"

I tried to nod but it hurt so I just said, "Yeah," but I wanted to sleep. He sorta shook me but not enough to hurt.

"I mean it, Girl, you have to stay awake, OK?" He got in the car then and don't you know he turned that radio up loud as it would go and just started singing at the top of his lungs?

I had to laugh a little even though it hurt 'cause he sure couldn't sing a lick. But he kept right on singing till we got to the hospital then he got me out and carried me in. I didn't really care what they did to me as long as they'd let me go to sleep soon.

TWENTY-ONE

That was kinda the last thing I remembered about that day. Or it was the last thing I *wanted* to remember. That doctor poked and poked on me and he hurt my nose something awful. He shined a light all in my eyes and made me stay awake till I was ready to drop. The he finally said it was OK for me to sleep. He gave me a bunch of shots too, but by that time, I didn't even care. I was in a bed that raised and lowered and any other time I would've wanted to play with it but I just wanted to sleep, so I did.

I don't know how long I was asleep but when I finally woke up, I was laying there on my back and my arm was strapped down to my side so it wouldn't move. My head still hurt so I reached up and felt my nose and there was a big bandage on it and also one at the side of my head and there was something on the back of my head. I felt back there and it felt funny, like wires, and it was real sore.

I'd never been in a hospital before and I wasn't sure I liked it. It smelled funny. There was a bed beside me but nobody was in it. There was a TV on a little dresser but it wasn't on. I looked down to see what I was wearing and it was a pink nightgown. I don't know where it came from but it sure wasn't mine. I didn't have any nightgowns. I didn't know what day it was or what time it was, but I knew I sure was hungry.

The door opened then and a nurse came in. She was carrying a silver tray and I looked at it hard to make sure there weren't no shots on it.

"Well, hi there!" She said, "We were beginning to think you were gonna sleep for a week!" And she laughed.

"Can I get up? And go home?" I asked her.

"Soon. But we want to make sure you're good as new before then, OK?"

"I guess," I said.

"Good! Are you hungry?" She asked me and I said, "Yeah! Real hungry!"

She laughed again and said, "That's a good sign! That means you're getting well. Hold on just a minute and I'll bring you something to eat, OK?" Then she came over and checked something on my head and she looked at my nose and she nodded her head. Then she handed me a little bitty cup that had some pills in it and told me to take those and she gave me another cup of water to wash them down with.

"I'll bring you a tray in a jiffy, OK?" And then she was gone.

I wondered where everybody was. I thought about Chuck being dead. It was kinda a good feeling, knowing he was gone for good and wouldn't ever hurt me or anybody else ever again. But I knew that was probably wrong to feel that way. I was kinda lonely and I wished somebody would come and tell me what was going on.

The nurse came back with something and she pulled a little table across my bed and set what she was carrying there. It was a metal tray and it had a little metal lid on the top and she took it off and opened up a carton of milk. I saw there wasn't nothing but a bowl of soup and some Jell-O. Well, I tried the soup, and even though I was real hungry, I wasn't about to eat that. So I ate the Jell-O and took a swallow of milk but it was plain white milk and I didn't like that kind. I pushed the tray back after I finished off the Jell-O and wondered what I was gonna do till I got to leave. Then I wondered who would come get me. Tracie was probably not gonna do it and I didn't know where Bettes was. Maybe they'd forgot about me.

I had just convinced myself I needed to go see if I could find somebody when there was a knock on my door. That nurse hadn't knocked so I knew it probably wasn't her. I didn't say anything and they knocked again.

"Come in?" I asked cause I didn't know why they were knocking. A lady with a hat on peeked her head around the corner and I saw it was Mrs. Miller.

"Hey!" I was real glad to see her.

"Well, hi there Miss Girl. How are you feeling?" She came in smiling at me and she was real dressed up in a brown dress with a brown hat, purse and shoes. I'd never seen another lady who always dressed as nice as she did.

"You look pretty! I'm feeling pretty good."

She walked into the room where I was and sat down in one of the orange chairs that was by the side of my bed. She reached out and took my hand, the other one, not the one strapped up, and gave it a squeeze.

"That's good to hear, you gave everyone a scare."

"Yeah," I said. "Did you come here to see me?"

"Well, yes, I'm here, but I've been here most every day for a week or so."

"Why?" I asked her.

"Brady's here in the hospital, too."

"What's wrong with him?"

She didn't say anything for a second then she told me. "He was beaten up by...some men." And just like that, I knew.

"Chuck and his brothers beat him up, didn't they?" I asked her.

Well, she stared at me then. "How did you know

that?" I shrugged.

"I knew he beat somebody up and I heard something him and Tracie were fighting about." I remembered that day they were screaming and Chuck was crying and he said something about someone stealing something out of his car. Now I knew that he blamed Brady for what I'd done. I felt so bad I wanted to cry and tell Mrs. Miller it was my fault but I didn't.

"Is he gonna be alright?" I asked her.

She smiled but it was kinda sad. "In time, yes, he'll be fine."

"Well, Chuck won't hurt him anymore. He's dead." I told her and she nodded so I guess she knew. "He beat me up, too, he was bad."

"Sometimes people are bad. But there are more good than bad. Just remember that."

"Yeah."

"Well, Girl, I need to go sit with Brady but I'll come back to check on you. When are you getting to go home?"

"I don't know," I said, and she rubbed my cheek.

'I'll come by tomorrow to see if you're still here." She turned and was walking to the door.

"I know about Antoe being my daddy," I blurted out. She turned to look at me.

"I see," was all she said.

"And I know Rosie was my momma. And you were Rosie's momma. So that makes you..." But the way she was standing there, so still, I couldn't say it.

"Your grandmother. Yes." She didn't sit back down, but she didn't leave either.

"So, I was thinking..."

When I stopped, she said, "Yes?"

"Could I come live with you? Maybe? Me and Cerese get along good and I'm a big help, and you could call me Corrine, 'cause it kinda matches with Cerese." I was talking real fast 'cause I had to say it before I couldn't.

She took a deep breath and looked down at her shoes, then she looked up at the ceiling, then she came over and sat back down in the orange chair.

"You've been thinking about it," she said.

"Yeah, I tried to ask Tracie but she wouldn't tell me nothing. How did Antoe know Rosie?"

"A long time ago, I used to work for your other Grandmother...Mrs. Brown. And Rosie would come with me and she and Antonio would play together. Then, when they got older..." She stopped what she was saying the way grownups always did whenever they were about to talk about sex or something.

"And had me," I finished for her, just to let her know I knew about babies and how they were made. Well, I really didn't but I knew it had something to do with a boy and a girl and a bed. I guess Antoe had known about it too, which kinda surprised me.

She smiled. "So could I live with you maybe?"

"What about Tracie?" She asked me, "It seems like she might need you now more than ever."

"Tracie ain't ever wanted me around. She sent Antoe away and she'll probably send me somewhere next." I waited. "You don't want me to live with y'all do you?"

"Baby, it wouldn't work out. It's too complicated and you're too young to understand right now. Someday you will."

I looked away from her then 'cause I was mad. I wasn't too young to understand anything. I'd run away from home, found Antoe when I didn't have any idea where he was, and I'd caused Chuck to die. I was plenty old enough and I thought about telling her that but my head was beginning to hurt again so I just laid back against my pillow and closed my eyes.

I felt her rub the side of my face again, and then she said, "I'll see you again, soon." I heard the door open and she was gone.

I opened my eyes when she shut the door and I got even madder. It sure did seem like nobody wanted me around much. Then I wondered where Brother Joseph was. It seemed like he might've at least waited to make sure I wasn't dead. But he was gone too and he said I couldn't live there at the castle, either. Just when I was getting all worked up the door opened and this time it was a man. I remembered him from when I'd first got there; he was the doctor.

"Well, what have we here?" He asked, and I didn't answer, I just watched him 'cause I was remembering all those shots.

He picked up something from the end of my bed and looked at it then he came to the bed where I was and put a round metal thing on my chest and listened to it. He unstrapped my arm and it hurt some, but not too bad. Then he felt around on my nose and on my head.

"Well, young lady, I think we'll let you stay with us tonight, then tomorrow we'll send you on your way! How're you feeling?"

"Hungry!" I said, and he laughed.

"Well, we have you on a liquid diet just to make sure, but I'll see if I can't round you up a milkshake, would you like that?"

"Yeah! I love milkshakes, especially chocolate ones." He laughed again and he put my arm in a blue thing that went around my neck and kept my arm still.

"Now, you have to wear this until your arm is better, OK?" I nodded and he left and it wasn't long till a different nurse came bringing me a chocolate milkshake. Well, that was just about the best thing ever, and I sucked it down so hard I got a pain right between my eyes.

Another nurse came and took the empty glass away. I asked her if I could have another one, but she said it would ruin my supper. I didn't tell her if she gave me the same stuff as lunch I'd be glad to have it ruined. She turned on my TV, though, and showed me how I could change the channels with a little box.

I had the best time watching TV up in that bed and changing the channels one right after the other. It made the rest of that day go by real fast. There was a window on the other side of the room and it was getting dark out. I wondered why Bettes or Tracie hadn't come, 'specially Bettes.

A different nurse (there sure were a lot of them!) came bringing another tray, full of the same nasty stuff from lunch. But this time there was pudding so I ate that, and they brought me chocolate milk this time. When she handed me two pills and a cup of water, I asked, "Can I go see a boy named Brady? He's here too. I know him and I just wanna say hi to him."

"Oh no, you can't do that. No children can visit each other's rooms on the children's ward."

Well, I figured that but now I knew he was somewhere close by, I'd take my chances on going out and trying to find him.

"OK, but I'm real lonely and bored."

"Well, we have a playroom at the end of the hall that has puzzles and books to read. You could go down there if you want?"

"Yeah, I'd like that, only, I can't wear my nightgown can I?"

"Yes, you can, all the children who go down there

have theirs on too, but I'll find you a robe and some slippers to wear, OK?"

"OK!" I grinned at her. She came right back and handed me a blue robe and some blue slippers. I put the slippers on but I had to just put one arm in the robe on account of the thing on my arm. She led me down the hallway towards the playroom and as we were passing by those rooms, I could see there were names on the doors, on both sides of the hall. The first part of the hallway was all girls and toward the end I started seeing boy's names. There weren't but three and the very last door before we got to that playroom said "BRADY MILLER."

I went in that playroom and no other kids were there and I was sure glad. There were some chewed up looking puzzle pieces and some HIGHLIGHTS magazines that I picked up and looked through, but they were dumb and silly. I went to the door and looked out and I didn't see any of those nurses wandering around. I started down the hallway, and before I got too far, I saw the door that was Brady's open. I turned around and hurried back to the playroom and peeked out to see who it was and it was Mrs. Miller leaving.

I ducked back so if she turned around she wouldn't see me and waited and watched her walk all the way down the hall, stop at the desk up front where all those nurses were, then go on out the doors. I waited to make sure nobody else was leaving and started down the hallway again. I got to his door and heard the TV going. I knocked on the door. He didn't say anything so I knocked again.

"Yeah?" I heard him say so I opened the door and stepped in his room. His face was a mess. It looked like a piece of squashed fruit and his leg was all in a cast and it was up in the air. He had the same sort of thing on his arm like the one I had. Now that I was in his room, I didn't know what to say and he was staring at me.

"Hey," was all I could think to say.

"Hey, white girl."

"Do you remember me? I came to your-"

"I know who you are, white girl, but what you doing in my room?" He asked me, but it didn't sound like he was being mean or wanted me to leave, so I walked a step closer.

"I was in my room here, and your momma stopped by to see me, and she said you were here so I wanted to say, hey."

He didn't say anything, so I kept on, "I'm sorry Chuck did that." I pointed towards him.

"Yeah, well, it's always something, huh? Who beat yo ass?"

"Chuck. But he's dead now. And you can't tell nobody, but I think I killed him."

He stared at me and then laughed and laughed. He

held out the palm of his hand flat and I thought he wanted me to shake it, so I tried, but he showed me he wanted me to slap his palm then he showed me how to turn mine over so he could slap mine.

"You'll learn," he grinned, and I grinned back.

"I gotta go before they catch me, bye Brady!" I opened the door carefully and nobody was there so I walked as fast as I could back down to my room and crawled back in the bed and clicked those TV channels and thought.

I was glad Brady hadn't been mean. I didn't know why he was mean when I went over there, but I think it maybe had something to do with me being white. If my momma was black, what did that make me? I didn't look black, not like the Millers did, so I wasn't sure. It was something I'd like to ask about but I knew people sometimes got funny when you started asking questions about black and white. If Brother Joseph had been there, I would've asked him. It seemed like I'd known him for a real long time, but I hadn't, not really. Now that he was gone I wondered if I'd ever see him again. I laid there in that bed and thought and thought and you know, I just didn't have any kind of plan. I guess I'd have to see who'd come to get me and what would happen once I got home.

TWENTY-TWO

It was real early when that nurse woke me up the next morning. She checked on all my bandages and then looked at my arm and it wasn't long before the doctor came in to look too.

"Well, young lady, I think you're on the mend and you can go home today!" He poked around on my head some and then he said I could leave as soon as someone came to get me.

Well, I sure didn't know how long that'd be 'cause I hadn't seen a soul. I wondered if maybe Mrs. Miller was in Brady's room and she could take me home. I was just about to go looking for her when the door opened and Bettes came in. She looked real pretty, too, she had her hair all down and she didn't usually do that. I loved her hair. It was straight and jet black and there was just so much of it.

"Hey, baby, how're you feeling?" She came over to my bed and put her hands on my face. "You still look banged up, but not as bad as you did!" And she kissed me on my forehead.

"I feel pretty good; I just wanna get out of this bed," I said.

"Well, I'm here to get you, here's some clothes for you, get dressed and I'll go see what I need to do to spring you from the joint." She handed me a sack and left.

I dumped it out on the bed and there were some new blue jeans and a shirt and some new tenny shoes! I yanked that nightgown up and put on those blue jeans under it. And they fit! I knew Bettes had bought them too,' cause the jeans had flowers going up and down the legs and there were real big at the bottoms. She knew I'd been wanting some like that forever. The shirt was white and kinda thin and it had flowers around the neck and the sleeves were real big and had flowers around the edges. But I didn't know how I was gonna put it on with that blue sling. I didn't even know how I was gonna get the nightgown off.

"Hey, you not ready yet?" Bettes flew back in the room. "You're all ready to get out of here!"

"I need help," I said, pointing to the blue sling. She unhooked it from around my neck and took off my nightgown then put the new shirt on being real careful with my arm 'cause it still hurt some. Once she got my arm through the sleeve she put the sling back on and I was all set. She picked up my nightgown and other stuff and put them in the sack and held out her hand for me. I grabbed it and we went out past where all the nurses were and they all told me bye and to take care of myself. It sure did feel good once we got out of those doors. Seemed like it was a long, long time since I'd been outside.

Bettes' car was right up front and we got in and she started it up.

"Are we going home?" I asked her and she nodded.

"Well, we're going to my house. That alright with you?" She asked.

"Yeah."

"Is Tracie alright?" I asked 'cause I kinda thought she might come to get me. Or at least come with Bettes.

Bettes glanced over at me and said, "Not really. She's...not really."

We didn't say anything else for a second or two then I had to tell her something that was bothering me. "Bettes?"

"Yeah?"

"I'm not sorry he's dead."

She kinda laughed, kinda snorted. "Well, baby, truth be told, I ain't, either. He was a batshit crazy motherfucker."

"Yeah," I agreed, "batshit crazy."

"But he wasn't always like that. Back when we were in high school, he wasn't like that."

"You went to high school with Chuck?" I asked, kinda surprised at this.

"Yeah, we all did. Tracie, me, Chuck. He was just like everybody else. Tracie was so in love with him...it liked to killed her when he was drafted. Then when he got home...she didn't wanna see what he'd turned into."

I was busy trying to figure all of this out. Tracie had known Chuck for a long time. And he wasn't always batshit.

"Did you know Antoe was my Daddy?'

"Tracie told me you found out."

"Why didn't you ever tell me? You tell me stuff."

"Yeah, well, it didn't seem like that was something you really needed to know."

"Why didn't Antoe ever tell me?" This was something that'd been bothering me since I found out.

"You know...you know Tonio isn't like us, right?"

"Yeah, it's like when I was teaching him his ABC's and he'd know them one day then he wouldn't know them the next."

She nodded. "Well, he was kinda the same way about you. When you were a baby, we'd tell him and he'd be happy about it but then he'd forget and wonder where the baby came from."

"But why was he living with Tracie?" And why was I?" I asked, 'cause I *knew* Tracie hadn't ever really wanted to take care of either of us.

"He's her brother," Bettes said. "So Tracie's your Aunt. When your grandmother died...the other grandmother...Tracie came back and took care of y'all."

"I don't remember that grandmother," I said.

"No, you were real little when she died."

"Rosie was my momma. Did you know her?"

Bettes shook her head. "Not really. I only saw her when you were born. She passed away the same day."

"I killed her?" No wonder Mrs. Miller hadn't wanted me to live with her if I killed her daughter.

"No! Nothing like that, she was just real young, and there were other things I guess. But she's the one who named you Girl. She was real happy about you and kept talking about her baby Girl. Whenever the nurses asked her your name she would yell Girl! Girl! Girl! So that's what they put down on your birth certificate."

I was quiet for a little bit then I remembered something else. "What were those balloons?"

Bettes sighed. "They were bad. Real bad. You didn't do anything with them, did you?"

"Like what?"

"Oh, like taste of them or anything? Or what was inside of them?"

I made a face at her for even thinking I was so little I'd put stuff in my mouth "No, I wouldn't do that. I did open one though and it was just gross stuff. Why were they bad?"

"They just were." We'd gotten to her road and were bumping down it. When we got to her driveway she turned off her car and turned to me.

"Listen to me for a second. The body—Chuck's gonna be brought to your house. And there's gonna be a lot of people there, and you don't have to go, but I think it'd be good for Tracie if you did, what do you say?"

"He's in our house? Dead in our house?" Well, I wasn't sure I liked the thought of that.

"Yeah, when somebody passes, they bring them to the house, and people visit and stuff and somebody'll sit up with the body...with Chuck all night. I don't know why, it's just what people do."

"Do I have to stay there all night? I don't think I'd like that."

"No, you're gonna come back here and stay. I just thought it'd be good to go for a little while. But like I said, you don't have to."

She got out of the car then and came around to open my door since my arm wasn't working. I thought about going back to our house and that didn't bother me so much, but seeing Chuck dead did. I remembered how his eyes looked.

"Will he look like he did in the floor?" I asked her as we were going up the steps to the house. "No, he'll look just like he's asleep," she said.

She headed towards the kitchen and I followed.

Without even saying it, she knew I was hungry and she made me a whole bunch of waffles with holes in them. I ate every last one, too.

"I miss Antoe," I said.

"Are you still mad at me for that?" She asked.

I thought about this. "I guess not. But I'm still mad at Tracie. She's the one who sent him, she just made you take him."

"She really did think she was doing the best thing for him. You'll understand when you're older."

"Hellshitdamn! I understand plenty now! I'm not so young. I know about lots of things. Like I know Antoe and Rosie had to do sex to get me here and I know that's the same thing Tracie and Chuck did when they said they were sleeping! Sleeping don't make that much noise!"

She stared at me like she didn't know what to say then she started to laugh. She laughed and laughed and pretty soon I started laughing too. I couldn't help it; no matter how mad I was I couldn't help laughing when Bettes got started.

"Oh, Girl, you're one in a million. I'll never, ever think you're too young ever again." And she kept right on laughing as she was washing the dishes.

I wandered in the living room but I didn't much feel like watching television and I wasn't sleepy at all. It felt like I'd had more than enough sleep to last me for a week or two.

Bettes came out of the kitchen and went down the hallway so I followed. She was gathering up towels and stuff from the bathroom then she went in her bedroom and dumped them in a clothes basket she had in there. Her bedroom looked like it always did: clothes everywhere and a mound of covers all on the mattress that she slept on.

"Did you like Brother Joseph?" I asked her.

"Yeah, he was nice. Kinda weird though, that he lives in a house with a bunch of other men and won't ever get married. But to each his own, I guess."

"When did he leave? I wanted to see him again."

"He stayed with you in the hospital the night he took you, then all the next day but he left that night." She was in her closet now and was dragging a bunch of clothes out and laying them on the mattress.

"I was asleep that long?" I asked and I was real surprised. I didn't have any idea I'd been there two days.

"The rest of the day and night he took you, all the next day and night, and then they called and said you'd woken up around noon yesterday and were doing fine. That's why nobody came up there."

"I wondered."

She looked at me then looked back at the closet. She was acting kinda funny, not like she usually did. But maybe she didn't wanna go see dead Chuck either.

"When do we have to go to my...to the house?"

I asked her as I was heading down to the bathroom. I wanted to get a real good look at my bandages and stuff. There wasn't a mirror I could look at in the hospital.

"Five o'clock," she said.

My nose was all covered with a white bandage and there was another one on the side of my forehead. My eyes both had black and purple circles all the way around them and I looked like a coon. My hair was a mess, too; I picked up the hairbrush and one of Bettes' pony tail holders and took them back to her bedroom and handed them to her. She motioned me to sit down in front of the mattress and she sat down and started to brush my hair. I loved for her to fix my hair 'cause she didn't pull like Tracie or Mrs. Miller did. She was real careful of my sore head, too.

"Did you happen to notice Chuck's leg anywhere? Did he have it on when he hit you?" She asked me and I had to think for a second what she was talking about. "Yeah, he did then, but when he came back he didn't. He was using his cane." I'd almost forgot about hiding his leg under the house.

"Why?" I asked her so she wouldn't think anything.

"Well, Tracie couldn't find it anywhere. It wasn't in the bedroom where he usually left it. I thought maybe you'd seen it somewhere."

"No, I didn't see it." I was glad I was in front of her 'cause Bettes could always look at me and tell when I was lying.

I saw she had taken out most of the clothes that were hanging in her closet and she had them all piled up here and there around the room.

"There!" She was finished and now I had a ponytail in the back. "Go see if you like it."

I ran back to the bathroom to look at it and it was perfect. I ran back to tell her and she was standing in the middle of the bedroom looking from one pile of clothes to the other then she looked at the alarm clock that was setting on the floor beside her mattress.

"Oh, fuck it, let's go do something fun!" And she grabbed her keys and held out her hand and you know, I didn't have a problem with that at all.

Well, we ran all over the place. We drove down to the lake and watched the boats, we went to the Dairy Queen and ate ice cream, and Bettes even took me to the library and used her library card to check me out five Nancy Drew books. I'd been begging Tracie to let me get a library card ever since I'd found out kids could get them too, but she said she didn't like the bitch that worked there. Bettes told me I didn't need one that she'd check out whatever I wanted. When she handed the lady the library card, the lady looked at the books and then she told Bettes that if I tore those books up Bettes would have to pay for them. Bettes just rolled her eyes at the lady and told her to put the books in one of those bags for me, and the lady didn't say a word, but put my books in a sack.

We went back to her car then, and Bettes asked, "Well, what do you wanna do next? We've still got a couple of hours."

"Could we go back home so I can read?" I asked her cause I'd read one Nancy Drew book from school and I couldn't believe how lucky I was to have five.

She laughed and said, "Sure thing." And we went back to her house and I curled up on the couch and read and read and read. I made up my mind that whatever happened to me next, I was gonna be just like Nancy Drew; she wasn't scared of a damn thing and she didn't take nothing from nobody.

TWENTY-THREE

Bettes came back to the living room where I was reading, a whole lot later, and told me we had to leave soon. She'd changed her clothes and braided her hair so it wasn't all over the place. That's what she said. I didn't have anything to change into and she said it didn't matter. We got in her car and took off towards my house.

When we got there I saw there were a bunch of cars and trucks in the driveway and even lined up down the driveway.

"Who're all these people?" I asked her.

"Don't know," she shrugged. "People who knew him, I guess. Or maybe people from his church."

We pulled in the driveway real slow so we wouldn't hit any cars setting there, and Bettes drove all the way around the house and parked her car by the clothesline.

"I don't want anybody scratching my paint," she

said, and winked 'cause her car was so messed up even if somebody did scratch it, you wouldn't be able to tell.

We went in the back door, through the washing room and into the kitchen. I saw somebody had cleaned up all the junk in the washer room, too. The pieces of the dead washer were gone and the floor looked real clean. I tried to see what I had bonked my head on but nothing was there. The kitchen had been cleaned too, and there was food setting everywhere. Cakes, pies, stuff in big pans, fried chicken, you name it and it was there.

"Who's all that food for?" I asked Bettes when we were in the kitchen.

"Everybody. People've been bringing it over all day."

She herded me through the people in the kitchen, I didn't know any of 'em, and through the front hall, and the first thing I saw was a big coffin sitting right there on the other side of the stairs. Well, I didn't much wanna go look at that so I stopped in my tracks, but Bettes had her arm around my shoulder and she pulled me with her. The front hallway had been cleared out too, all the tables and the coat rack and all the junk was gone and now there was a bunch of metal chairs with people in them. People were everywhere. Some were even in the front room.

In order to keep from looking at that coffin, I looked around to see if I knew anybody. I saw Mr. and Mrs. Per-one were there, and some of those people I remembered seeing that time at Chuck's church. The big lady who'd had a fit and gobbled was there and she waved at me so I waved back. Tracie was sitting in a chair right up beside that coffin and she looked like hell. I don't mean she wasn't dressed nice,' cause she was, in a dress I'd never seen her wear before, or that her hair was a mess, it wasn't, but her face looked almost as bad as mine did. Her eyes were swollen and red and she didn't have a lick of makeup on. Bettes went over to her and leaned down and hugged her tight. I was standing right by that coffin and I had to look.

Chuck was laying there looking like he was asleep. He was wearing a suit and a tie, and somebody had cut his whiskers so they weren't all wild and long like they normally were. He was holding a book that said HOLY BIBLE and he looked different than I'd ever seen him look. I tried to look down and see if I could tell he wasn't wearing his leg, but part of that coffin was over his lower body. He was laying on what looked like a fancy pillow. I just kept staring at him 'cause he was the first real dead person I'd ever had a chance to look at. I thought dead people were supposed to be scary but he wasn't. He was a lot scarier alive.

Bettes stopped hugging Tracie and both of them came around to stand on either side of me. Bettes put her arm around my shoulders and sorta squeezed me, like she was telling me to chill like she did sometimes.

"You know he thought of you as his own daughter, don't you?" Tracie said, staring down at Chuck and I yanked my head up to stare at her and Bettes squeezed me a little harder.

"You know that, don't you?" she said again and looked down at me. I didn't know what to say 'cause I wanted to say that batshit crazy bastard was no daddy of mine, but she looked so sad and just not right that I nodded my head.

"You know he didn't ever mean to hurt you. After you left, he was so worried about you and he bought you a new radio, but I don't know where it is now."

"He didn't ever mean to do the things he did." It seemed like she was trying to make herself believe what she was saying. I really wasn't mad at her, but it seemed like I couldn't let her know that just yet.

"Hey, why don't I take Girl outside, so we can talk?" Bettes said, but she wasn't looking at me, she was looking at Tracie. Tracie looked over at Bettes real quick and they just looked at each other and then Tracie nodded.

"C'mon Girl, let's go outside," Bettes said, and I was glad to get out of there. On the way to the door I waved at Mrs. Perone but Bettes still had ahold of me and kept me moving. We got outside and more people were coming, but we headed down to where the bag swing was. Seemed like it'd been a long time since I'd been on it and I wrapped my legs around it and held on with my good arm.

"You know how you told me you were old enough to understand a lot of things?" She asked me and I nodded. "Well, I need you to be old enough to hear what I'm gonna say and not get upset about it, OK?" I looked at her. "I was planning to move, even before all this started, I was gonna go to California. There's not much for me here and I just wanna try something different."

"You're leaving?"

"Yeah, it's time for a change. But I'm gonna call you, and write you tons of letters and I promise you can come visit me in the summer, OK?"

"I guess," I said, but I couldn't believe Bettes was leaving. The only person I'd have left was Tracie and I wasn't sure how much good she'd be from the looks of her in there.

"I promise, Girl, we'll never lose touch, OK? You're not gonna be able to get rid of me that easily, OK?" And she pulled me off the swing and thankfully I held my hurt arm down or she might've torn it off.

"You're stuck with me for life, you hear me? I'm never having kids so you're gonna be all of mine, even when you're old and grey and I'm older!" And she laughed, but it sounded kinda funny.

I held on to her with one hand and hugged her hard. Then she let me go. I thought we were gonna go back in, that she'd told me what she wanted to tell me, but she hiked up her long skirt and sat right down on that swing.

"There's something else, too." I waited.

"See, now that Chuck's gone—" She stopped and I turned to look at what she saw that made her stop, and it was Tiny, the youngest of Chuck's brothers walking over towards us.

"Shit," Bettes said, but quiet so Tiny didn't hear.

"Hey, Tiny, good to see you. Well, I'm gonna go check on Tracie," she said. She whispered in my ear, "We'll finish later, 'kay?" I nodded.

Tiny stood where he was, not saying anything, and now that I thought about it, he really didn't talk much. It was Dale and Richie who were the loud ones.

"Where's your brothers?" I asked, 'cause I really didn't wanna deal with them tonight and if he said they were here somewhere, I was gonna go in the house right quick.

"They got sent off. What happened to you?"

"Chuck...I fell down some stairs." I don't know why I said that, 'cept I remembered Chuck *was* Tiny's big brother, so maybe Tiny didn't know he was batshit.

"Where'd they send them to?" I asked.

"Juvie," he said.

"What's that?"

"It's jail for kids."

"Why'd they go to jail? Cause they beat up somebody?" I remembered they helped Chuck beat somebody up that night and now I knew it was Brady.

"Na, they don't send you to juvie for that. They was doing bad stuff. Delivering drugs and stuff."

"Oh." I really didn't know what exactly delivering drug was, but as long as they were locked up I wasn't gonna worry about it.

"Could I swing some?" Tiny asked, and I felt bad for him so I got off the swing and even pushed him once even though I couldn't do it good 'cause of my arm.

Tiny got himself going real good and I was standing there watching when I heard a loud car coming. It sounded like a gun shooting and when it came in sight don't you know it was that old rusted van of Brother Joseph's! I couldn't believe he had come back and I was so excited I just took off running towards it.

He stopped it and turned the motor off and jumped out and grabbed me. He was wearing his brown dress, too. I had to remember to ask him why he wore it sometimes and not other times.

"Hey, slow down! You've been in the hospital remember?"

"Yeah, but I'm better now. Why're you here?" I asked him, 'cause he hadn't known Chuck and I really don't believe he would have liked him much.

All of a sudden Bettes was there and she must've been watching out the window to get out so fast.

"Hey, Brother Joseph, long time, no see!" she said.

"Hey, good to see you again." He looked at me.

"You have your stuff ready?"

"What stuff?"

He looked over my head at Bettes. "You haven't—"

"No," she said.

"I'll tell her. If that's OK?" He asked, and she nodded, yes.

"Well, I'll let y'all visit. C'mon in and have something to eat, there's a ton of food in here." She went back in the house.

"Can we go somewhere and talk?" He asked me, and hellshitdamn, what else were they gonna tell me? Bettes was leaving, and now Brother Joseph wanted to talk, and I knew no good thing ever came out of somebody wanting to talk to me.

"We could go to the swing," I pointed to it, "but Tiny's swinging on it now."

"What about around back?" He asked.

"Yeah, there's an old table around there," I said.

"Let's go check it out." I should've told him the old table was rotten and really wasn't fit to sit on but he was heading around the side of the house so I went with him. When we got back there he saw that the table was all lopsided and he looked at it and kinda grinned and don't you know he went over and just took a seat on the ground, so I did too.

"Are you leaving too?" I asked him. "And I'll never see you again either?" I picked up a stick and started poking around in a crawdad house that was on the ground beside me. Sometimes I could make them come out.

"Did Bettes tell you she was leaving?" he asked.

"Yeah. She said she'd write me all the time but I don't think she will. She forgets things."

He smiled. "So. Tracie's going to be pretty lonely, huh? With Chuck...and Bettes leaving."

"I guess so."

"You'll want to stay and keep her company?" He asked.

I shrugged. I really didn't know what it was gonna be like with her acting so weird and all.

"Or, would you like to go to school somewhere else?"

"To California?" I asked but I didn't even know where that was. The only thing I knew about California was that was the place the Beverly Hillbilles went to.

"I don't wanna go to California."

"No? You don't think that would be fun, to move to a different state far off?"

"Would Antoe come too?" 'Cause if Antoe was going then maybe it wouldn't be so bad.

"No, he's going to stay where he is."

"Then I don't wanna go...Brother Joseph?" He looked at me.

"I'm not sure I wanna stay here anymore." I kept poking around in the crawdad hole and he picked up a stick and helped me. We saw a big ole crawdad's whiskers sticking up from the mud, but we tried and tried and just couldn't get it out. After a long time Brother Joseph said,

"Well, how about this, then. I know a place where you can go to school, and you can even stay there, how would that be?"

"I'd live in a school?"

He smiled. "Well, no, not really." And then he went on to explain how there was this school and it was run by these women, he called them nuns, and he said that a few students were able to live there with them. He called their house a convict, and he said that all I'd have to do is help them out around it. He told me it was a house kinda like the one he and his brothers lived in. He also told me it was in Little Rock, which was where Antoe was, and he said he was almost positive I'd be able to visit him some. And he even told me I could visit at the castle, that Father Bonaventure had said it would be OK on Sundays.

Well, you could've knocked me over with a feather after hearing all of this. One thing I did know, though, Tracie didn't want me, just like she hadn't wanted Antoe. And really, that was the main reason I didn't wanna stay. Seemed like it might be good to have a change and be where maybe people wanted me to be.

"Well, what do you think?" Brother Joseph asked me when I hadn't said anything.

"Well...when would I be going?" I asked, 'cause I

was gonna have to find some way to wash clothes and pack and a lot of other things.

"I thought, if you want to, of course, that we could leave tonight and you could stay with us, then tomorrow I would take you to meet the Sisters."

I didn't know all this would be happening so fast. But I really didn't wanna stay without Antoe, and it seemed like instead of Tracie looking out for me, I'd be looking out for her just like I used to do with Antoe.

"We're leaving tonight? But I haven't packed anything and I know my clothes are all dirty."

"We'll figure it out," he said, "shall we go back in?" I nodded and we started walking towards the house.

"Brother Joseph?"

"Yes?"

"If I'm going to a new place, then I don't wanna be called Girl, OK?"

He smiled. "What do you want to be called?"

I shrugged. "Could you help me find a good name?"

"We'll find a great name for you, and you can keep Girl as your middle name, how about that?"

I thought about that and then nodded and we went back in the kitchen. Nobody was there, and all that food was still out, so I got one of the paper plates that were on the table and looked around till I saw a chocolate cake, cut me a huge piece, and slapped it on the plate. I was gonna ask Brother Joseph if he wanted some but he had gone to the front room. I sat there eating chocolate cake that was so good I was gonna get me another piece, but I changed my mind and got apple pie instead. It was good, too. Then I had a cupcake. It was yellow with white on top and I thought about my birthday, a long time ago, when Tracie said she was gonna get me pink cupcakes.

I was working on a second cupcake when Tracie, Bettes, and Brother Joseph came in the kitchen. Tracie was carrying a suitcase and she handed it to Brother Joseph then touched the side of my face and turned right around and went back to the room where Chuck was.

Bettes kneeled down and hugged me tight. "Remember, I'm gonna write you every week, and you gotta write me too, OK? I love you, Girl." She squeezed me one more time then she turned away and I could see she was crying.

Brother Joseph was holding the suitcase and said, "Well, are you ready?"

"Is that mine?" I asked, 'cause I'd never seen that suitcase in the house.

"Yes, Tracie bought you some new clothes. Just a few because you'll wear uniforms to school and we'll take care of those when you get there. Do you want to say good-bye to anyone else?" He asked me, and I shook my head but then I thought about the Perone's and I ran out to the front room and saw they were leaving. I followed them out and said, "Mr. Perone, Mrs. Perone, I wanted to tell y'all bye cause I might not see you again, well, not for a long time anyway."

"Well, hey there, Miss Girl, I hear you're going off to the big city to go to school!" Mrs. Perone leaned down and hugged me. "You don't forget us, y'hear?"

I promised her I wouldn't. Mr. Perone put his arm around my shoulder and told me to tell Antoe Hi the next time I saw him and I said I would. I followed them out to their car and watched while they got in and started to leave. I waved bye till I couldn't see their taillights anymore.

"Are you ready?" Brother Joseph was right behind me.

"Yeah," I said. "Hellshitdamn! I gotta go get something!" I had forgot all about that money upstairs in my room and I wasn't about to leave without it. I ran back to the house and in the front door. All those people kinda jumped when I opened the door so fast but I couldn't help it. People were standing on the stairs, talking, and I had to weave in and out to get up them. When I got to the top I ducked in my room real fast and slid under my bed, felt around till I felt the piece of wood that was loose, and stuck my hand in the hole to pull out the bag. I opened it up and made sure the moneybag was still there and it was. I turned on the light then to see if there was anything else I might need and there were those beads and the white lady statue laying there on my bed. I figured since I'd had them before, I might as well take them with me now. I looked around and there wasn't anything else I needed to take so I headed back downstairs and I didn't even look around to see if Tracie or Bettes was standing there. I got back to the van and Brother Joseph was standing there, waiting for me.

"You know, we are going to have to do some work on that mouth of yours. You'll give Sister Agatha a heart attack, and then she'll wash your mouth out with soap!" He opened the door for me and made sure my seatbelt was fastened and then he got in. I turned around to watch our house as we were leaving the driveway and I felt real, real funny. I'd left my driveway thousands of times, but I always knew I'd be back. Now, I was leaving for good. I didn't exactly like the feeling.

"You OK?" Brother Joseph asked, and I turned back around to look straight ahead. Bettes once told me there wasn't no goddamn reason to ever look behind you, 'cause once it was behind you, it didn't matter worth a shit. Now that I thought about it some, I kinda understood what she was talking about.

THE END